Thomas V. Stumpf

Bathsheba Monk was born to a family of Pennsylvania coal miners. After being discharged from the U.S. Army, she lived in Europe. She recently settled in Allentown, Pennsylvania, where she is writing her second book.

www.bathshebamonk.com

NOW YOU SEE IT . . .

NOW YOU SEE IT . . .

STORIES FROM COKESVILLE, PA

Bathsheba Monk

PICADOR

SARAH CRICHTON BOOKS

FARRAR, STRAUS AND GIROUX

NEW YORK

www.picadorusa.com

Picador® is a U.S. registered trademark and is used by Farrar, Straus and Giroux under license from Pan Books Limited.

For information on Picador Reading Group Guides, please contact Picador.
Phone: 646-307-5259
Fax: 212-253-9627
E-mail: readinggroupguides@picadorusa.com

Designed by Cassandra J. Pappas

Library of Congress Cataloging-in-Publication Data

Monk, Bathsheba, 1966–
Now you see it . . . : stories from Cokesville, PA / Bathsheba Monk.
p. cm.
"Sarah Crichton books."
Includes index.
ISBN-13: 978-0-312-42610-1
ISBN-10: 0-312-42610-0
1. Pennsylvania—Social life and customs—Fiction. I. Title.

PS3613.O529 N69 2006
813'.6—dc22

2005022284

First published in the United States by Sarah Crichton Books, Farrar, Straus and Giroux

First Picador Edition: December 2007

10 9 8 7 6 5 4 3 2 1

For Uncle Mike,

Paid in Full

CONTENTS

NOW
YOU SEE
IT . . .

Small Fry

1980

AFTER SAM BLEDSOE DIVORCED ME, I decided to cut my ties with Boston, where I had lived for ten years, and move to Los Angeles. I stayed with Theresa Gojuk, or "Tess Randall," as she was known in the business. I was trying to break into screenwriting, and she was trying to break out of an alcohol and pill habit. We'd been friends since high school, the type of friends who could drop in on each other without any notice. So I did.

"You want my advice, Annie?" she asked, even though I hadn't asked her. "You want my advice? Go back home. It's better to be a big fish in a small pond than, well, the other way around. You know."

She reached for a glass, but the counter was empty. There was no booze in the house, she said. She kept apologizing for that, even though I told her I didn't drink much anymore, either.

"Still," she said, "I should keep some for company."

She looked around the bar by the pool where we were sitting. Her fingers tapped the stool, then the counter again. I got the feeling she didn't want to be here, that she didn't want to be anywhere, because she didn't even want to be in her own skin.

Since I'd last seen her at her father's funeral, Theresa had divorced Jason, her sometime co-star, and married a lawyer named Phil. "I need a lawyer, let me tell you," she had said on the phone when I told her I might be coming to L.A. "Lawyers are God in this town." The next time I spoke with her, a month later, she'd said, "You'd think if I married a goddamned lawyer, I'd get some free legal advice, right? No! The bastard charged me! He charged me!"

By the time I made it out to the coast, she'd divorced Phil. Her only male companion seemed to be an illegal El Salvadoran, William, who cleaned her pool and who, as far as I could tell, didn't speak any English. She was so desperate for cash she'd taken a job as hostess on *Alien Visitation*, a show that highlighted videotapes of aliens that viewers had recorded.

"Every creep in America has a camcorder," she told me. "They're skulking around the bushes at night, recording God knows what, and they just happen to see aliens. So what the hell, right? Turn the camera on them. Most of them have sex with the aliens, too."

"You don't believe that."

"This is Los Angeles," she said. "Look around! Alien spawn is the most logical explanation I can think of."

William came out to the pool with drinks on a tray. I sipped mine and felt a tang. It had tequila in it. William winked at me and offered one to Theresa. Soon Theresa stopped giving me advice I wasn't going to take and we started having fun. Like old times.

"If Cokesville's such a hot town," I asked, "and I should go back, why don't you go back?"

"Didn't they bulldoze that fucking place?"

She moved the beach umbrella so her face was in the shade. No one wanted to look at a wrinkled face on television, even if it was only introducing aliens. William, bored with bringing trays of drinks, set a giant pitcher of margaritas between us.

"The furnaces are shut down," I said.

Theresa squinted into her drink. "Bastards," she said. Her father, Bruno, had fallen into a vat of steel four years ago, but the company had refused to compensate the Gojuk family for his death, saying he'd committed suicide. They claimed to have witnesses who saw him jump, actually take a dive into the pot of molten steel. By the time Theresa sent her lawyer husband to see what he could do, Cokesville Steel had shed its last seven thousand employees and had been bought and sold so many times there was nobody to sue. It was as if the three-hundred-acre plant had never existed. Now you see it. Poof. Now you don't.

A theme park subsidized by the Smithsonian Institution, Grace Landing, was there instead. For twenty-five dollars, an entire family could walk around exhibits that explained how steel was made and coal was mined. They could watch a film showing bridges, like giant Erector sets, being assembled. They could crowd into open train cars that miners rode into the earth. But without the possibility that the hot metal would explode or a mine would collapse, it was as exciting as a bronze plaque. After six months, only Japanese tourists came, buying licorice I-beams and black jelly beans, standing reverently in front of the carcasses of the blast furnaces their own steel industry had bested.

"I know!" Theresa jumped up, her drink welded to her fist. "Write a screenplay for me. My agent says I just haven't had the right vehicle. All I need is the right vehicle. You can do that. You're a writer. Write me a nice little vehicle."

She flung off her sunglasses and plunged into the pool. She stayed at the bottom for a long time, and just as I was considering whether or not to save her, she popped back up to the surface. She whipped her head around to shake off the water.

"We'll get started right now," she shouted.

She swam gracefully to the edge of the pool and hoisted herself up. Whatever negative things people could say about her acting ability, they had to give her credit for her body. And the rumors about the breast implants weren't true.

"Remember Small Fry?" Theresa toweled off and rearranged herself under the umbrella. "Do something with Small Fry."

The Small Fry gig was Theresa's first foray into showbiz. Three short fat geezers in fishing gear did fly casting at sports shows and they needed a "chick" for a prop. Theresa squeezed into a blue spangled gown and pranced around the stage, seducing the audience away from the motorboats and snowmobiles, the main attractions at those events. Her job was to hold a cigarette between her lips as the anglers cast their lines, tipped with lead weights, to knock the ash off. Sometimes she held a hula hoop, and they would cast through that into a bucket of water.

When I was a senior in high school, I'd traveled to St. Paul in the dead of winter to see her do one of her last shows with the Small Fry. She was in a tizzy over the decision to go or stay with them, because a pair of Canadian log rollers, guys who walked on top of a spinning log in a swimming pool, were trying to lure her away from the anglers. As amazing as that skill was, no one wanted to look at two scruffy woodsmen in plaid shirts. They needed a "chick," too.

"I've never seen Canada," she'd said. "But it's hard as hell to stay on that log. You have to keep running or you fall off. And I feel so tired lately."

When she picked me up at the St. Paul bus station, I'd noticed the purple circles under her eyes, but it wasn't until that evening as she shimmied under the civic arena lights in her spangled blue dress that I saw her rounded tummy. Not much, but enough, so I knew.

"Dr. Carter could do it," I'd told her later as she undressed backstage. Dr. Carter was the only doctor in Cokesville who gave out birth-control pills to girls our age. All you had to do was tell him you were engaged. He would also do abortions, and you didn't have to tell him anything.

"I don't know. I think it's too late for that," she'd said. "I could go to a Canadian bad girls' home and have the little bugger."

"It wasn't one of them, was it?" I'd asked, pointing to the room where the Small Fry were changing into clothes suitable for a big night in St. Paul.

"God, no!" she'd laughed, wrapping her arms around herself. "It was just, you know, some boy."

Although we were supposedly best friends, she'd never told me who the father was.

"Remember that dress they made me wear?" she asked now. "They told me I looked like a stream full of trout." She laughed loudly. "Write that down," she commanded, when she saw that I wasn't. She started singing: "Small fry, struttin' in the poolroom. Small fry, da da da da da duh. How the hell did that song go?" She hummed, then sang, "My my, put out that cigarette." She stared off into space, trying to remember. "Oh hell, if it becomes a movie, someone can look it up. They have people especially for that."

William refreshed our pitcher of drinks and disappeared into the bathhouse. We started talking about her life and the baby she gave up for adoption, which turned out to be a bad idea, because soon she went on a crying jag that got me crying, too.

"I can't do anything with this," I told her. "Your life is a freaking mess. We need a happy ending here. What's the plot? Small fish flops into big pond. Flounders. What?"

"Fix it," she said. "Fix my life. You're a writer. Or aren't you good enough?" She looked at me meanly, then shrugged. "Make it come out right. Life never comes out right, but you can fix it. Give me a neat life. Something with pink in it."

She did a dance to the pool, clowning at the side, pretending to totter. She turned to smile at me and I gave a foolish, drunken wave. It occurred to me that I was her only real friend. Like her, I picked friends who couldn't see through my protective camouflage. How could the two of us possibly help each other?

She stood by the edge of the pool and spread her arms to dive in again, but by this time I was too drunk myself to save her.

"I can't save you," I shouted.

"What?" She lifted her hand to her ear in a graceful motion.

"I said I can't save you!"

She smiled and nodded as if she understood, but a second later she dove in.

Hocus-Pocus

1949

AT FORTY-FIVE, Theodore Cheslock is miserable. The most miserable man in Cokesville. Can anyone be more miserable than a man who wakes up on his forty-fifth birthday knowing that today will be as disappointing as yesterday and that tomorrow will be exactly like today?

"Every day the same," Theodore complains to his friend Felix Gojuk. "We go down into the ground when it's dark and come out when it's dark. Then we scrub our backs, eat our bread, and go to bed. Where is the adventure in that?"

"Why do you want adventure?" Felix asks. "You have everything you need. You're the luckiest man I know."

"Yes, I have a lot," Theodore admits, confused. He's the strongest man in the mines. He married Anna Herling, the most sought-after woman in Cokesville, when she was still in widow's weeds, one month after meeting her at a dance at St. Cunegunde's. Anna, née Plaskonos, had been married to a Jewish mine owner in the Dnieper and was reputed to have a fortune. By daring to marry outside the faith, she had done the unspeakable and was shunned by both her own family and her husband's after his death. To escape the opprobrium, she had put an ocean between herself and her past. She'd kept to herself after arriving in Cokesville, and with each passing month of seclusion, the size of her late husband's fortune doubled and trebled in the telling. By the time Anna appeared at that dance, she had a golden glow, which would have enhanced the plainest woman, which she was not. Anna's beauty pleased Theodore, but it was the thought of her fortune that made him propose. After Theodore married her, he discovered that Anna didn't have money. Mr. Herling's family had made sure that the bulk of his fortune stayed with them. But she did have a trunk of her dead husband's books—all in English, because he had planned to emigrate to America with his shiksa bride—from which Anna read to Theodore every night: stories of Knights of the Round Table and Arabian Nights and navigators of the globe: adventures that Theodore had begun to believe should be his. And yet, fate—or God—has decided that Theodore squander his life digging holes in the ground and pulling out coal.

"I might as well be Lucky," Theodore says, referring to the donkey that carries coal from the mine to the breaker every day and is beaten every night for his trouble by the mine foreman, Devlin. "That's me. An ass." He bares his teeth and brays at the sky.

"Stop it!" Felix scolds, looking over his shoulder. "Someone will hear you."

"How am I any different?"

"God has a plan for you. He doesn't have a plan for Lucky."

"Some plan! I might as well be digging my own grave. Why didn't God just make me a donkey? Eh?" He grabs Felix by the lapels and pulls him close, then shoves him away.

"It's bad luck to talk like that." Felix crosses himself to make sure God knows he doesn't approve of his friend's blasphemy.

"You're just superstitious." Theodore punches Felix on the shoulder.

The smaller man staggers theatrically, clowning to dispel his friend's evil mood.

It's Saturday morning in late winter, and to save the nickel bus fare, the friends are walking over the strip-mined hills to Warrenside, the nearby big city, on Theodore's whim, ostensibly to look for other work. "Anything," Theodore says, "where we don't have to scrub with lye every night. We're still strong, eh? Look at this." He flexes his huge muscles through his thin coat. "Not bad, eh?"

By the time they reach Warrenside, the streets are clogged with horses, cars, donkeys and their drovers. The sidewalks are mobbed with shoppers, widows hurrying to Saturday confession, and people swarming out of the matinee at the Rialto, where *The Third Man* is playing. Theodore tugs at his work clothes self-consciously and reties the red bandanna around his neck like a cowboy he saw in one of Anna's books.

"We should have brought Anna and Ilonka," Felix says.

"Next time."

Theodore is angry at Anna. Yesterday, without consulting him, she had told their two sons, Mike and Steve, to pack up and leave. They had refused to work as breaker boys in the mines like other sixteen-year-olds and had fallen in with mobsters from Hazelton. Men in double-breasted suits would whisk them away in the back of black sedans, and when they returned, they made a show of stuffing rolls of twenties in Anna's teapot. Their gangster-movie antics pleased Theodore in a perverse way, but they drove Anna mad. She stopped reading to Theodore and would lie awake at night fingering her rosary, praying in Ukrainian, until finally he could stand it no more and moved a cot into his sons' room, where he now slept alone.

"Where should we go?" Felix asks.

Theodore points to a saloon. A sign on the door says THE AMAZING SUSAN BUTTERFLY PERFORMS TODAY *ONLY*. "I haven't seen that place before. Let's go in and wet our whistles."

"We told Anna and Ilonka we were looking for work."

"Just one," Theodore says, crossing the street. "It's my birthday."

The saloon is full of men drinking shots of homemade house whiskey. Those who aren't smoking meerschaum pipes have cheeks full of tobacco. Little paper bags resembling mail pouches, filled with tobacco, are on almost every table.

The place is brightly lit by glass chandeliers, and a white marble railing lines the fancy oak bar. Theodore and Felix lean on it, and the bartender pours them shots from a ceramic jug.

The tables in the back of the saloon have been pushed together to make room for a stage. An accordionist sitting at one of the tables lethargically plays the theme from *The Third Man*.

"So," Theodore asks the bartender. "The Amazing Susan Butterfly. Is she any good?"

"I haven't seen her act," he says indifferently.

The accordionist picks up his pace. The lights go off and one lone spotlight shines on the back door. It opens and a blond woman in a long, iridescent cape steps onto the stage, her cape shimmering in the watery light.

The accordionist sweeps his hands toward her and declares, "The Amazing Susan Butterfly."

Susan Butterfly spreads her arms wide, and the cape drops to the floor behind her, revealing a tight red strapless dress and skin so pale it glows. She pulls a playing card, the king of diamonds, from her bodice and holds it in both hands, looking around the room until she has everyone's attention.

"I love magic," Theodore whispers excitedly.

Felix crosses himself. Magic is the work of the devil.

She opens her hands and the released card wavers in midair before it rises slowly out of the spotlight, then, a little too quickly, flutters back into her hand. A few men, including Theodore, applaud. Those closest to the stage snicker. They can see the guyline attached to the card. Susan Butterfly smiles and bows. She reaches into the darkness behind the spotlight and produces a top hat. She turns it over and slowly circles the stage, making sure everyone can see that it is empty. Then she smiles, flips it over three times, touches it with a wand, and slowly pulls out a red silk handkerchief, and then another one knotted to it, and then another, until twenty-four handkerchiefs are coiled like rope on the floor. She stuffs the handkerchiefs back in the hat, flips it over, and touches it with the wand, and this time a white dove flies out. Everyone applauds.

"Amazing!" Theodore shouts.

Susan Butterfly plucks a violin from the darkness and begins playing with the accordionist "The Blue Danube," a dreamy song that pulls on Theodore's soul. She steps off the stage and walks around the barroom, playing to each table. When she comes to the bar, she stops in front of Theodore and plays right to him, never taking her eyes from his. Theodore is shocked: he knows her.

"She looks familiar," Theodore whispers.

"There are hundreds like her," Felix answers.

She tosses her hair and walks back to the accordionist. The two musicians pick up the tempo, working themselves into a frenzy, when suddenly Susan Butterfly steps out of the spotlight. The spotlight turns on the audience, and there is a loud moan as they are blinded. When the lights come back on, Susan Butterfly has disappeared!

The men whistle and clap. The accordionist resumes his heated playing. Theodore claps his hands to the beat. Felix shuts his eyes tightly. He can feel the devil in the room.

"Let's go." He pulls at Theodore's sleeve.

The accordionist wanders from table to table, slowing his tempo as he nears the front door. He stops playing, looks at the audience, then opens the door, and there is . . . Susan Butterfly, finishing the song with a flourish. She raises instrument and bow in the air to foot-stomping applause.

Theodore is on his feet, whistling. "Wonderful!"

Susan Butterfly snaps a top hat out of the air and bows in front of each table until they drop some money in her hat.

Felix slides his money off the bar into his pocket. When she comes to him, he won't look at her. She steps in front of Theodore, who sweeps all his money into her hat. She looks at him curiously before walking to the back of the saloon and slipping out the back door.

"Ignoramus!" Felix says. "Now you can't take the bus home!"

"Bah!"

Felix puts a hand on his friend's arm. "Let's go, Theodore. I don't like this place."

Before Theodore can answer, Susan Butterfly is beside him.

"Did you like the show?" she asks in thickly accented English.

"I liked watching you."

She smiles. "Buy me a drink."

Theodore elbows Felix. *"Daj mi beniaze!"*

"Nie. Nedam ti nic," Felix says.

She signs to the bartender to bring a round, then looks at Theodore intently. "You are a miner."

"That's right."

"And you are sick to death of black."

"Are you a mind reader?" Theodore says, astounded.

She looks from Felix to Theodore. "I have some powers."

"Can you tell the future?" Theodore asks.

Susan Butterfly studies the creases around Theodore's eyes. Coal dust is embedded in them, but the skin is red and raw as if he scrubbed with lye every night, instead of weekly like most men. She had spent the first twenty years of her life as Hannah Bineki, separating coal from slate in the Hazelton mines, and she knows how long it takes to get coal out of your skin. She smiles at the cowboy bandanna around Theodore's neck. She also knows firsthand the telltale signs of someone who is unhappy with his fate. "I can tell *your* future."

"Tell it to me now!"

Susan laughs. "I can't do it on demand. I need some"—she rubs her thumb and forefinger together—"inspiration."

"I gave you all my money! Please, tell me my future." He looks pleadingly into her eyes and recognizes . . . himself! It's like he's looking into a mirror.

"I have another show at six o'clock. Be my assistant. Then you will know your future." She glides away.

Felix is distraught. "I don't like this place. I've never seen it before, have you? Let's go home."

"I can't go home. I want to know my future."

Felix scowls. "You know what your future is! If you don't go back to work, they will deport you!"

Theodore pats his friend's shoulder. "They just say that to scare us. They can't deport us. Now go catch the bus. You can make it if you run."

"Here, I have enough for both of us. We can ride together."

"Go! I'll come later."

"What will I tell Anna?"

"Tell her I'll be home later."

"What if you aren't? What will I tell Devlin?"

Theodore laughs and pushes Felix out the door. "Tell Devlin to find another donkey!"

But Felix can't bear to leave his friend. He watches the Cokesville bus roll down Main Street, then walks disconsolately around to the back of the building to wait. The accordionist is sitting on a barrel, smoking. He grins at Felix and squeezes the bellows on his accordion tunelessly and laughs. Felix shudders. He pulls out his rosary beads, and, fingering them frantically, recites Hail Marys, one after another.

Just after six, he slips back into the saloon. All the seats are taken, so he stands near the stage with a rowdy group of miners. The Amazing Susan Butterfly shows them the king of diamonds, then opens her hands to let it go. It rises out of the spotlight and flutters back into her hands. The miners guffaw. Her new assistant hands her a top hat. She shows them it's empty, then touches it with her wand, and twenty-four handkerchiefs coil like a rope at her feet. She stuffs them back in the hat, twirls it around, touches it with her wand, and out flies a dove. The miners applaud. Theodore hands her the violin. She walks to the edge of the stage, smiles down at Felix, and begins to play a sad Slavic folk tune. "Hail Mary, full of grace, the Lord is with thee," he prays aloud to drown out her music.

She breaks away, and as she and the accordionist quicken the tempo, Theodore begins to dance. He dances in circles around the stage, clapping his hands overhead. He winks at Felix as the spotlight follows him. The barroom chandeliers go off. The spotlight shines directly into the audience, and for a moment the stage is dark. When the lights come back on, Theodore has . . . disappeared!

"Mother of God!" Felix whimpers. He has heard that when a magician makes you disappear, you go to hell until you reappear. And if you aren't a believer, the devil will make you stay there forever. "Please come back, Theodore. Don't leave me."

Susan Butterfly steps off the stage and fiddles her way to the barroom door. Felix holds his breath. She flings it open to reveal . . . a donkey!

The men in the saloon go wild, laughing and banging their glasses on the table.

The donkey bleats at the confusion, then turns and runs away. Felix bolts out the door after it. The donkey runs down Main Street, heehawing, Felix running after it. At the edge of town, out of breath, he stops, sits down on the ground, and starts to cry. "Theodore! Come back. Don't leave me, Theodore!" he yells as the animal runs into the hills. He sits there until the sun comes up. When the church bells start ringing for early Mass, he slowly gets up and starts home across the barren hills, praying for Theodore's soul.

Theodore watches Felix all night from the flat roof of a carriage house. When his friend is out of sight, he climbs down and walks back to the saloon. He enters through a side door where there is a room with a single iron bed. He nudges the Amazing Susan Butterfly awake and tells her that he's leaving.

She reaches under her pillow for a satin purse and pulls out some money from the show. "Do you know where you're going?" she asks.

Theodore shakes his head. "I haven't thought about it."

"You can still go home."

Theodore takes the money and bows to her. "Why would I go back?"

Flying Lesson

1957

SELLING YOUR SOUL implies an after-hours pact struck with a man in red patent leather twirling a handlebar mustache: a flamboyant one-shot deal with payback a dark day in the distant future. With my mother, Connie Kusiak, the sale was a couple of hasty transactions for which she didn't think she would be held accountable at all. She didn't believe in the devil's collection agency, because—and this was a secret she told me once, then denied—she didn't believe in the devil. She didn't believe in God, either. She didn't believe in anything she couldn't touch or smell or hold a two-way conversation with. I think she thought that unbelief kept her invisible; that she was flying under the radar.

And in any event, should the devil come looking for payback, what was a soul worth? You couldn't pay the mortgage with it; you couldn't buy a new dress or suit for Easter with it. She didn't think a soul was worth much at all. Which is probably why she got such a poor price for hers.

The spring when I was four, my mother got a job at the pajama factory on Seneca Street. Mary Gaydos from the Portuguese church worked there and told her what to say to get past the receptionist, who, it was rumored, was the owner's mistress. A lot of Portuguese women worked there, and Connie didn't see any reason why she couldn't, too. She could sew. Mary Gaydos said Mr. Zuckerman, the owner, was very cranky but would give you a chance if you were willing to work hard. Work hard? Isn't that what she had done all her life? She might as well get paid for it.

Connie had dressed in her church clothes, a beige veiled hat and heels and white gloves. Even though it was early spring and still cold, she didn't wear her winter coat, because she thought it spoiled the effect. She climbed the long, narrow stairway to the second floor of the old brick factory building. She paused a moment to consider the sign NOT HIRING hanging from the door with ZUCKERMAN MILLS stenciled on the frosted glass before she pushed it open and entered. The odor of hot oil and the loud clacking of sewing machines ambushed her and she winced, but she recovered to look pleasantly at the woman behind the front desk.

"I have an appointment with Mr. Zuckerman," Connie lied.

The woman, a blonde with dark eyebrows wearing a tight sweater, frowned and examined the desk calendar.

"He didn't tell me," the woman said.

"I ran into him yesterday. He probably forgot," Connie said.

"I don't know . . ." the woman said.

"Just tell him Connie Kusiak . . . from Market Street. He'll remember me." She held herself very straight, her clutch bag clamped under her arm, which was damp with nerves. She would have to keep her arms down so they wouldn't betray her.

The woman got up and opened the door to the office behind her. Through the half-opened door, Connie could see a figure in a white shirt working behind a fancy oak desk.

She strained to hear while the woman spoke to Mr. Zuckerman. A chair scraped against the wooden floor and the woman scurried back to her desk. A large man appeared at the office door. He was taller than six feet, lanky, with a lot of black curly hair on a big head. His tie was loosened and he was adjusting it when he saw her and smiled. "Mrs. Kusiak," he said, putting out his hand for her to shake. "Come in, please." He pulled her in and closed the door behind her.

Connie, who almost never smiled, did. Then she laughed. "I'm sorry," she said, tilting her head toward the receptionist.

Mr. Zuckerman waved his hand. "I like chutzpah," he said.

"What?"

"Nerve. You got nerve!" He laughed. "Please, sit down."

An open book was turned over on his desk. The wall behind his desk was lined with books. Storybooks. A dreamer, Connie tsked to herself. Like her mother, Anna. Like her husband, Frankie, dreaming about other worlds instead of paying attention to the one right under their feet.

She took off her gloves, and she caught him looking at her hands, which were lovely and white despite her hard work. She blushed.

"We make pajamas here," Mr. Zuckerman said. "It's piece rate. If you're fast, you can make a lot of money."

Connie leaned toward the desk. "I am very fast."

"Do you know how to sew?"

Connie stood up and turned around. She had made the dress herself from a Butterick pattern. It was cotton gingham: a fitted bodice embroidered with strawberries and a full circle skirt with yards and yards of material that floated like waves when she twirled around, which she wouldn't do now, of course, but she was sorry he wouldn't get the full effect of her handiwork.

"I made one just like it for my daughter, Annie. She's four. So it would be a size 6X. So I can sew children's clothing as well."

Mr. Zuckerman nodded, looking at her waist, which was still small despite two children.

"I sewed all the curtains in our house," Connie said. "Lined. Pleated."

"We use machines that cut and bind at the same time," Mr. Zuckerman said. "Three needles. If you misjudge a seam, you've ruined the garment."

"I see."

"Have you ever used one?"

Connie looked at the books on the shelf behind him, thinking how to lie, but she couldn't. She started to put on her gloves and stopped herself. "I can do anything. Just show me how to use the machine. I won't ruin any of your garments. If I do, I'll pay for it myself. Let me try. One pair of pajamas. No mistakes."

"We're not hiring," Mr. Zuckerman said.

"I'm a very good worker. You can't afford not to hire me," she said.

Mr. Zuckerman laughed. "You got a lot of nerve. Ten cents a bundle. Give a quarter to the union every week. It's a closed shop. Everyone has to join the union. Start tomorrow at seven-thirty. I like your nerve."

He walked her to the stairway, past the receptionist. "Is your husband on strike?" he asked.

The steelworkers had been on strike for three months. "They can't agree on anything," Connie said.

"Wish him good luck for me," Mr. Zuckerman said. He went back into his office, closed the door, and turned over the book on his desk.

"EVERYBODY ELSE IS DOING OKAY on the union stipend," Frankie complained when she came home and announced she was going to work.

"We're not everybody else," Connie said. "We have a big mortgage."

My parents had bought a detached home with three bedrooms on the north side of town a year ago: Frankie because he wanted more children; Connie to leave gritty downtown Cokesville behind. "You may have to work in the mill," Connie had told him, "but we don't have to live in it." The house was in a block of homes originally built for managers in the mill, but they had deserted them for the new development houses being built in the suburbs. The house needed some work, mostly cosmetic. Any repairs that had to be done, she had promised Frankie, she would learn how to do herself.

It pleased my mother no end that our neighbor in the house next door was a doctor, albeit one who had lost his admitting privileges to St. Luke's, the local hospital, and who, I realize now, was an alcoholic. But still, a doctor! We were living with rich people. Behind our back fence was an old strip mine. Occasionally, it was still detonated to dislodge coal; and when that happened, the crab apples fell out of our trees and the holy statues on the dressers jumped. But Connie thought it was a natural setting, almost bucolic. "At least we don't have to look at the smoke from the blast furnaces," she said. Connie began drinking her morning coffee on the back porch, looking at the strip mine but seeing only the white birch trees and huckleberry bushes that grew through the slag. She was happy, I think. At least she smiled. She stopped smiling when the steelworkers' union went out on strike. She was not going to lose her beautiful home. She would go to work to save it herself.

"Well, I'm gonna try it, no matter what. Babba will have to help around here during the day," Connie said to Frankie.

"Yeah, sure. Babba."

They said some other things loudly, and soon, from my perch on the windowsill on the second floor, I heard the porch door slam and saw my father walk over to the bench in the backyard and put his beer down. He took his wooden clarinet out of its blue fur-lined case, screwed it together, wet his reed, and began to play. My father played with a local group, Jolly Joe Timmer's Polka Band, for weddings and dances at the church; but when he was by himself in the garden, he played a different kind of music, and the songs he made up—wistful voyages up and down the scales—had no names.

That evening he sent seductive notes into the twilight to do his bidding, like Pan in the primeval forest. And soon my mother came out and sat beside him on the bench. I stood up on the windowsill and stretched, holding on to a limb of the big maple tree whose giant branches embraced my room.

"Annie?"

I turned around to see Babba in my doorway. She sat down on the bed.

"Come in. Let's read a story."

MY MOTHER AND I wore our matching dresses to church that Easter, and I wore a pair of cherry red double-strap Mary Janes, which I admired continually; so much so that my mother told me it was foolish to regard myself so highly. I hadn't started speaking yet, so I didn't defend myself. And anyway, because I wasn't talking, my mother never listened for an answer.

After Mass, my aunts and uncles and cousins came to eat with us, and while the women were preparing the meal, my father played his clarinet in the living room and I showed my cousins how my skirt twirled up when I spun around, dancing to his music. I was in mid-twirl when my mother grabbed me and slapped me hard across the face.

"Keep your skirt down," she said, and sent me to my room.

After a while, my older brother, David, came and told me I could come downstairs again. I was sitting on the windowsill and shook my head no. He pulled on my arm, but when I looked like I was going to start crying, he said, "You're crazy, you know that?" and left.

My mother's brothers, Mike and Stevie, were in the backyard with my father. Like my uncles, my father had taken off his suit jacket and rolled his white shirtsleeves to his elbows. He wore navy blue suspenders and his church tie: a piece of navy blue silk with sky blue dots. He had another tie with a hula dancer under a palm tree painted on it that he wore under a sweater vest when he played with Jolly Joe, and when he put it on, he would ask me to dance the hula for him, and he would laugh and hug me and say when he took me to Hawaii I would put the hula dancers there to shame. My mother would roll her eyes and say the closest he would ever get to Hawaii was that tie. But once, he took me into their bedroom and showed me a picture in a brown cardboard frame that he kept under his socks of him in a sailor's uniform with a real live hula dancer, so I knew he had been there and my mother just didn't know about it.

I listened from the windowsill as my father and uncles talked about the strike. "You need some muscle," Uncle Mike said. "The only things those bastards understand is muscle." My father said the strike couldn't go on much longer. The steel company was losing money, same as the workers, but Uncle Mike said, "They have deep pockets. They'll wait until your children are big enough to work in the mills and take your place." He poked a finger in my father's chest. "They don't give a damn. They need to be shown who's boss." My father took a swig from his beer bottle and looked up. When he saw me, legs dangling from the windowsill, he smiled.

"Hello, Annie," he said.

I stretched my arms out like I was going to jump.

"Wait, I'll catch you." He put down his beer bottle. "Don't move."

Right then, my mother came out to call them in to supper and looked up at me.

"Get down from there."

"Don't make her afraid," my father said. "I'm going to catch her."

"Are you crazy? She'll hurt herself. Get down from there right now," she yelled up at me. "Put your legs back in your room and come downstairs. Right now." She turned back into the house, her brothers following.

My father waited until they were all inside, then he opened his arms. I held out the hem of my gingham dress. And jumped.

MY MOTHER CAME HOME at four-fifteen every afternoon from the pajama factory with a paper bag full of scraps that Babba twisted into rag rugs. She would toss the bag on the dining-room table, then go out onto the back porch and stretch. Everyone thinks their mother is pretty, but Connie wasn't that. Her leanness would be fashionable in ten years, but it wasn't then. Her honey-blond hair and brown eyes were nice enough, but nothing special. But she had a way of looking people in the eye that made them think she could see way down into their soul. Men were mesmerized by that look. My father's union brothers were always asking him if Connie had a sister, and when he would tell her, she laughed derisively. "Which one was that again?" she would ask, only half listening for the answer. Before I knew what the word meant, I knew my mother was sexy.

When she stretched on the porch after work, it was from her fingertips to her toes; unself-conscious and full of delight in her body. If she saw me then, spying on her from behind the porch rocker, she would laugh. "Come here, Annie. What are you doing out here?

Where's your *babba*?" she'd say, and tell me about her day. I think she told me because, as a presumed mute, I couldn't pass on her confidences. Not that there was much to tell. She was stiff, she said, from sitting all day at a sewing machine. The Portuguese women all complained that she was ruining their rate by working too fast. Morty Zuckerman had singled her out to sew a special gift for his wife. "But I did one for myself, too. Look," she said, pulling a light blue chiffon peignoir from a brown bag. It had aqua smocking gathering it in around the waist and aqua polka dots embroidered over the skirt. Like raindrops, I thought. She slipped it on over her dress and frowned. She was pregnant and it wouldn't close around the waist.

On warm days, the doctor next door, Dr. Gresh, would be in his yard, dozing on an old chaise lounge. He and my mother had only exchanged pleasantries since we'd moved in; but toward the end of the summer, from my perch on the windowsill I saw my mother go over into his yard and rouse him. She sat down next to him on the chaise lounge and began talking to him in earnest. At first he seemed startled, but then he sat up and answered her, his face close to hers, as if they were old friends. He patted her hand when she left.

She started working overtime after that, not coming home until eight at night, when she would be too tired for the dinner that Babba had made. If my father wasn't home, and he increasingly wasn't, she would go to sleep.

My father's polka band had begun taking out-of-town gigs, and he came home later and later. From my room, I could hear them fighting when he came in. The same fight every night. "I'm doing it," he would tell her, "so you don't have to work."

"You can make more money in a factory. You're doing it because you love to do it."

"I have to hate what I'm doing?"

"We're going to lose the house," she said. "Music doesn't pay enough."

"You got to trust me."

"Music, Frankie! They're hiring at the silk mill."

The silk mill was next door to the pajama factory. Some of the strikers worked there part-time, watching the sixteen giant spools spinning jacquards. When a thread broke, you had to tie a knot while the machine was still clacking away. And the knot had to be invisible in the pattern or the bolt was ruined. It was tedious and nerve-racking, and most of the workers drank to get through a shift.

"We won't stay out forever. And your brother said he would loan us some money."

"Hah!" Connie said. "You want to be beholden to him? You want him to own our house?"

"He's your brother, Connie. You got to relax. You're working too hard. You're going to hurt the baby."

"How can I relax?"

But then we got a television with the money my mother made working double shifts. Usually, she fell asleep as soon as we turned it on. When Elvis came on *The Ed Sullivan Show*, my father held his hand out and asked, "Dance?" but she pointed to her belly and shook her head.

The strike dragged on, and the union slush fund was running dry, so my father switched to a traveling swing band, the Tri-Tones, to make more money.

"Why can't you work at the Banana House?" Connie asked him. The Banana House was a warehouse, owned by two Greek brothers, where they gassed green bananas, then loaded them onto trucks for delivery around the county. "Mary Gaydos's husband says they're hiring. Why can't you work there?"

My father didn't answer, because that wasn't really the question.

He patted her belly and left for Harrisburg, a five-hour drive away, to play with the Tri-Tones. My mother slept on the couch, waiting for him, but he didn't come home until nine in the morning, and she was already at work.

David started second grade at Sacred Heart in September, and in October I said my first sentence to my mother. I was on the back porch with her when I said it. It was a beautiful evening, and she had come home from work early. She was telling me that she didn't know where we would live if she had to quit her job because of little Frankie when I interrupted her with my demand. "I want to go to school."

She squatted down beside me and looked at me peculiarly, as if a dog had just asked her to pass the rolls. "What did you say?"

She yelled for Babba to come out on the porch and made me repeat what I had said.

Babba listened, indifferently. "So send her to school," she said.

"She talked!"

Babba went into the house and came back with a storybook, *The Arabian Nights*, that we'd been reading together when we'd seen my mother coming up the street from the living-room window. She handed it to me and pointed to the page where we'd stopped.

The passage was about a flying carpet that transports the hero "whithersoever" he wants to be. I hesitated over the big word, sounding it out, then said it again, thrilled with the sound. "Whithersoever he desires to be."

Connie stared at me in disbelief. "She's too little." The horror on her face made me feel ashamed of myself instantly. "It's your fault," she accused Babba. "We can't afford to send her to school now. Not now."

Babba slept with me, and one evening as I was looking over her shoulder in bed, the squiggles on the page she was reading aloud had started to line up in formations that marched to Babba's words. So it wasn't Babba's fault.

"The church will pay her tuition," Babba said, as if that settled things, and went back in the house to start dinner. "Don't be so proud."

I stood frozen next to my mother on the porch. She was crying, but the enormity of my crime made me unable to even touch her hand. When Babba called out that dinner was ready, I slipped away.

Babba and David and I were eating in the kitchen when my mother walked past us, went upstairs, and locked the bathroom door. We heard the water running and running. Babba banged on the door and said she couldn't do the dishes because my mother was using up all the hot water. I was sitting on the floor outside the bathroom when my father came. He called an ambulance.

Connie had to stay in bed for a week. David wasn't allowed to go back to school because we were in mourning, and I spent most of my time in my room looking out my window, pretending I was somewhere else. Which was where I was when they sent David to find me. "You can stop looking." He opened the window and stuck his head out. "*Sputnik*'s not there anymore," he said, as if I had been looking for it, too. "It was on television."

The next day, the President of the United States made the steelworkers return to work, because we couldn't let the Russians beat us to the moon. My mother announced that she was going back to the pajama factory. What if the steelworkers went out on strike again? She couldn't count on my father.

"We could go on the road with the Tri-Tones," he said.

He was kidding, of course, but Connie was incredulous. "With a band? Where would we live?" She motioned at the house as if it were the Taj Mahal in a coal patch. "And the union just got you a raise! Ten cents an hour, Frankie. For God's sake, stop dreaming."

My parents stopped fighting after that, and I went to school, where we were afraid that Russia would use the moon to lob bombs at us. When the air-raid sirens went off, we hid under our desks to protect ourselves from shattered glass. I couldn't stop crying, and the nuns pinned a note on my blouse for my parents saying I was too immature for school, but David ripped it off and threw it away on the way home.

We had a great Christmas, because both my parents were working. The biggest present was the hi-fi my mother gave to my father. It was a console model, made of blond wood with closed-in shelves on the sides for records. The giant speakers were so loud they rattled the windows. My father acted pleased and played jazz records on it. After New Year's, my mother decided the hi-fi made the rest of the living room look shabby. While we painted, Babba went to live with Uncle Mike for what was supposed to be a month, but it turned into fifteen years. We stored the old furniture in the attic, and that, along with my father's clarinet in the blue fur-lined case, became just some stuff I was surprised to find, and had to get rid of, when I sold the house thirty thousand light-years later.

Slam Book

1968

My brother, David Kusiak, is marrying Beatrice Marzak today. I am one of the bridesmaids and Theresa Gojuk is the maid of honor. We are both wearing seafoam gowns and carrying bouquets of tiny pink roses, which we have momentarily laid on the radiator in the bathroom while we hover over a kneeling figure in white chiffon throwing up into the toilet bowl. I pick at a nonexistent splinter on the palm of my hand. Theresa plucks a tissue from the box and thrusts it under the pouf of white.

"I'm all right," Beatrice says, getting up and wiping her mouth carelessly on the back of her hand, smearing her red lipstick. She looks in the mirror. "Jesus, I look like the wrath of God." She grabs the bottle of Listerine and takes a swig. Then she laughs.

"You just have to make it through the Mass," Theresa tells her, rearranging her friend's headpiece and tucking a blond curl under the cap. "People will be too drunk to notice at the reception."

"I'm usually okay by noon," Beatrice says.

We pick up our bouquets and file toward the stairs.

Theresa turns to look at me. "Are you all right, Annie?"

I nod, although I always feel like throwing up when I hear someone else doing it.

Theresa reaches into the satin purse tied around her wrist and pulls out a red-and-white mint wrapped in cellophane.

"Eat it," she says. "It'll make you feel better."

I look at it dumbly.

"It's only a mint, for God's sake. Here, Beets." She pulls out another one for Beatrice. "You smell like the gates of hell."

They laugh. They are best friends. Even though Beatrice is in twelfth grade and Theresa is in tenth with me, she and Theresa are the same age. Theresa was sick for most of the first grade and had to repeat it. She couldn't get the hang of long division and had to repeat third grade, too.

"All right, then," Theresa says. "Are we all ready?" She grabs Beatrice by the arm and they walk down the stairs. I trail behind, carrying the train of Beatrice's dress. We join the ocean of seafoam waiting in the living room. There are ten other bridesmaids, Beatrice's clique. All the popular seniors. Our dresses are long, belted tunics over floor-length skirts. When we were in the bridal shop trying them on, Beatrice made a big deal about how we could wear the dresses again by just slipping off the skirts. I laughed at the thought of twelve of us in these ridiculous dresses showing up at the same time at some function, like a flock of cartoon birds. Beatrice gave me a dirty look, but Theresa said, "She's just a kid, Beets," and everyone ignored me.

When we join the bridesmaids downstairs, they all make a fuss over how beautiful Beatrice looks; then we pile into the cars, decorated with pink crepe paper and dolls wearing the same dresses as us sitting on top of the hood ornaments. I ride in the backseat of the last car. The driver, Kurt Devlin, is the halfback on David's football team. Another teammate, Barry Murphy, closes the door for me and hops in the passenger seat.

"Beets looks good," Barry says.

"His life is over," Kurt says.

"He can finish school. That doesn't change," Barry says.

"Everything else does," Kurt says, referring to the football scholarship to Penn State that David will have to turn down because he has a family to support. Kurt meets my eyes in the rearview mirror. I quickly look out the window. Kurt is angry because my brother was the big hope of their circle of friends. A scholarship to Penn State. Maybe the pros. He would escape the cycle of mine, mill, and mortuary. But now he's let them down. Kurt shifts into gear and we join the slow procession to the church. "Throwing your life away for a piece of ass. What an idiot."

AFTER THE WEDDING, Beatrice moves in with us. The school officials at Warrenside think it will corrupt the morals of the other students if they have to study geometry alongside a pregnant, albeit belatedly married, woman, so Beatrice is forced to drop out. But because David is the captain of the football team, which is on its way to winning the division championship, they decide it won't corrupt anyone to be around him.

Theresa comes over every day after school to see Beatrice. They go into David's room and shut the door, laughing and giggling until David comes home.

Tonight, though, when I let myself in, Theresa comes to the top of the stairs.

"Oh, it's you," she says.

"Hello to you, too," I say.

"Where's David?" she asks.

"How should I know? At practice, probably." On the banister there's a note from my mother, who gets home late from her job at the pajama factory, for Beatrice to start dinner. But my mother doesn't want to cause trouble with David by asking her directly, so Beatrice doesn't do anything. I'll have to make dinner again, which is bad news for anyone eating at our house.

Theresa glares at me.

"What?" I ask.

"Never mind." She turns back to David's room.

I put my books on the dining-room table and tiptoe up the stairs. The door to David's room is open, so I walk over softly and look in. I haven't been in his room since the wedding, and I am surprised to see that it looks as if he doesn't live here anymore. Dresses are thrown over the closet door. Slips and shoes are everywhere. On the nightstand, where there used to be a statue of St. Francis of Assisi that my mother bought after our brother Frankie died, is the bride doll from Beatrice's car. Even the Day-Glo crucifix that used to hang on the wall between the twin beds is gone. Beatrice is on one of the beds, sobbing.

"Is she okay?" I ask. Beatrice has never actually said anything to me since she moved in, so I'm not used to addressing her directly.

Theresa shakes her head and pats Beatrice on the shoulder. She picks up a notebook from the bed and, putting a finger to her lips, closes the door and leads me away from the room. She hands me the notebook.

"What's this?" I ask, opening it up. It's full of loose-leaf pages. Each page has a name at the top with stuff written underneath it. "What is it?"

"It's a slam book," Theresa says. "Look."

She turns to a page with *David Kusiak* written at the top and hands it back to me. "Nice ass!" I read aloud, then laugh and make a face.

Theresa taps the page and I read on. Mostly comments about what a fantastic guy David is, blah, blah, blah; then at the bottom of the page, underlined twice, "Great kisser!" I feel like someone's punched me. I know Beatrice didn't write it.

"Maybe it was before the wedding," I say.

"The book was started this week. Somebody saw him at the slag heap with Franny Giordano after practice," Theresa says. The slag heap is a deserted area outside of town. Carts filled with coke wind through the mill on train tracks and are hauled to the top of a hill. One by one, the carts tip over and spill their molten contents down the slope. Because the lava show is so spectacular, it's the most popular make-out place in Cokesville. It's probably where David got Beatrice pregnant.

"What's she going to do?" I ask.

"What can she do?" Theresa says. "She's screwed."

I wince and turn the page. *Loretta Symms* is written at the top, and I read about Loretta's (the head cheerleader at Warrenside) deft handling of the defensive line. I flip through the pages to see who else I know. The front door opens. It's David.

"What a bastard," Theresa whispers.

I hand her the book, but she shoves it back at me. "Take it."

"What am I supposed to do with it?"

"Just get it out of here. It's like fat on a fire."

I clamp the slam book under my arm. David waits at the bottom of the stairs to let me pass. Although David and I have never had a conversation as equals, he usually kids around with me. He's two years older, and our interaction is limited to him rescuing me from the wrath of our parents: like when he intercepted the note the nun pinned to my blouse saying I would Burn in Hell for All Eternity if I didn't stop drawing snowmen on the cover of my math book. David tore up the note. "That stupid bitch is the one who's going to hell for scaring a little kid," he said.

After that, he convinced our parents to transfer us to public school, even though my mother worried that being with a bunch of Protestants would endanger our immortal souls. My parents do anything he wants, because he's the golden boy, the one for whom everything will turn out perfectly. I'm not immune: I worship him, too.

But since he brought Beatrice home, he's been silent in a way that scares me. I want to warn him about what I've just read, but I know I can't, so when he's halfway up the stairs I give him a wolf whistle.

He turns and smiles. "Hey, Annie."

I stare at him, willing him to read my mind.

He looks concerned. "What's the matter, Annie?"

Nothing comes out, and finally I fake a laugh. "Nice ass," I say.

DAVID AND BEATRICE'S UNHAPPINESS permeates our house. After I'm asleep, the sound of Beatrice's crying wakes me up. My parents' bedroom is at the end of the hall facing the street, next to David and Beatrice's. Then mine, next to the bathroom. I strain to hear what they're saying, but the twin beds are against the opposite wall and the thick maple doors muffle their words. One thing I know for sure: what they used to do every night, what they did to get Beatrice pregnant, they aren't doing anymore.

David stays later and later at school, not even making it home for dinner. Beatrice refuses to come down for dinner, until finally my mother makes me bring her dinner to her room. "It's not for her," my mother explains, in case I'm getting any ideas about what kind of behavior I can get away with. "It's for the baby."

"It doesn't matter to him whether the baby lives or dies," Beatrice says, sullenly picking at the food. "Why should I care?"

I'm supposed to stay until she finishes all her food, which is really boring, so I open a book I brought with me.

"Annie, I'm talking to you," Beatrice says sharply.

I look up, surprised. "What?"

"The kids at school. What are they saying?"

"About what?"

"About *me*!"

"I don't know," I say. The only person who talks to me about Beatrice is Theresa's sister, Margaret, and that's just to find out for Mrs. Gojuk what Theresa does when she comes to our house, because she thinks Beatrice is a bad influence. "Nothing."

"Who's going to say anything to you? Your nose is always in a book." She slams down her fork. "Well, they're not the only ones who can have opinions. I have a few things I can say about them, too." She looks at me slyly. "Did Theresa give you the slam book?"

I squirm. I'd put it between my mattress and box spring and tried to forget about it, but it was like a bogeyman under my bed. "No," I lie. My face turns red.

Beatrice pushes the tray away. "Your mother is a terrible cook. What is this supposed to be? Some kind of fish?"

"It's chicken croquettes," I say. I got the recipe from my mother's *Family Circle* magazine, which she never actually reads. "That's the way they're supposed to taste."

"Well, if you find out what happened to the slam book," she says sarcastically, "let me know. I have a few things I can say about them, too." She throws herself on the bed and buries her face in the pillow.

I pick up her tray. I'll have to throw the food down the toilet so my mother doesn't see she didn't eat anything.

Theresa is coming up the stairs as I go down.

"Beatrice wants the slam book," I tell her.

"No, no, no, no, no! It'll make her crazy." She puts her finger to her lips. "I'll get it from you later."

But she doesn't. She leaves almost as soon as she arrives. The next day at school I hear that she went to the movies with Doug Grace, who is home from Andover for Thanksgiving. I don't even know who Doug Grace is, and at lunch, when I ask Theresa's younger sister, Margaret, she looks at me as if I couldn't name the Pope.

"Douglas *Grace*?" she says. "His father is only the boss of the whole steel company."

"I thought Mr. Heiman was the boss."

"Mr. Heiman is a foreman."

We eat our sandwiches while Margaret lets the enormity of her sister's coup sink in.

"Theresa's going to marry him," Margaret says.

"He asked her?"

"He'll ask her at Christmas. They'll move to New York City so he can work at a bank, and then we'll probably never see her again."

That night, after Beatrice and David's fighting wakes me up, I pinch a dime from my savings can and tape it to the back of the Infant of Prague statue that has been on my bureau ever since I can remember, and say a prayer that Theresa won't marry Douglas Grace and go away.

AFTER FOOTBALL SEASON, David drops out of school. No one is surprised. What's the point of finishing high school if he can't go to Penn State? He gets a job in the meat department at the Acme supermarket, and right before Christmas he and Beatrice rent an apartment, the third floor of a half double. They come to our house for Christmas Eve. Beatrice wears a black velvet maternity dress, which highlights her blond hair and makes her look less whale-like. She flashes a small diamond ring, which David bought her with money he earned at the Acme. She lets her left hand linger on everything, for everyone to get a good look at it. We smile at David approvingly, but he isn't paying attention. No one can get David's attention. It's like he's away on vacation and forgot to take his body.

After dinner, we sit in the living room, eating walnut *kiffel*s and watching the Liberace Christmas special on TV. My dad plays with our new automatic antenna until my mother finally says, "For God's sake, Frankie, if you can't fix it, please just let it alone." There is an urgent knocking on the door and David gets up eagerly to answer it. Theresa rushes in and stares at Beatrice, and together they bolt into the kitchen, murmuring excitedly.

"Switzerland!" Beatrice says suddenly and loudly from the kitchen. "Doug's family is going *skiing*! For *Christmas*? Why didn't he ask you?"

My mother gets up and turns up the volume on the TV. Soon they're talking so low, I can't hear anything anyway.

"Well, screw him!" Theresa shouts. "Screw *him*! *Screw* them *all*!"

My mother looks at me, quick as a hawk, and I reexamine my mound of doughy *kiffel*.

In April, Beatrice and David have a baby girl, Monica. In May, Theresa's brother Steve Gojuk and Paul Szewczak, their next-door neighbor, come home on leave from Vietnam. Paul's parents surprise him with a new Mustang convertible, and every day Paul and Steve pick up David after work and the three of them spend hours driving around town in it. Beatrice spends a lot of time at our house complaining about that to my mother. Complaining about her colicky baby. Complaining about how fat she's gotten, although as far as I can tell, all she does is eat.

Steve Gojuk asks me to go to the sophomore dance. He was the fullback on the football team, so I know David made him ask me.

"You should see the women over there," Steve tells me as he leads me around the dance floor, eyeing my classmates. "They wear silk pajamas that float around their bodies in the breeze."

I tug at the tunic part of my seafoam bridesmaid's dress. My mother took the hem up, so it's a miniskirt, but only a typhoon would make it float in the air. "They wear pajamas in the street?" I ask.

"They're very delicate people," Steve says. "It's a different world there."

Theresa is at the dance with Paul Szewczak, and they go out every night until it's time for him to leave. We double-date with them once. Theresa laughs and jokes like she's having a good time, but I think it's fake. A week after Steve and Paul return to their units, David joins the Marines and volunteers for Vietnam.

"Beatrice and Monica will be fine here," David says to my parents. He shows them the forms that forward his pay into Beatrice's bank account and give Beatrice and the baby free medical benefits. Beatrice and Monica will move in with Beatrice's grandmother Mrs. Herbinko to save on the rent. She'll have to help take care of Mrs. Herbinko, but Beatrice says she doesn't mind. She's seems relieved that David's going. My mother gives him a medal, Our Lady of the Immaculate Conception, which he puts around his neck, but it isn't there when he leaves. He and my dad hug like men do, without any hands. He even kisses me when he says goodbye.

And then he's gone.

The next morning I pull the slam book out from under my mattress. I put it in my book bag and take it to Theresa's house. Margaret answers the door and lets me in.

"Theresa?" I ask.

She points upstairs and shouts, "Theresa! Annie's here."

Theresa comes to the top of the stairs.

I hold up the book. "I have this."

She looks at it blankly. "What?"

"It's the slam book," I say, taking it out of the bag and waving it.

"You can just throw it out," she says.

"It isn't mine," I say.

"Just throw it out."

"I can't."

Theresa comes halfway down the stairs. "Just throw it out. They make new ones all the time."

"They do?" I laugh nervously, then start crying.

"Of course they do." Theresa is beside me suddenly. "What's the matter?"

"Did you see it?" I ask.

"What?" She sits down on the bottom step and pulls the book out of my hand. It's folded back to her page, which I had reread a hundred times. She reads the long entries calling her a slut—actually a stupid slut—slowly. She throws the book on the floor. "Who cares what they think? They'll be here changing diapers and cutting coupons long after I've left this town."

"You can't leave," I say, sick with guilt over my part in it. "If Douglas Grace isn't going to marry you."

Theresa snorts. "You think I have to wait for that jerk to decide I'm good enough for him? I'm leaving by myself."

This idea is new to me. Most of the boys in Cokesville leave one way or another, but the girls just hang around waiting for them to return. "What are you going to do?"

She straightens up. "I'm going to be an actress."

"Don't you have to go to school for that?"

"You just have to look a certain way." She looks pleased with herself. "And get one lucky break. One good role," she says. "Then you're in. I'm not worried at all."

Theresa grabs the slam book and smacks it closed. "They won't be saying 'stupid slut' in three years. They'll be watching me on television getting academy awards. *Begging* for my autograph."

To expose yourself to the rejection of the entire world seems breathtaking to me. I laugh foolishly.

"You don't believe me?" Theresa asks.

"I believe you, Theresa."

Congratulations, Goldie Katowitz

1970

THEODORE CHESLOCK, my *zedo*, came home today. He deserted the family twenty-one years ago, right before the mines shut down. He got up one morning saying he was going to look for work, pulled on his steel-toe boots, packed a lunch with two cheese sandwiches and an apple, walked through the door, and never came back. That was before I was born.

We had no place in dinner conversations for reminiscences, so it was as if he never existed. But he did. Does. He's here now.

His appearance makes me rearrange my idea of family, but also my room, because the equipment he needs to survive will be stored there: oxygen tanks, catheter bags, rubber gloves. We all have to make sacrifices to ensure Zedo's happiness.

I have another grandfather, of course: my father's father. He had a fatal heart attack soon after the mines closed, leaving us warm memories of him as a provider. He went to work every day, did chores at night, went to Mass not only on Sundays but also on feast days. Then he died before he became a nuisance.

In the family's book, he became the standard by which grandfathers are judged. Zedo, if for no other reason than he is still alive, could never measure up.

That is, until yesterday, because that's when he won the lottery. He won the big boy, the entire state treasury. One million dollars. Uncle Mike bought the ticket for him.

"I bought it for him," Uncle Mike said. "So it's part mine. He wouldn't have had the wits to buy one himself. So really, it's part mine."

The big surprise to me was that for the past year Zedo had been living only forty minutes from our house in the state mental institution. The big surprise to Uncle Mike was that, since Zedo was an official ward of the state, his winnings would go to the state hospital system to ensure his care in perpetuity.

"But who," Uncle Mike asked, as he made arrangements for the burden of that care to be shifted from the state, "could better care for a man than his own family?"

Uncle Mike and Uncle Stevie bore Zedo home on a forest green velveteen-finish BarcaLounger in the back of Uncle Mike's new pickup truck. They strapped him in with bungee cords, then they secured the chair to the truck with more bungee cords so the whole thing wouldn't fly out. They put Uncle Mike's sunglasses on him, for appearance's sake only, because it didn't matter if the sun got in his eyes, as he was blind. They put one end of a straw in a can of soda and the other in his mouth to keep the bugs out and then wrapped his hand around the can.

"Clutch on to it, Pop," Uncle Stevie had instructed him, and Zedo must have held that can as if it were his anchor, because it took both uncles and my mother's wheedling to pry his fingers off later.

They'd bought the BarcaLounger with Zedo's winnings.

"Why not?" Uncle Mike said. "He's a millionaire. A rich man. He has the right to park his butt on a nice chair." He rearranged his blue-striped seersucker suit and straightened his tie from the morning's exertions. Uncle Mike was the only man on either side of the family who dressed up for work. What, specifically, that work was, I had learned not to ask.

They'd bought the pickup truck with Zedo's winnings, too. Although, besides the ride home, it wasn't clear how it would benefit Zedo. But Uncle Mike said that from now on it was important that we spend as much of the lottery money as possible, because the state doled it out in an annuity that stopped the instant Zedo died.

"Spend, spend, spend," Uncle Mike instructed us. "It's Zedo's money, and as soon as he dies, that's the end of it. So get him whatever he needs. You, too," he said to my mother. He pulled out a wad of bills that he always had in his pants pocket, peeled off a couple, and put them on the kitchen table. "Get yourself something. Frankie, too," he said, referring to my father, who was working another double shift. I was sure Frankie wasn't going to like his father-in-law roosting in the living room, no matter how much money it meant for us. But Uncle Mike didn't bother asking him. Uncle Mike never consulted anyone.

My first impression was that Zedo wouldn't contribute much to the household besides cash. He had had a series of strokes that left him speechless. Diabetes took away his sight. He was a big man, but he couldn't walk, because his muscles were atrophied from disuse, and although we poked around, we couldn't tell if something was organically wrong or if he just had nowhere to go. He responded to us with a low guttural laugh that turned into a coughing fit, which seemed to propel him out of his new chair. We decided to keep him tied up with bungee cords to control his whereabouts.

After my uncles settled Zedo in the living room and discussed with my mother his care and feeding, we stood around, examining our new boarder.

"It's going to be a lot of work," my mother said.

"You got Annie here to help you," Uncle Mike said, pointing at me.

He went over to his father and kissed him on the head. "Good to have you home, Pop."

"Good to have you home, Pop," Uncle Stevie repeated.

The men looked out the back window to the alley where Uncle Mike's "associate" stretched against the truck, his open leather jacket revealing the holster strapped under his left armpit. We never invited Uncle Mike's associates in for hospitality, because, as Uncle Mike stressed, they were on duty. Uncle Mike checked his watch. "Gotta run, kid." He put on his straw fedora.

Both men left without a backward glance, leaving my mother and me with Zedo. My mother looked at him with a coolness I found interesting. She didn't share her brothers' affection for their sire.

"Well," my mother said, turning brusquely to finish her laundry, "talk to him. He's your grandfather."

I had just graduated from high school, and it was my summer vacation. And although my most ambitious plan was to lie in the chaise lounge reading, I was concerned that entertaining Zedo was going to occupy too much of my time.

"Do you like Irwin Shaw?" I asked. "I'm reading Irwin Shaw now." Irwin Shaw was one of the selections of my father's Great Books subscription series. "I'll get my book and I can read to you. Would you like that?"

He didn't respond, so I got my book and began reading to him. Soon a new noise came from him: snoring. I laid my book open over my chest. As he was sleeping, I thought I could risk a little disrespect and ask him the one question that had been on my mind ever since I learned that he was still alive, that he had won the lottery and was going to live with us.

"Where the hell have you been?" I asked.

Zedo wasn't asleep. He let out a long, low laugh that turned into a coughing fit that I knew would be the musical accompaniment to my summer.

THAT SUMMER I was seventeen. I had no employment offers, no marriage prospects, and, because I had no money for college tuition, no hope of learning how to write. My friend Theresa Gojuk had already run from Cokesville to Hollywood to be an actress. We had made a pact. When I figured out how to do it, I would join her in Hollywood and write memorable screenplays for her to star in. But even though I was overwhelmed with emotion and conflicting desires—the stuff of great literature, I was sure—those feelings hadn't yet formed into words.

My passions found an outlet, instead, in the arms of Dagomar, a local loser whose only qualification for winning my heart was a lack of friends in whom to confide his conquest. Dagomar lived with his family by the armory, in public housing. We never went anywhere. Early each evening, I dodged bouncing balls and lounging elders to get to the two-story barrack he shared with four siblings and his eccentric mother, a redhead with a weakness for cigars and exotic men. Her children were fathered by several different men. At first I thought they were adopted, but they were hers. "The fruit of Maura's loins," Dagomar had introduced them to me, without getting specific. His own father was Maura's high school sweetheart. "Her first love," he confided smugly, showing me a photo of a blond, tattooed man sitting in the saddle of the Harley-Davidson he'd probably zoomed away on when he heard about his firstborn. In a different social set, with more money and education, Maura would have been considered a free spirit. But there's no such thing as a free spirit in public housing.

"Going out tonight, honey?" Maura asked me from the bottom of the stairs as I slipped up to Dagomar's room. She wore something similar to a muumuu, but cut from ethnic cloth. A cloud of cigar smoke surrounded her head.

"We're working on music," I said.

"I want to hear it," she said, moving back to the living room, to her own evening's entertainment—a pediatrician-resident from India who had tended to one of her kids at the clinic earlier that day.

Dagomar looked up briefly from his electric guitar when I pushed open the door. He patted the place next to him on the mattress while he picked out a new composition. He sang in a wavery voice. The song was as amorphous as my writing, but I said I liked it.

He nodded. His white-blond hair fell down his face, and he played a bit more, letting me appreciate his genius before he put the guitar down and got to work on me. We necked for a couple of hours, sucking and moaning until it became tiresome. We had agreed not to go all the way, not to screw up our lives like that. It was evidence of our lack of chemistry that I didn't feel the urge to screw up my life. I thought that somewhere in all that slurping and groaning, I would find the words for my inarticulate passions. I thought I would find the secret to life, so I could write about it. Isn't sex what life is all about? It makes life, so there is a connection. Maybe sex had to be accompanied by something else, but what, I had no idea.

Dagomar reached for his guitar and picked up where he'd left off.

"My grandfather came to live with us today," I said, making conversation, hoping to take our relationship to the next level, maybe imbue our sex with some meaning, if that's what was required. I straightened out my blouse and zipped up my jeans, which were moist despite the lack of chemistry. I made a note of it. My body could be in gear while my heart was in idle. That was important to know, wasn't it?

"My grandfather," I repeated. "I thought he was dead. And there he is all of a sudden. Living with us."

Dagomar nodded, so I knew he'd heard me. But he continued strumming as I let myself out the door.

I BROUGHT the chaise lounge indoors and pulled it close to the BarcaLounger so Zedo could hear me read. I had managed to fob off the more onerous chores, like changing Zedo's diapers, onto my mother. But I figured that as long as I was reading anyway, I might as well read aloud to Zedo, who seemed to like it. And the time I spent reading to him counted as one of my chores.

"How about this?" I said to Zedo, holding up a library copy of Dante's *Inferno.* "It's about hell, which is kind of interesting."

Although it might be rude to read a book about hell to a guy who was headed there, that summer I wanted to read everything: every book I had ever heard someone praise or even refer to in passing. Most of them were from my father's Great Books subscription series. Some I found in the library. Anyway, I thought that perhaps the secret of life and my writing might be in the writings of other authors. It would be a shortcut, especially to finding out how it all ends. When you're seventeen, you know how the story begins, but not how it ends. And you need to know the ending to make sense of what happens in between.

I skimmed the book jacket blurbs. "It's a romp through the highly charged political world of the Guelphs and Ghibellines in medieval Florence," I informed Zedo. My eyelids flickered at the thought of finding something relevant to my cause in medieval Florence. Zedo was doing no better. He grunted. I sighed and opened the book, then closed it again before Beatrice had even tied the blindfold around Dante's eyes.

"It must have been different when you were young, Zedo," I said. The thought that Zedo had had a young life was jarring. I couldn't picture him with all his senses open, married to Babba, going to work, having children. Could this person who was stumbling around, feeling the walls of life for the exit, ever have felt love? Or longing?

Uncle Mike came in just then and, without greeting his father or me, asked where my mother was.

"I was going to ask you about money for tuition," I started. Now that we had some money, it seemed that maybe I would be able to go to college after all. At least there I could bide my time until I figured out how to write.

"We have a lot of details to iron out," he said.

"School starts in a month."

He nodded as if he were listening, reaching for the cellar door. "Under no circumstances do you let anyone in who you don't know," he commanded me. He went down the stairs where my mother was shoveling coal in the furnace for the hot water heater. I heard them argue, then Uncle Mike came back up. He took off his straw fedora and wiped his forehead and double chin with a white handkerchief, and took off his sunglasses to mop his eyes, mole-like orbs that regarded me dispassionately.

He breathed heavily. "No one at all. I know what her angle is."

He patted Zedo on the hand and tousled my hair as if I were a child. I followed him out the door.

"I could use a little spending money until we get the tuition thing straightened out."

He pulled out his wad of bills and flipped through them until he found a suitably small one. He stuffed it in my hand.

"Taking care of Zedo is taking up a lot of my time," I said.

Uncle Mike reached in his pocket and pulled out a couple of rings, taken from one of his clients in lieu of payment. He offered them to me in his outstretched palm. I shook my head. He shrugged and got out his roll again, slipping off a larger bill. "If she comes here, just don't even let her in. Okay? I'm counting on you. We're all counting on you."

I had no idea what he was talking about, but I nodded, pleased with the larger denomination, and went back in the house to continue reading to Zedo. My mother was spooning applesauce into his mouth, using a napkin to catch the part that drooled out. She looked up warily, continuing her task. I pocketed the bill that Uncle Mike had given me.

"Who am I not supposed to let in?" I asked, picking up my book, intending to earn my booty.

"Zedo's wife."

"Babba?"

Zedo smiled at us dumbly.

"No. Someone else. He met her at the hospital. She's a patient. Puerto Rican."

"Puerto Rican! What about Babba?"

"This woman claims she married Pop. She has a license. Until we get it straightened out, the money from the lottery is hers, too."

This was big news. I thought about the fallout from this information. I didn't think she would take the BarcaLounger. After all, that was clearly Zedo's. "What about the truck?"

"That depends on how much she likes going for rides."

I felt the magic carpet of a college education take off without me. I was going to be stranded in some gray life, dyeing my hair red and disgracing myself with colorful men. "What about my tuition?"

"I guess that depends on how she feels about educating you."

"I JUST CAN'T picture them doing it, you know?"

Dagomar was blowing on my left nipple, licking and breathing hard, causing goose bumps to appear on my breast. "Hmmm."

"I mean, they're like retards or something." Maria Esposito, Zedo's supposed wife, had moved into my brother's old bedroom. It was either that or forfeit the lottery money, so Uncle Mike said we had to accommodate her. If I wanted that tuition money, I would have to be nice to her. Maria was a sweet enough woman, with graying hair and black eyes, which she kept closed most of the time, even when she was talking to you. She kept saying she didn't want to cause any trouble, and she didn't. She watched television all day, eyes closed, with Zedo, patting his hand in a familial way that made me jealous at first. I mean, he was my *grand*father, and this woman was a stranger. Well, Zedo was pretty much a stranger, too, but we were connected by blood, however watery that glue. Anyway, he laughed more now that she was there. So she was good for his health, and I didn't have to read to him anymore. Books couldn't compete with television. I made a note of that, too.

Still, when I tried to picture Zedo and Maria cementing their marriage, I just couldn't see it.

"Do retards do it, do you think?" I asked Dagomar, who was still gamely trying to excite me. "Try the other one."

Dagomar obediently shifted his attention to the right breast. He lifted his mouth only to say, "Retards love sex! They don't have the same moral censors that we do."

I snorted: moral censors. Dagomar's conversational gambit, since I forced him into it, was that I had too many moral censors. That if I were really the questing spirit I claimed to be, I would want to have sex with him.

"How do they even know how to do it?" I asked absently. I liked the nipple sucking, but it didn't force life to give up its secrets. My attention kept drifting. Maybe I was expecting too much out of sex.

Dagomar lifted his head. His fair face was blotchy, his eyes were hooded. He pointed to his crotch. "Please," he said.

We shifted awkwardly on his twin mattress. Dagomar was anxious to give up his secrets. But I was deaf or something. I just couldn't hear what he was saying.

MARIA TOOK CARE of a lot of Zedo's needs, feeding him like he was a giant doll baby. She was less meticulous, however, than my mother in making sure that a certain percentage of food found its way to his gullet. Maybe it was because she had her eyes closed and couldn't see her target. He lost a lot of weight quickly.

They laughed a lot together. It was a messy laughter, full of spit-out food and spasms of hilarity they were unable to control. My job became massaging them both to normalcy, rubbing Maria's back until she finished hiccupping and sputtering. I never found out what they found so funny, but it seemed to be what they had in common. They both loved to laugh.

Uncle Mike said he saw no reason why I couldn't proceed with my plans to attend the University of Scranton in the fall. He made his peace with Maria when it became clear she didn't give a damn about the money. She was just happy to be with Zedo. She would agree to finance my education. As I had bad grades and no teacher willing to give me a recommendation, I asked Uncle Mike to make good on his promise to get me admitted as well. He claimed that he had some "chits to call in" at the university and that it would be "no problem." "Just wait for the admissions letter," he said, reaching in his pocket and pulling out a ladies' watch, at least thirty years old, with *Waltham* on the old-fashioned cream face and minuscule diamond chips imbedded in the silver-plated band. I held it to my ear and could hear a reassuring tick. "It's a beauty," he said, curling my fingers around it, and scurried to the car before I remembered to ask for money.

So while I continued with my reading program, I spent most of my time planning my school wardrobe. I figured Maria and Zedo wouldn't mind springing for a little something extra there, too. I wanted to discuss it with Maria, but she had no interest in it. Most of the time, I didn't think Maria was really retarded, as they thought. Glimpses of her seemed so normal. But then she loved Zedo. How normal was that?

And she was cagey, too: she carried her marriage certificate in a pink plastic tube, originally meant as a case for tampons, on a cord around her neck. She never took it off and would clasp it to her if any of us got too close. The same nurse who bought her the case and told her never to let it go told us that Maria had been an orphan in Puerto Rico. But as her town had no orphanage, she was raised in the local insane asylum. It was hard to tell, the nurse said, what part of Maria was all hers and what part she learned from the patients of the asylum.

I found this interesting and would have liked to discuss it with Maria, but when I brought it up, she stroked Zedo's hand, and before long they were lost in their own world of comedy, blocking me out.

I tried to imagine Maria as a normal kid in an insane asylum, but the gray-haired old lady in front of me wouldn't move over for that little girl. All I could see was Maria's mouth opened wide in endless mirth, her eyes closed to the wrong worlds she found herself in, thinking that maybe laughter would transport her to the right place at last.

THAT SUNDAY, Uncle Mike and I sat on the bench in back of the house. On the other side of the alley behind our garden was a ninety-foot-high mountain of strip-mined dirt and slag pockmarked with stunted birch trees and huckleberry bushes. Our own garden, defined by a fence of mismatched boards, smelled of wet wood and the cinders that my father put between rows of tomatoes to keep the weeds down—Cokesville gardening techniques. Maria fussed over Zedo, who had been moved to the backyard to enjoy the late-summer afternoon. They seemed unnaturally content, not laughing for once. If you glanced at them, you might mistake them for a normal couple. My parents were in the house taking a nap. Uncle Mike and I drank beer companionably, right from the bottles. We swung our legs, which didn't reach the ground, hitting the woodpile beneath the bench. I heard little after-movements and knew we had disturbed a mouse family.

"How do you like the truck?" I asked him. It was parked in the alley. His driver leaned against it, occasionally stretching, bored.

"It's not a smooth ride."

"Trade it in."

He shrugged. "In case we have to take Pop somewhere, I should hang on to it."

It was the first time I had heard him express a genuine concern for his father, and after letting that sink in for a moment, and warmed by the beer, I was moved to confide in him my own concerns.

"I don't think I can be a writer," I said.

Uncle Mike took a swig from his bottle. "You can be anything you want. This is a great country. Great opportunities. All you need is hustle. I'm going to see Monsignor Zybatko at the university on Tuesday." He grabbed the beer bottle with three fingers and pointed at me with the same hand. "Tell him about you."

I nodded, not doubting that he would. "Opportunity is one thing," I said. "Hustle is one thing. But writing fiction is like lying. You have to lie and make stuff up, and I don't know if I can do it.

Lie. About people." It was true. Every time I tried to imagine the lives of people I knew, it was like creating fanciful, useless additions to structures that couldn't support them. The whole thing crumbled.

Uncle Mike listened. Although his role was family adviser, it seemed odd to be confessing my moral dilemma to a man who—let's face it—was a hood. Lying was the least of his sins, if there was a hierarchy of such things. We surveyed the bleak landscape of our backyard and the strip mines beyond. The muscles in his face moved. Several times I thought he was going to say something. Finally he did.

"I only went to the sixth grade."

I waited for him to continue with his point, but that was it.

He put his beer bottle on the cinder pile. "Let's take Zedo in. Give your mom a break."

Uncle Mike lifted Zedo from the chair and carried him into the house. Maria let me lead her by the hand. I didn't ask Uncle Mike for money and he didn't offer any. Instead, he kissed me on the forehead and pulled out a charm bracelet from his pocket. It had obscenely large gold charms on it. The charms were engraved with the significant dates and occasions in the life of Goldie Katowitz. One was an old-fashioned typewriter with a moveable carriage. I knew she was a secretary, but Uncle Mike probably thought the typewriter would inspire me to write. He put the bracelet around my wrist. "It's big."

It was big, all right. I shook my wrist and the charms sounded startlingly loud, as if they wanted attention.

"Pure gold," Uncle Mike said.

He straightened out his suit jacket and walked down the path to the alley, where his associate came to attention when he approached. Uncle Mike jerked his head, and they climbed into the pickup and drove off.

I WOKE UP at three o'clock that morning to an absolute silence, like after a gunshot in the woods.

I slipped down the back stairs to the kitchen and opened the door. An August stillness. The full moon gave our garden dignity, highlighting voluptuous contours and hiding the rags that tied the tomato plants to the stakes, hiding the splits my father had sliced into the plants to make them think they were dying so they would produce more fruit before the frost.

Autumnal decay had already begun. I breathed in the tangy air, aware for the first time that the earth's atmosphere enveloped me and was part of my body. It wasn't off in the sky somewhere. It surrounded me, was in me. Life wasn't something that I had to stand on tippy-toe for and steal from the shelf. I was looking in the wrong direction. I just had to reach inside myself, because I was part of everything. In the same way that everything was part of me.

I was part of everything, and everything was part of me. It was the first fact I was ever completely certain of.

I heard a small muffled crying, like a kitten's, and as the night had made me feel as if everything emanated from me, I thought it was me. But then I figured out it was coming from the living room. I turned from the screen door and went to check on Zedo. The moonlight illuminated his figure in the hospital bed we had rigged up for him there. Maria was lying with him. They were naked under the covers. Her black eyes were wide open for once, sparkling with tears. I knew, without checking, that Zedo was dead.

I rubbed her shoulder, trying to imagine what her life would be without Zedo. When a lover departs, does it leave an empty space? Or are you always filled with that person, your soul getting bigger and more beautiful with every person you love? I didn't know.

"He died," she said.

"I know."

She sobbed. "I can't leave him." The pink plastic capsule containing her marriage certificate rested on her exposed breast. "I can't leave him."

I smoothed her hair, which had unraveled from its usual bun. "Maybe you don't have to."

COLLEGE WAS OUT of the question, of course. We had lost our money. If it was ever really ours. Shortly after Zedo's funeral, Uncle Mike was investigated for manipulating the state lottery. His name was in the paper and he went to Florida to lie low. Monsignor Zybatko sent me a personal letter saying that I was a strangely misguided young woman if I thought that the way to negotiate life was via the machinations of a criminal. He quoted a few New Testament passages and tossed in some Aristotle just to make me feel bad. He was a Jesuit, after all. If I wanted to attend the university, I could apply like everyone else. As it was, he would do his best to forget that I was associated with Michael Cheslock when he got my application.

MARIA STAYED with us for a while. She helped my mother keep house, and at night she slept in Zedo's bed. One morning she was sitting in the kitchen, waiting for us to wake up. She was dressed in her good dress, with her belongings packed in the laundry bag she had brought with her from the hospital. She wanted to go back where she knew people and had happier memories. Since Maria had started running around the house naked, moaning her grief, it was okay with my parents. She wasn't a great housekeeper anyway.

Her eyes were shut during the entire ride to the hospital. They stayed shut while she hugged and kissed me goodbye, and she then ran ahead of me into the building, back to another wrong place.

AFTER LABOR DAY, the statute of limitations on my idleness ran out. My father insisted I get a job. And as there isn't much out there for a seventeen-year-old with no skills and the misleading sense of life I was acquiring from the Great Books subscription series, I got work at the pajama factory. My mother coached me: I was to tell the owner that I wanted to sew pajamas until I dropped dead. "Don't tell him you want to go to college," she said. "He won't hire you." Why would he waste time teaching someone to sew who wanted to work only until she had a baby or went to college? My mother herself worked there until she had forced the steel union to admit her last year. She was afraid that because she quit before she dropped dead, our name was tainted with the owner's son, who now ran the place. If he saw me as an undependable character, however, he showed no sign of it when he hired me. "I knew your mother," he said. "You don't look anything like her."

In fact, the owner's son, Richard Zuckerman, was a Harvard graduate who studied literature before coming home to run the family business. He held a Great Books discussion every Friday with the two girls who were saving money to go to the state teachers' college in the winter semester. Since I'd made it clear that I wanted to sew pajamas for the rest of my life, I was excluded. One Friday, one of the college-bound girls announced that Mr. Zuckerman had a question about literature and he would give to whoever could answer it matching funds for one year's tuition. The would-be college girls chirped around, anticipating the question. A year's tuition was a big deal for girls who were earning that tuition at a pajama factory. But they came back from their discussion disappointed. They couldn't answer the question, which was, to me, an amazingly simple one: Who was Tom Wolfe and who was Thomas Wolfe?

"You didn't know that?" I interrupted the girls in the bathroom at break time. "How could you not know that?"

They ignored me. I was invisible.

It was piece rate. I earned ninety-five cents for every bundle of baby-doll pajama bottoms for which I sewed the left-side seam. The material was pink or green, satiny on one side and brushed to a fuzz on the other. The lint got in my nose and mouth, and in a month I was sure I had tuberculosis. I imagined the giant fuzz ball they would find in my lungs. "No wonder!" the doctors would say. "She was much too delicate for this kind of work."

But I didn't have to worry about a premature death. The sewing machines had three needles, which cut and bound the seams at the same time, and I continually broke all three needles at once, redoing lumpy seams, trying to get them straight.

"No one ever broke all three at once," the technician told me.

"Yeah, well."

"You're going too fast," he said, whispering. "The others won't like it if you go too fast. You'll ruin their rate." He jerked his head at the other women, mostly Portuguese and Puerto Rican wives of steelworkers, who deliberately paced their work to keep the price per bundle up. "You'll ruin it for everyone."

Between ruining the rate and breaking the needles, I was soon fired. On the way out, I was reprimanded by the quality-control woman, Francie, a large woman without teeth who wore sleeveless shirts and whose complicated odors blended into a breathtaking stink. "Look at this." She held up a pair of the baby-doll bottoms that I had sewn. "What human being can wear this?" The hole for the left leg was at least two inches smaller than the hole for the right. "What were you thinking of?"

"It's straight," I said, defending myself. "Look, my seam is straighter than the other one."

Since I was fired for cause, I couldn't claim unemployment. I collected my back pay from the office manager, who gave me advice about learning to fit in; then I went to Marzak's bar around the corner to plan my next move. The bar was owned by Gloria Marzak, the mother of Beatrice Marzak, who had married my older brother, David. A Polish woman with a compact figure, starched housedress, and a stiff blond hairdo, she put out a shot and poured me a beer without bothering to card me, then went back to emptying the ashtrays on the bar. She adjusted the antenna on a little black-and-white television on the counter. The Reds were playing the Orioles in the World Series. Various men around the bar drank in silence, grunting when one of the ballplayers did something noteworthy.

"I don't know why they put him in," the man next to me said. "He can't hit. Why would they put someone in the last inning of a critical game who can't hit? Huh? Will you tell me that?"

I didn't know. It seemed so obvious that they shouldn't. The man turned his attention back to the television.

"Buy another one for the lady," he told Mrs. Marzak.

I picked up the extra shot of whiskey, threw back my head, and drank it, washing the taste away with a sip of beer. I coughed.

"You get used to the taste, honey," the man said, without really looking at me.

I might as well, I thought. What was I going to do now that I had proven myself unfit for even the humblest employment? What was I left with?

"You a secretary?" the man asked.

"What?"

He pointed at my charm bracelet. I had never taken it off since Uncle Mike gave it to me, even though it got caught on everything and the clanging charms caused some rude remarks. The gigantic typewriter with moveable carriage dangled from the bottom of my wrist.

"No, I'm not a secretary," I said.

"Oh."

I rubbed the typewriter, and like a genie, the specter of the bracelet's previous owner appeared to me out of nowhere, scolding me for ignoring her.

"I'm right here," she said, wagging a finger, making a racket with her charm bracelet. "*Mein Gott!* Are you blind or deaf?"

She was a small woman with excellent posture and tight black curls who wore stiff hats and white gloves long after it was chic to do so. Who tsked over bad grammar and declining standards. Who could type 85 words per minute on a manual typewriter, 110 on an IBM Selectric. Who had worn red ever since the first grade, when her teacher took her to all the other classes in the school to show them how pretty she looked in the red corduroy jumper her mother had sewn for her. Who cared for her aging mother until her mother died, and then she herself became aged and regretted defining her life by other people's roles for her: Mr. Lerner's secretary, Mrs. Katowitz's daughter, Tommy McLaughlin's girl, until Tommy got tired of waiting for her to live out her other obligations and married Goldie's best friend, Sarah.

I told the man, "I'm between jobs."

Goldie threw up her hands. "Can you *hear* yourself talking?"

"Okay. I'm really a writer." It was the first time I had ever said I was already one, not that I wanted to be one. It didn't feel like a lie. "Okay?"

"That's nice," the man said. "A writer."

"Yeah."

He stuck out his hand and introduced himself.

"What's your name, hon?" he asked when I didn't volunteer it.

I turned my wrist so he could see the charm.

"Goldie?" he asked.

"That's right. Goldie," I said. "Goldie Katowitz."

Little Yellow Dogs

1970

IN THE END, Mrs. Szilborski was glad when they came to take away Mrs. Wojic's little yellow dogs. She was sorry that Mrs. Wojic got depressed about it, but if she couldn't control them, she had no right to keep them.

They terrorized the neighborhood, going in Mrs. Szilborski's flower beds, tearing things up. Howling at night. God, they made the most awful noise. They had no room to run. It wasn't fair to the dogs, Mrs. Szilborski said.

She never actually told Mrs. Wojic that. They were neighbors for more than thirty years, but they didn't speak often. Until the end that is, and that was so crazy it doesn't really count.

It wasn't Mrs. Szilborski's fault. She had always been very friendly and had coffee with every woman on their block, passing time and exchanging news. She got along with everyone, too, and didn't gossip much. Except about Mrs. Wojic. From the day the Wojics moved into the neighborhood, thirty years ago, everyone gossiped about Mrs. Wojic. She brought it on herself. She never had time for *anyone*, not just Mrs. Szilborski, who, as Mrs. Szilborski told everyone, graciously invited Mr. and Mrs. Wojic over when they first moved in. *He* looked like he had wanted to come. He had an eager, friendly way about him, but Mrs. Wojic just smiled and guided him back to the house.

The Wojics were a good-looking couple. He was big and blond, worked in the mills with Mr. Szilborski. She was small and had all these lovely black ringlets. She was very attractive. Beautiful, actually. She was always having children. Nine, she had. You'd think it'd kill her as tiny as she was, but she seemed to thrive on it. She would come back from the hospital in two days and start cleaning windows and beating rugs.

All the Wojic children looked alike, Mrs. Szilborski thought, and she couldn't even tell you how many girls and boys there were; that's how much they resembled each other. Mrs. Wojic didn't pay much attention to them, either, although Mrs. Szilborski thought it wasn't any of her business. Mrs. Szilborski admitted that they all turned out okay, but if Mrs. Wojic was always cleaning, how could she look after the kids? Mrs. Wojic gave her children names from the old country, too: Szczepan, Tekla, Grzegorz. Everyone was trying to blend in, and she was doing her best to stay apart. Why would she want her children to stand out in such a pointless way? The women in the neighborhood talked about that quite a bit.

Mrs. Wojic tried to keep her children away from everyone else, too. You never saw any other children going over to the house to play with them. They played by themselves in the backyard. A few times a ball came over into the Szilborski yard. Mrs. Szilborski would always good-naturedly toss the ball back, and ask them if they would like a piece of cake. Although all the women in the neighborhood prided themselves on having a cake on hand for company, Mrs. Szilborski was known for her chocolate cake, whose secret ingredient was strong day-old coffee instead of milk. She always had one ready in case someone dropped by or for when the paperboy collected his money. Mrs. Szilborski had a son from her first marriage, but she and Mr. Szilborski weren't blessed with children, so she always liked it when children stopped by for a visit. And they sure did love her chocolate cake. But the Wojic children wouldn't stay. They would thank her very nicely for the ball and say their mother didn't allow them in strangers' houses. Can you imagine? They were practically living in each other's backyards and she calls Mrs. Szilborski a stranger.

Mrs. Wojic had those kids cleaning, too. You'd think the Pope was coming for a visit the way they cleaned that house. Not just inside. Mrs. Szilborski (or anybody else, for that matter) never actually saw the inside of her house until the dogs came. But the outside! Mrs. Wojic would hose down the aluminum siding and scour the sidewalks once a month. All those kids were out there, too, sweeping and swabbing and taking care of the garden. The place was never dirty. That's why it was so odd that she kept those little yellow dogs, because they certainly made a mess.

You'd never see the husband much. There was so much work at the blast furnaces he probably worked double shifts. Mr. Szilborski was turning down double shifts all the time. They didn't really need the money. It was just the two of them, since Mrs. Szilborski's son was grown up. They had already saved enough money so Mr. Szilborski could retire a couple of years early. They were going to go to Florida to live, but he died of liver cancer before they had a chance to go. So Mrs. Szilborski stayed put. She thought about going all the time, though. She had some cousins there. They were always writing that she should come down. She couldn't decide.

Mr. Wojic worked right up until the end. He couldn't afford to quit with all those kids. Got them all through college, though. Mrs. Szilborski admired that. Her own son had gone to Vo-Tech.

They were hanging their sheets out one morning when Mrs. Szilborski asked Mrs. Wojic what she planned to do when her husband retired. Mrs. Wojic's dark eyes got shiny. She said they just wanted to enjoy themselves. Alone for a while. Her gorgeous black ringlets had only a tinge of gray in them, and Mrs. Szilborski thought how youthful and pretty Mrs. Wojic still was. Mrs. Wojic seemed so friendly and talkative that Mrs. Szilborski invited her over for some cake, and she probably would've come over, too, if a black Chrysler hadn't pulled up in front of the Wojic house. It was a company car, you could tell by the plates. Mr. Wojic was supposed to retire the next week, so Mrs. Szilborski thought it had something to do with that. But it didn't. It was the company man telling Mrs. Wojic that her husband had had an accident at the mill and wouldn't be coming home. Mrs. Szilborski didn't know that then. She found that out later. She waited in the yard for Mrs. Wojic to come back and have some cake with her. But she didn't. She went into her house and closed all the curtains. Mrs. Szilborski was miffed at the time, but got over it when she found out what had happened.

It wasn't that Mrs. Wojic and Mrs. Szilborski became great friends after that. They didn't. But Mrs. Wojic did come over and talk to her when they were both in the yard. Nothing personal. Just the weather and their gardens. Things like that. She did tell her, though, that since Mr. Wojic was flattened by the beam that came crashing down on him, they didn't wake his body. It would be like waking a pancake, she said. She told Mrs. Szilborski that with very little emotion, even though Mr. Wojic had been dead only a few months. It took Mrs. Szilborski almost a year after her husband died not to cry when someone mentioned him. But Mrs. Szilborski thought that Mrs. Wojic was a stronger person than she was. Sometimes small people can amaze you with their strength. And Mrs. Szilborski thought her neighbor was doing okay, really, and when the little yellow dog came by the Wojic house, and Mrs. Wojic sort of adopted it, Mrs. Szilborski thought it would be good for her. To be honest, Mrs. Szilborski often thought of getting a dog herself, but she wasn't raised with animals and she didn't know how to take care of them. But they sure looked like a lot of fun, and to tell the truth, Mrs. Szilborski had been a little lonely since Mr. Szilborski died, so she was glad when the little fella came to Mrs. Wojic's house.

Mrs. Wojic didn't have much time to speak to Mrs. Szilborski after the dog came. She was always walking him, or feeding him, or brushing him, or talking to him. She never paid much attention to her children, so it seemed a little odd that she spent so much time with this mutt.

She didn't spend as much time cleaning, either. She never hosed down the house or scoured the sidewalks after that dog came. She didn't get dirty or anything. She didn't. She just seemed to lose interest.

Mrs. Szilborski was thinking that maybe she should go to Florida to live with her cousins when the damnedest thing happened. Another little yellow dog came to live at Mrs. Wojic's house. It had that same friendly and frisky quality the other one had, and Mrs. Szilborski thought they might be from the same litter. She asked Mrs. Wojic about it, and Mrs. Wojic said the dog just sort of appeared on her doorstep and looked at her with these big eyes. What could she do? Mrs. Szilborski told her she should call the animal shelter, that's what she should do. Mrs. Wojic was shocked. You know what they do to animals there? she asked Mrs. Szilborski. They kill them, she said. Mrs. Szilborski told her she knew that, but Mrs. Wojic couldn't be expected to take care of every stray that happened by. The other dog had already eaten up Mrs. Wojic's garden, and at the risk of sounding unneighborly, Mrs. Szilborski told her the dog was making trips into hers. Two dogs would overrun them. Mrs. Szilborski told her she did think it was kind of funny that the only kinds of strays that wandered onto her property were little yellow dogs. Mrs. Szilborski laughed, but Mrs. Wojic looked at her neighbor solemnly and put her hand on Mrs. Szilborski's arm. She asked if she could come into Mrs. Szilborski's house and talk to her in private.

Mrs. Szilborski was delighted. She had just baked a cake that morning. She baked a cake every week, but usually had to throw them away when no one came to visit.

She was doubly glad she had cleaned the kitchen yesterday. She motioned for Mrs. Wojic to take a seat at the kitchen table while she put on a pot of coffee. The new chocolate cake was like a jewel on the cake dish in the middle of the table. She was so proud of how everything looked, but Mrs. Wojic didn't seem to notice. She had her hands folded in her lap and was staring at them. Mrs. Szilborski thought she must be thinking of her poor dead husband, and went over to her and hugged her gently. Mrs. Wojic looked up at Mrs. Szilborski hopefully. She asked her if she'd noticed anything unusual about either of the dogs. Mrs. Szilborski didn't know much about dogs and told her that. Except for the fact that they looked so much alike, they seemed like ordinary dogs to her. Mrs. Wojic looked truly forlorn. That's just it, she said, they looked so much alike. She wasn't sure, and this is where it got really unbelievable to Mrs. Szilborski, Mrs. Wojic wasn't sure which one was her husband!

Well! Mrs. Szilborski asked her to explain. Maybe she misunderstood her. They'd had a discussion in bed, Mrs. Wojic said, only a few months before Mr. Wojic died. All the children had made homes of their own and he would be retiring in a little while and they would finally have time to enjoy each other and enjoy life. They were so happy. So happy, she said, that she was scared something would happen to take it all away from her. And she started to cry. Mr. Wojic tried to reassure his wife, but nothing could shoo the black fog that had come into the room. He tried to make her laugh, she said, and said she wouldn't be so lucky to get rid of him like that. He would come back as something else to be with her, he said.

Then they started making up animals that they looked like and she finally started to laugh. She told him he looked like a yellow mutt. They both thought that was funny, and laughed until Mrs. Wojic was able to fall asleep.

Mrs. Wojic hadn't thought about it again, she said, until the first yellow dog appeared at her door. She was scared, she said. After all, she was a good Catholic and didn't believe in this sort of thing. She didn't even take it in at first. She slammed the door when she saw the dog out there when she went to get the morning paper, and then she prayed her Rosary. But it was just the sort of dog she thought Mr. Wojic would look like, and when it was still there at suppertime, Mr. Wojic let it inside. Everything was just fine, she said, until this *other* yellow dog showed up. Now she didn't know which one was Mr. Wojic.

Well! If this wasn't the craziest thing Mrs. Szilborski ever heard! She wished her Stanley were alive. He would have known what to say. But she sure didn't. And now she had this batty woman right there in her kitchen. She told Mrs. Wojic she had a hairdressing appointment downtown and had to run, but would talk to her later. Mrs. Wojic went back to her house a little happier, but Mrs. Szilborski never spoke to her again. After that day, whenever Mrs. Wojic was in her yard, Mrs. Szilborski made sure she was in her house with the curtains pulled. She kept watch, though, to make sure Mrs. Wojic didn't do anything crazy to her property.

She never did do any harm to Mrs. Szilborski's property, but those two mutts of hers sure did. They completely overran her garden and went to the bathroom everywhere. They kept her up all night, too, with their yapping. Mrs. Szilborski wasn't the only one complaining, either. Almost everyone on the block had asked Mrs. Wojic to do something about them, but she wouldn't discipline them at all. Finally, Mrs. Szilborski couldn't take it anymore and called the animal shelter. She figured Mrs. Wojic probably didn't have licenses for them, and she didn't. The truck came to get them while she was working in her garden. You've never seen such a carrying on. Mrs. Wojic never even cried like that when her husband died. Mrs. Szilborski felt a little sorry for her, but what could she do? She really should've been in a home, anyway, she was so crazy.

Mrs. Wojic never came out to her garden anymore. Mrs. Szilborski hardly ever saw her again after that, to tell the truth. The curtains were always pulled, and if Mrs. Wojic went out, Mrs. Szilborski stayed inside.

It wasn't long after that, a couple of months only, that Mrs. Wojic died. Bad heart. Mrs. Szilborski never knew she had a bad heart. Of course, Mrs. Szilborski didn't know her very well.

The other day, the craziest thing happened. A stray mutt came to Mrs. Szilborski's door. It was small, with dark curly hair and the brightest black eyes you've ever seen. Mrs. Szilborski would've kept it. She kind of liked the dog, actually. But she wasn't raised with animals and wouldn't know how to take care of it. She called the animal shelter and they came and got it. They said they were having a real problem with strays lately.

That year Mrs. Szilborski's newspaper boy graduated from high school, and nobody else was willing to take the route. She would have to buy her newspaper at the 7-Eleven. It was just as well, she said, because he was the only one who ate her chocolate cake and she was getting tired of making it.

Annie Kusiak's Meaning of Life

1972

I WAS SURPRISED to wake up that morning, because I had taken precautions against it the night before: a dozen sleeping pills, a fifth of vodka. At midnight, I'd poured out three bowls of food for Roosevelt, my dog, in case it took them that long to find me, then deliberated before deciding on clean pajamas as appropriate attire, hoping attention to detail would give me an edge in the afterlife that I hadn't enjoyed in this one.

At first I wasn't sure I was alive. My stupor felt like a swim through a polluted, dark canal. The sun cutting through my dreams could have been the light at the end of the tunnel I had read about. But instead of loved ones beckoning and welcoming me into Paradise, silhouetted against the glare, I saw Roosevelt. He was pawing at the door, whining to get out. I felt more hungover than dead. After a blurry moment, I realized the phone was ringing. If I was dead, I wasn't in heaven.

"Okay, boy. I'm coming."

I wrapped my green terry robe around my soiled pajamas and shuffled toward the door, my feet sliding on something wet. Roosevelt had peed on the floor. He looked up at me sheepishly.

"It's okay, boy."

I opened the door and Roosevelt rushed out. Three copies of *The Boston Globe*, my employer since I'd dropped out of Tufts last spring, were on the stoop. The *Globe* had fired me for falling asleep in a city council meeting I was covering. Not only did I fall asleep, I fell off my chair. I gathered up the newspapers. The latest was dated August 15, 1972. I had knocked myself out for three days with the pills and booze, becoming incompetent in death as well as life. A feeling of shame and futility overwhelmed me. The ringing telephone persisted.

"All right!"

I let the papers drop on the porch and went into the dining room to look at the phone, willing it to stop. It didn't.

"For God's sake." I lifted the receiver. "What?"

"The phone rang fifteen times. No one lets the phone ring fifteen times before picking up. What's going on over there?"

It was Ben. I sat down. In the two weeks since he'd told me he needed to marry a Jewish girl and we would have to get on with our—separate—lives, I had gone through all the stages of grieving I could remember, even making up this last one of suicide. I resented him intruding on me, trying to make me feel anything at all, even if it was just guilt.

"I know you were fired, Annie. I called the paper. What's going on? I'll never forgive myself if you fall apart over me."

I flicked dried vomit off my collar. He thought I was falling apart over him, which wasn't true. He was handsome, but my heart didn't flip when I saw him. Not anymore. And he possessed specific faults that I'd noted even when we were talking about marriage last year, when we were supposedly blindly in love. For example, I found his liberal politics patronizing. His driving drove me nuts. He actually obeyed the speed limit, not even giving himself the ten miles per hour the cops allowed. Mostly, though, I hated the way he was right that our plan to refashion me into a perfect Jewish wife would be a hard fit. When the ghettos of Poland were being trampled, my ancestors were on horseback; his were on foot. The difference in seating arrangement had eventually proved insurmountable.

It wasn't Ben I missed, though. I missed being with a nice Jewish man who gave me entrée into a special and defined club. Jews were a definite thing. They ate gefilte fish, the most horrible food on the face of the earth, and they all knew it, but they stuck by it, because it was their fish. I liked that kind of loyalty. They questioned everything: right and wrong; the nature of a God who could treat His chosen to such an astounding variety of cruelty, which they accepted as proof of His special attention to them. God was with them. I wanted to be part of a people who had access to that kind of attention.

I stared at the phone. I used to imagine that people killed themselves in a fit of passion. Who would have thought it could be the opposite? That it was possible to feel so little that taking a lot of pills and booze only ratified a done deal?

"I'm not coming over. You're just doing this to make me feel guilty. I know all about guilt tricks."

It was mean of him to rub it in. He was Jewish, and I wasn't.

But if I wasn't Jewish, what on earth was I? My life had no meaning. When I'd enrolled at Tufts two years ago, I took care to erase the footsteps behind me. I couldn't go back. But I hadn't moved forward. If my suicide had succeeded, my obituary would have read: "Annie Kusiak, 19, was found dead today," followed by two inches of white space.

"I love you, Annie."

"What are you talking about?"

"I don't mean 'I love you' love you. I mean, I love you like a friend."

"Thanks."

"You need help, Annie. You're taking our breakup much too hard. You should see my cousin Mel."

"You never mentioned a cousin Mel," I said, thinking he was trying to fix me up.

"He's a psychiatrist."

Roosevelt was scratching on the door, trying to get back in, and for a moment I tried to see myself through my dog's eyes. He probably saw me as some sort of magician. A door-opening, food-dispensing magician. A PEZ dispenser for canines.

I opened the door and Roosevelt ran in with the same enthusiasm with which he'd run out. I envied his ability to be happy, even while at the mercy of a fickle magician. I envied my dog. Maybe I did need professional help.

"I'm going home for a few days, Ben." I thought of it right then, but said it as if I were already packed. That's what a normal person would do, I thought. When you need to regroup, you retreat to the familiar.

"Do you think that's wise?"

"They're my parents, for God's sake."

"They're peasants."

"God, that's so arrogant."

"I just mean they have no idea who you are. They don't know the real you."

I stroked Roosevelt. "And that would be who?"

"What do you mean?"

"Nothing. Just a joke. Really, I'm okay. I'm going to be okay." I forced a laugh, disappointed that Ben didn't have a synopsis of the real me handy. "You weren't that devastating, you know."

"The sex was great," Ben said, whispering so his father, with whom he shared an office in the family's medical supply company, wouldn't overhear.

"You're so romantic," I said.

Now that I had decided to go home, for whatever feeble succor that would provide, I wanted to be there immediately. It was a six-hour drive from Boston to Cokesville.

"I can be there in ten minutes," he said.

I had an awful image of myself married to Ben, running out of excuses not to have sex with him, just like I'd heard Jewish women did once they were married. "I want to hit the road," I said, and hung up, and then, as if it made things final, unplugged the phone.

THE RIDE FROM Boston to Cokesville, Pennsylvania, is all turnpike and interstate until exit 68 on Route 80; then a fairly old two-lane through rolling farm country. Everything seems pastoral, when suddenly the trees become stunted, the houses crabbed, and the sky turns cadmium orange, like on Mars. After a sharp curve, the road begins to descend along a ridge looking down into the Catawissa River valley. The riverbanks are lined with monstrous smokestacks and brick buildings whose windows flash with sudden blasts of burning light. Dry gears and rail switches grate. It's as if the earth opened up to reveal Cokesville Forge, which runs along the river to the horizon, the town behind it dwarfed and incidental. I drove down the mountain, and when I got closer to the mills, I turned up my car radio to drown out the moaning of cooling steel. Why had I come back?

Seventeen church spires probe into the brown atmosphere of the downtown—looking for God, but finding soot, which rains like manna on the southside row houses. An inch of soot on the windowsill means a regular paycheck. Two inches means a fat one. As I drove across town, I expected to see Annie Cheslock, my *babba*, who had moved back in with my parents when I left, scrubbing the sidewalk like the other old ladies. But she was in the kitchen, peeling potatoes. Potatoes were everywhere. Pots of white tubers lined the counters and stovetop. Cold water from the faucet splashed over a colander into which Babba plopped another spud.

We would have to clean up the mess before my mother, a spare woman who hated excess, got home. I hugged my grandmother around her thick belly. "Babba."

She continued working. "I know you're there, Annie, but I got to finish this before your mother gets home. She's so changeable. I thought it was a good idea this morning, but by the time she gets home, well." She sighed and looked up from her work, scared of her daughter's chameleon nature. "It will be wrong." She put the peeler on the counter and peered at me, trying to decide if I was flesh and blood or the phantom who regularly conversed with her. "Annie. My dearest, most precious angel."

I took her hands in mine. My mother said Babba had been "good" lately, which meant that she hadn't displayed the obsessive behavior I was witnessing now. Once she got started on something, she couldn't stop. My mother would have Babba back on the seventh floor of St. Luke's Hospital tonight if she saw any signs of this.

"Let's slice the potatoes," I said. "We'll make French fries. And freeze them. What do you say?" I said it brightly, as if I had looked forward all day to slicing cold potatoes instead of putting my head in Babba's warm lap.

Babba looked at the potatoes as if seeing them for the first time, fear in her face. "I had a dream about you last night," she said. "Every time I went to sleep, I had the same dream. You were in trouble." She held up a potato and peeler, searching for the magic they'd possessed moments ago, "I thought these would save you." She shook her head. "I'm just a stupid old woman."

AT FIVE-THIRTY the next morning, I stood sleepily in the kitchen doorway as my mother packed lunches for herself and my father. My parents were working double shifts at the mill and I'd fallen asleep by the time they came home the night before. My father grunted hello and went outside to wait in the car.

My mother poured coffee into two thermos bottles. The red plaid one was mine from grade school. "You don't call for a month, then suddenly you're here. Why aren't you at work?" She put the bottles and sandwiches in two tin lunch boxes. She pressed my arm, because I wouldn't look at her. I shook her off.

"I'm on sabbatical."

THERE WAS no reason not to become Jewish just because Ben and I were no longer getting married. Why did I need to marry a Jew to become one? I went to see Rabbi White, resident at the state university extension school in Cokesville. He carried himself casually, athletically, not with the studied awkwardness of the rabbis I had met during my year and a half with Ben.

"Do you know what it means to be a Jew?" Rabbi White asked.

"Jews are the chosen people. That's impressive."

"Chosen?" he said. "Some chosen. People hate you just because you're a Jew. They kill you. Just because you're a Jew. Have you forgotten the Holocaust? And when they're not killing, they're hating you, anyway." He made a swirling motion with a hand, trying to scoop up the goyim's hate. "Why in God's name would anyone choose that for themselves? Is there something wrong with you?"

"I wanted to marry a Jew."

"Ah, marry. That's different. When do you want to get married? Do I know this boy?"

"We're not getting married anymore."

"So then, why?" He spread his hands out in front of me.

"I just want to convert."

Rabbi White narrowed his eyes. "Jewishness is culture, not just a religion. What's wrong with your own culture?"

"That's the part I love. The culture. Jews have that modern-art thing. It's so rational. You don't hang pictures on your living-room wall of saints holding their own heads in their hands. You don't have glow-in-the-dark virgins spying from your dresser. You don't have . . ."

He wagged his finger. "You can't get just the culture. You have to take the religion."

"I don't mind the religion."

"What about Jesus?"

I looked at him, dejected. Didn't they want more players on their team? Catholics were always laying traps to convert people. Didn't he want to bag a convert who wasn't forced into it by marriage?

He leaned forward, searching my eyes. "I'm converting another woman from Sacred Heart parish. Mrs. Szilborski."

I knew Mrs. Szilborski, a sour old woman who lived across the street from the Gojuks. She had never tipped Steve Gojuk when he'd delivered her newspapers, and she poisoned dogs that peed on her shrubs. "Why are you converting her?"

"She doesn't really want to." Rabbi White shrugged. "God appeared to her and told her to convert."

God was appearing to Mrs. Szilborski. What were God's criteria for choosing people? "Is there anything I can do?"

He opened and clapped shut an appointment book. "Come

back tomorrow at four o'clock. You and Mrs. Szilborski. I'll do you together."

FOR A WHILE when I was four, a kindly gentleman would wake me up in the middle of the night. He sat on the rocking chair by the window. The wind through the maple tree just outside my window blew the curtains and obscured his face, but I never thought to ask who he was. When I heard his voice—"Annie? Annie, are you awake?"—I would look for the alarm clock to see the time, but it was never on the dresser where it belonged. It would be on the floor by my bed or on the windowsill. Once, it was on the dresser, but the dials were spinning round and round. I remembered that I laughed. He told such funny jokes. He always asked me about my day, talked about the things I wanted to. I laughed so hard I would hiccup.

I wasn't frightened while he was there. It was only after I casually mentioned my visitor at breakfast one morning and saw the panic in my parents' faces that I cried.

"What's the matter? What's wrong?" my father asked as I sobbed and struggled to remember every detail for his benefit. He was scared, I know now, that he had sired a fragile creature who would forever need tending. Like Babba.

"David didn't see anybody, did you, David?" he asked my older brother.

My mother shoveled more bacon onto my father's plate. "Annie reads too much. She's only four." She looked accusingly at Babba, who was crocheting yet another elaborate dress for the Infant of Prague statue on her dresser.

"I didn't teach her to read," Babba said. "She taught herself."

"You're reading to her all the time."

"Reading, yes," Babba said. "Teaching, no."

"No more reading."

"Too late," Babba said. "She can do it herself."

My parents gave me chores to divert me from my perplexing vice. I had to sweep all the rooms upstairs. But under each bed I hid a book. Every Saturday morning I walked with David to the library and exchanged my five dusty books for five new ones, which I would have read by Sunday night, clasping each to my chest when I was finished, staring up at the slats of the bed frame, wondering at the worlds the author had whispered into my ear. My mother scrutinized me for signs of sensitivity. I had to clean downstairs as well. The excitement in my soul was dimmed with soapy water and dust bunnies. Everyone relaxed. I was going to be normal. Soon no one even remembered that I had ever had a night visitor.

"WOULD YOU MIND if I became Jewish?" I asked Babba.

Babba was always happy when I came to visit. We stayed in our bathrobes all morning, drinking pots of decaf and feeding anti-bad-breath biscuits to Roosevelt, who rolled around on the floor, belly up, hoping for a scratch. Babba seemed calmer, her restless hands content around a hot mug.

"Why should I care?"

"I thought it might mean something to you. No one in our family is Jewish."

"My first husband was a bear," Babba said, trying to be helpful.

"What do you mean, a bear?" I didn't know my grandmother had been married before she moved to America and married Theodore Cheslock, my *zedo*. "You mean he was hard to live with?" I asked, intrigued with the bear suddenly perched in our family tree.

"I mean he was a dancing bear. He came through our forest in the Dnieper with the Gypsies. Skinny old bear. A party hat falling off one ear." She chuckled, remembering her first love. "I gave him my bowl of turnips and that was that. He didn't carry food in his satchel like other bears. He carried books. He read me to sleep every night." She smiled like a young girl, like the famous beauty she once was. "No one moved through life like he did."

"I wonder how they train bear cubs to dance?" I asked.

"They make them walk on hot metal." Babba put up her hand impatiently. "He told me. Pretty soon, they know how to dance, and then they don't need it." She looked around the room for something else to occupy her hands, making a clicking sound with her tongue. Then she focused on me and seemed to settle down again. "I was just saying, though. Just because I married a bear, you don't see me becoming one myself."

MRS. SZILBORSKI AND I met Rabbi White at his office for our first lesson. I had brought Roosevelt, but he stayed in the hallway, barking.

Mrs. Szilborski squinted at Roosevelt. I knew that she carried Mace in her pocketbook, because a year ago she had blinded Roosevelt with Mace while I was home for a visit, walking him. She was lurking behind a bush and suddenly *pfish*, right in his eyes. She'd mistaken him for a dog that had peed on her azalea. After much shouting, Mrs. Szilborski finally admitted her error. But then she shrugged and put the Mace back in her apron pocket. "Who's to say he won't pee on my azalea tomorrow?"

"Is there some reason you brought your dog to a religious ceremony?" Mrs. Szilborski asked now, holding her pocketbook in front of her like a shield. "Animals don't have souls."

"This isn't a religious ceremony, is it?" I asked.

Rabbi White pulled his attention away from a book opened in front of him. His shoulders and eyelids drooped. "If you were a Jew in Europe in 1939, your names would be etched here. Mary Szilborski. Annie Kusiak. Your husband. Your parents. All your children." He held the book so we could see that he was looking at a black-and-white photograph of a Plexiglas wall covered with numbers: the Holocaust Memorial in Boston, the caption read.

"They would not have been," Mrs. Szilborski said. "We weren't Jewish, and neither was any of our family."

"I'm saying, if something like this happens again and you're Jewish, you will be up there." He looked closely at me and then at Mrs. Szilborski. "You will be marched to the chambers, the camps, and you will die. Just because you're a Jew. I want you to reflect on the implications. I want you to be clear about why you're doing this."

I only wanted an identity. Why was he making it so grisly?

Mrs. Szilborski puffed herself up. "Well, I'm only a convert. It's not as if I were a Jew forever. I was born a Catholic, and I have the papers to prove it."

"They won't make distinctions," Rabbi White said.

Mrs. Szilborski looked upward. "God told me to convert. Do you think He would tell me to do something that would kill me?"

"It's His specialty," he said. He went out into the hall and patted Roosevelt, then wandered away.

Mrs. Szilborski and I faced each other. I tried to feel kindly toward the older woman, whose first husband had died in Poland before she came to America and married Stanley Szilborski. Her only son, Joseph, was from her first marriage. He was as old as my father, and from a distance he didn't seem the type to give his mother much comfort. He was a big man who wore his blond hair in a buzz cut. It must be gray by now, I thought. He came to his mother's house on Sundays to cut the grass in the summer and shovel snow in the winter. Even in the dead of winter, he never wore a hat and was always taking clothes off, as if they oppressed him. Coats and shirts would be strewn carelessly on the lawn no matter what the season. Although I knew he was married, he never brought his family to see Mrs. Szilborski. It had never struck me as odd until now.

"I wouldn't be doing this if God hadn't specifically requested," Mrs. Szilborski said.

"I know, I know. God appeared to you." I was jealous of Mrs. Szilborski for being singled out for special treatment, for having such a clear mandate. "Did He say why He wants you to be a Jew?"

"It's not as if we have long conversations. I couldn't believe it myself. I didn't think I heard Him right. A Jew! What do I know about Jews? The only ones I've ever known were . . . I don't know . . ." Her voice trailed off. "I asked Him to repeat it, and He got quite testy. He's not the kindly old gentleman you'd think."

Rabbi White came back. "Do you ladies want to get a cup of coffee? Have you decided to go through with this? We should talk about something that Mrs. Szilborski brought up: Do animals have souls? It's a good place to begin our lessons."

ON FRIDAY my parents worked a single shift and returned from the steel mill early. Babba had dinner on the table. It could be any Friday, I told myself, smiling at my mother first, then my father, as they sat down. They smiled back. They can't tell, I thought with relief. I didn't want to hear how right they were that I should never have left Cokesville. I scooped a huge portion of French fries onto my plate.

"I got a call from Ben today," my mother said suddenly. "At work. They pulled me off the line to take his call. He said it was an emergency."

"Oh, Ben." I pushed a French fry into a pile of ketchup. "Did he tell you?"

"Tell me what?"

"Did he tell you we broke up?" There. It was out.

"He didn't say that. Did you? Break up?"

My face felt warm. "Did he tell you I was fired?"

"Were you? Fired?" She put her fork down and stopped pretending to eat. "Annie, what's the matter? What's happening?"

I wished I could tell them, but they would accept my failure as proof that they were right. Who did I think I was, trying to be something I was not? I started to cry and put my head in my hands. Babba started to cry sympathetically.

My mother put a hand on my arm, trying to calm me.

"What did he tell you?" I asked between gulps.

"He said you tried to kill yourself."

"What?" I stopped crying. "Why did he say that?"

"He went to your apartment and found the empty bottles by the bed. He said he knew something was wrong." She scrutinized me, looking, I knew, for signs of that dreaded sensitivity.

"What do you think?" I asked. "Do you think something is wrong?"

"I only know what you tell us."

"I know one thing," my father said. "You're not staying in this house unless you get a job."

"Fine."

"It's for the best," my mother said. "You get so introspective. It's not healthy to think so much. No one's ever accomplished anything by thinking. And it makes you so unhappy."

"Everyone in this house works," my father said. "No one is too good to get his hands dirty."

"You're too reflective. Too sensitive." My mother glanced over at Babba. "Maybe you should try something besides writing. Get out in the sunshine. That'll drive away the demons."

"You have to get a job," my father said. "You're too big to sit around doing nothing."

"I said, 'Fine.' "

BY THE TIME I was nine, I had read all the fiction in the children's section of the library and began grabbing handfuls of nonfiction and hiding them under the beds upstairs. One of these books was *The Child Philosophe* by Schmulig Ganz. It was written in 1953 and had been checked out only once. Schmulig asked lots of questions, and I spent a lot of time lying under the bed slats trying to figure out the answers. For example, if you saw a friend steal a quarter from another kid, was it right to squeal on him? Would you talk to him and tell him to give back the quarter? What if he wouldn't? What if it was a hot day and he stole it to buy a soda? What if the other kid was rich and wouldn't even miss the quarter? Was stealing always wrong? Was anything ever completely right or wrong?

That was an easy one: all that was at stake was a quarter. A harder one was this: If you were a gentile during the time of the Nazis, would you have helped your Jewish friends if the result was that you and your family might be killed? I didn't know any Jews when I was nine. Why were Jews people who had to be protected and hidden?

When I met Ben Livingston and his friend Marcia Bloom at Tufts, the word "Jew" fleshed out. They were like anybody else: like Italians without the great cooking, I thought, glad that they didn't need my protection and that I didn't have to make the choice.

I CALLED Ben.

"So, I saw a rabbi. He's at the state university right here in Cokesville."

I could hear him breathing, but he said nothing.

"I'm converting, Ben."

I waited a few seconds.

"Ben?"

"Yeah?"

"I said I'm converting."

"Are you crazy? Why do you want to do that?"

"Ben, can I come see you? I'm at my parents' right now and they're driving me crazy, you know? Saturday, my God, and they have nothing to do. Can I come over? I can be there in five hours if I drive fast."

"I have my evening planned out already," he said.

"So? Don't you want some company?"

I strained to hear what was going on in the background. "Is someone there?" I asked.

"Yeah. Marcia's here," he said.

"Marcia Bloom? So? It would be good to see Marcia."

"We're having a dinner party," he said, "with some friends."

"So? I'm your friend."

He took a deep breath and coughed. "I'm sorry, Annie." And then he hung up.

I KEPT my appointment with Rabbi White, but I told him when I arrived that this was the last one. I just didn't think I was cut out to be a Jew.

We faced each other across his desk, hands folded in front of us.

"Where is Mrs. Szilborski?" I asked finally.

The rabbi shrugged. "God appeared and told her to stop the lessons. 'Stop the lessons!' He says."

"And you believe her? You believe that God is actually talking to a woman like Mrs. Szilborski?" I was indignant.

"That's between God and Mrs. Szilborski. God doesn't tell me who He talks to or what He says."

"You're a rabbi. What do you think He's doing? Why's He spending all this time with her? She's a mean old woman who poisons animals and whose own family doesn't like her enough to come and visit. Why her?"

Rabbi White slapped his hand on the table. "Why *not* her? I'm a rabbi. I don't have the answers. I only have the questions."

I PACKED UP my few things and threw Roosevelt in the car to drive back to Boston. My parents were at work, so I didn't have to deal with tedious explanations. I couldn't see any future beyond my ride home. Babba seemed much better, swiftly cleaning the house from room to room, not staying in any one place or repeating one motion long enough to arouse suspicion. She was able to stop dusting and give me a kiss goodbye.

"My dearest, most precious angel," she said, stroking my hair.

"Whatever happened to Bear," I asked, "your first husband?"

"Ah, Bear. He went to Belzec with the Gypsies."

"But he wasn't a Gypsy," I protested. "He was a bear."

"I tried to tell them that." Babba wiped a tear with her dust rag. "But they didn't make those kinds of distinctions."

"How could you stand to lose him?"

"I stopped thinking about it," Babba said. "In time, I just became glad I wasn't a bear."

I STOPPED at a liquor store in Brighton on the outskirts of Boston and picked up a quart of vodka, the kind in a dark blue bottle. I set it on the night table alongside twice the number of sleeping pills I had taken last time. I put on clean pajamas and closed the curtains tight so no glimmer of hope would find its way into my room. I poured three bowls of food and water for Roosevelt and remembered to leave the back door unlatched so he could push it open and get out. He jumped in the bed with me.

I lay in the dark, looking up at the ceiling I couldn't see. God was probably yakking His ass off right now to Mrs. Szilborski, but He couldn't be bothered to answer a few simple questions for me or Rabbi White. Mrs. Szilborski probably even had Polaroids.

All night I lay with my eyes open, looking for a pin of light that would make sense of the darkness. If I was unfit for the life I was born into, why had God made it impossible for me to become someone else? My solitary cocktail party was waiting, but it was important to get all this stuff figured out before I did anything final. At dawn, Roosevelt nudged my arm. I hadn't come up with any answers. Like Rabbi White, all I had were more questions.

The room suddenly seemed oppressive, thick with despair. I wanted light. Maybe in the light of day I could ask the right questions.

I pushed Roosevelt off the bed. "Let's get out of here, boy." I got up and opened the curtains. The sky was overcast, but I still had to squint against the sun's glare. I pulled on my jeans and grabbed the leash. Roosevelt jumped around excitedly, submitted to his collar, and trotted after me to the front door.

THE PHONE RANG. It was my mother.

"We're taking Babba to St. Luke's," she said, out of breath. "She went over the edge as soon as you left yesterday. She ironed everything in the house. Ruined everything. Put a scorch mark in the middle of every blessed thing in this house. Curtains, shirts. Everything."

"Is she there?"

"She should never be out of that place. She can't function. A scorch mark in the middle of everything. Ev-er-y b-les-sed thing."

"Is she there?"

I could hear scratching and bumping as my mother passed the phone to Babba.

"I thought you were in trouble," Babba cried into the phone. "I kept thinking you were in trouble. I'm just a stupid old woman. I thought ironing would save you."

"I'll come see you next week, Babba."

"I thought you were in trouble. I thought I could save you."

My mother took the phone back. "You see. She can't even think straight."

"Put Babba back on," I said. "I have to tell her something."

"Your father's here now," she said. "You can tell her later."

"You saved me, Babba," I said into the dial tone. "You saved me."

Now You See It

1975

THERESA GOJUK MARRIED a black man just to piss off her father, Bruno. She was twenty-five years old and couldn't remember when making her father angry became more important than pleasing herself, but somewhere along the line it had become the only thing that mattered.

Theresa hadn't even noticed Jason, her new husband, at first. Hollywood was littered with handsome men. It was only when she found out Jason was half black that she pictured herself walking down Market Street in Cokesville with him—smiling at the hissing tongues and shaking heads. Positive proof that she wasn't one of them. Intermarriage in Cokesville was a Lutheran marrying a Catholic. A Polack marrying a black had no polite name.

"What do I say without sounding like it's the first thing I noticed about Jason? Like being black is his only defining characteristic?" she asked Annie on the phone before Annie flew out to the coast to be her bridesmaid. "God, I would be just as bad as my father."

"You don't say it. You just don't. How do you say something like that? God, what do they expect?"

They commiserated over Cokesville's unreasonable expectations and discussed what Annie should wear as matron of honor. "Something in black. A cocktail dress. No doodads, though. That's so Cokesville."

Since high school, Theresa and Annie had been in a conspiracy to leave Cokesville and never come back. Wash the soot from their hair and pretend Cokesville never happened to them. Annie tried writing her way out of Cokesville. Failing at that, she'd married Sam Bledsoe, a Boston tax lawyer who'd never heard of Cokesville or set foot out of Massachusetts. Theresa scrapped her Cokesville identity by becoming an actress, reborn and rebaptized with each performance. Marrying Jason was just another role, albeit a risky one.

At the reception dinner, Bruno Gojuk was shocked when he met Jason's father, who was, as he said poetically, "black as the ace of spades," and Jason's mother, who was Jewish. Bruno had never actually met a Jew. But he had heard rumors about them, and as he danced with Jason's mother, he sifted through those rumors, trying to find a stereotype to define her and save himself the effort of forming an original opinion.

Theresa's mother didn't comment on either Jason or his family, because, by this time, Helen Gojuk was less interested in her daughter's love life than in her Hollywood career. Helen herself once had had show-business aspirations. She wanted to fly to Los Angeles in 1957 to be Queen for a Day. She practiced telling the studio audience how hard it was to raise five children with her husband out of work. At that time, the steelworkers' union had been out on strike for five months, and the Gojuks had run out of money. Mrs. Gojuk was certain she could move the studio audience to clap so hard that the needle on the clap-o-meter would fly into the red zone, dwarfing the competing hard-luck stories. "They could show a little dignity," she had said. "Look at them blubbering. You don't have to do that to win." But she couldn't get the plane fare together; and so she stayed home and watched lesser talents walk away with the loot.

"We could've used the money," she told Theresa, reminiscing before the wedding.

"They weren't giving away money, Mom," Theresa reminded her. "They were giving away refrigerators."

"That's right," Mrs. Gojuk said. "And we didn't need a refrigerator."

"But you would have won," Theresa said. "You have a lot of talent."

Mrs. Gojuk smiled. "Do you think so?"

"Where do you think I get it from, Mom?"

When Theresa danced with her father at the reception, she noticed for the first time that his jowls were sagging.

"What do you think, Dad?" she asked, touching her own face uneasily.

"About what?"

"About *Jason.*"

"You made your bed," he said with the bluntness Theresa had always felt it her duty to defy. "Now lie in it."

Before she and Jason left in a white limousine for their honeymoon, she went into the ladies' room and stared at herself in the mirror. Annie found her there.

"Don't worry, you're still beautiful," Annie reassured her.

Theresa laughed and shook her head. "Do you think I look like my father?"

"Bruno? No. You look like Jason."

Theresa giggled. "That's a good sign, isn't it?"

"Do you need a sign?"

Theresa scowled and put some lipstick on, then threw it in her bag. "Come on, catch my bouquet."

"I'm married, remember?" Annie said. "Sam?"

Theresa snickered. "I'll aim for you. Just in case."

It wasn't that Theresa and Jason were a bad match. He seemed to really love her and Theresa loved who she was with him: part of an exciting, photogenic couple. They were sharing her excitement a few months later, when Theresa's brother Milos called to say that Bruno Gojuk had fallen into a vat of hot metal, becoming one with the molten steel he was cooking.

"Mom wants to know what to do with the one-hundred-and-seventy-five-pound ingot. Should they deliver it to the house or the funeral home?"

Jason jumped out of bed and pulled on his underpants. "Oh man. This is terrible," he said over and over again, until Theresa told him to shut up.

"Why one hundred and seventy-five pounds?" Theresa asked. "He weighed over two hundred pounds. Shouldn't we have a two-hundred-pound ingot?"

Milos told her that their father's job application listed his weight as one hundred and seventy-five pounds. They were entitled to an ingot that weighed that much.

"But he hasn't weighed one hundred and seventy-five pounds in thirty years," Theresa said. "We should get a two-hundred-pound ingot."

"I don't know," Milos said. "The company man said if his application says he weighs one hundred and seventy-five pounds, that's what we get."

No one was surprised to see an ingot in the casket instead of Bruno. Accidents happened all the time at the plant, and people found it as normal to view a *Made in the USA* stamp on a slab of steel as it was to view a face made up with lipstick to meet its maker. Not only had the people of Cokesville waked steel ingots, but over the years they had stood reverently in front of hunks of coal when mines collapsed on miners and the mines were sealed before they could retrieve the bodies. And sometimes all they had to look at was the American flag when their boys vanished in battles overseas. The people of Cokesville were used to their men leaving home in one form and coming back in another, like a cosmic sleight of hand.

No one at the viewing was really interested in Bruno Gojuk or the fact that he had changed into a two-by-four-foot steel rectangle. People, even those who didn't go to St. Cunegunde's, the Polish church, came to see Theresa Gojuk, who had become, in an even more mesmerizing sleight of hand, Tess Randall, star of the prime-time sitcom *Seattle*. Also, she was the only person they knew who'd married a black man.

Ordinarily, they would say it wasn't that they didn't like blacks, they just didn't know any. But that was only part of the truth, because by this time, blacks were working in the mill. Blacks and whites just didn't live next door to each other. As soon as there was a whisper that a black family was interested in buying a home, a neighborhood lifted its skirts and moved over a block or two. A black family, no matter how determined to move into a white working-class neighborhood, could never quite find it. The neighborhood moved past Maple, then past Elm, then finally to a different suburb entirely, leaving the black family, whose intent was to raise their children in a decent environment, wondering where the hell it went.

By the time of Bruno's accident, the white neighborhood had left the center of Cokesville altogether and was inching toward the underground seam of coal that had caught fire twenty-five years ago, when someone dumped a load of garbage down a mine shaft and it ignited. The fire cut a burnt path from the woods outside of town down Wayne Street, and its smoke was visible from the Irish Catholic church, Our Lady of Perpetual Hope, on Hayes Street. The Irish didn't mind living so close to the burning seam, because it divided them from their old neighborhood, which was now called "Dark Town."

Of course, Jason wasn't like any black the citizens of Cokesville had encountered. He didn't take their jobs through namby-pamby affirmative-action quotas, and he didn't actually look black. In fact, no one would have even known he was black if the tabloids hadn't repeatedly run pictures of his father, a superintendent of schools in Queens, New York.

So they came to the funeral wanting to claim Theresa, rub noses with her fame, and get a good look at this Jason guy. Maybe rub noses with his fame, too, if he would let them.

"So glad to meet you," they said, scrutinizing Jason for Negro features and eyeballing Theresa to verify the rumor that she'd had breast implants.

"How's Hollywood treating you?" they asked. "You look beautiful. Just like your mother!"

Theresa, leaning on Jason's arm at the funeral parlor, shook their hands solemnly and said to each one, "Thank you for coming. He would have been so glad to see you."

BEFORE THEY GOT on the plane in California, Theresa had told Jason that he didn't have to come with her. He had to read for a part in a new movie. She didn't want her father's death to get in the way of his career. He could just turn around at the airport and go back home.

"You'll just give the Cokesvillers something to gawk at."

"I'm used to it," Jason said.

"Trust me," Theresa said. "You wouldn't have liked my father. It's not like he can see down and know that you're there."

"How could I not love the father of the woman I love?"

He said it with such sincerity and kissed her so tenderly that Theresa felt bad about not loving him now that his shock value had become irrelevant. But she liked Jason and they had fun. Even as she was scripting her exit lines, they were decorating their house together, arguing over bathroom fixtures and floor coverings like a normal married couple. She liked him, really. That would make the inevitable much harder.

"There's nothing to do in Cokesville," she said. "You'll be bored out of your skull. Anyone with any life left years ago."

"You still have friends there. I'll bet they make a big deal out of it when you come home. They do when I come home. You should see." He smiled. Since they would be on the East Coast anyway, they'd decided to visit Jason's neighborhood after they cleaned up the mess caused by Bruno Gojuk's death. If there was a mess. He was such a meticulous person, Theresa couldn't imagine him leaving anything surprising behind.

They transferred to a puddle-jumper in New York. As they descended over the Catawissa River, Theresa could see a big gash in the earth where her uncles used to mine. Farther downriver was the steel mill, Cokesville Forge. It looked as if some giant, with a swipe of his hand, had knocked it over. The Japanese were buying it up piecemeal and sending the usable equipment to a mill in the Philippines. Theresa could see the small section that was still open. She pictured her father running from one rusting building to another, a step ahead of the bulldozers, until he was finally cornered above his cauldron.

The little plane banked left, and Theresa's stomach lurched. She grabbed for a sick bag. Then they landed. The other passengers in the twelve-seater were businessmen. As they filed out, one of them asked Theresa for an autograph.

"It's for my daughter, Morgan. Are you here to do a movie?"

Theresa scribbled the usual pap on the back of a photo of his daughter. "Are you a steel executive?"

"We're wrapping up the sale this week. Great news for Cokesville Forge stockholders."

Theresa let Jason lead her down the stairs and across the tarmac. Her sister, Margaret, clutching her purse to her chest, waved from the doorway of the terminal. Theresa waved back to let her sister know she saw her. But when she closed her eyes against the sun, she saw her father, backed into a corner, not hesitating as he jumped into his cauldron, because there was nowhere else for him to go. She strode over to where her sister waited, forcing the image away.

THE MOVIE THAT had brought Theresa and Jason together was *The Great Disappearing Howard Thurston.* At first the studio blamed the misleading title for the movie's failure. Howard Thurston didn't actually disappear. He made *other things* disappear, most notably automobiles.

The screenwriter, who had adapted the screenplay from her original biography of Howard Thurston, blamed the actors. Jason said that Laurence Olivier wouldn't be able to squeeze life out of the stiff she'd created. "Who talks like this?" he asked. " 'Now you see it. Now you don't!' That's the dumbest line I ever heard."

"It's how they talk," the screenwriter screamed at him. "It's a line that magicians use. What planet are you from?"

None of the finger-pointing could save the film. It opened and closed in one weekend. Now you see it. Poof. Now you don't.

It was to have been Theresa's big break, her launching pad from the television sitcom *Seattle* to the silver screen. No matter how bright her star shone in Cokesville, Theresa knew that if she couldn't transition, her acting days were numbered. And like anyone whose livelihood depends on physical beauty, she was aware of her short shelf life.

She asked her agent for more scripts. She did readings and film tests, but nothing panned out. Her career was taking the fall for that crummy movie. Everyone else had been exonerated. Even Jason, and he *was* the Great Disappearing Howard Thurston.

When she returned to the set of *Seattle*, she could feel the tectonic shift. She would get her script late, sometimes without the changes. The wardrobe girl handed her costumes as if they had cooties. There was talk the series would be canceled. The radioactive ring around her grew. No one wanted to be tainted by association with a failure.

Whenever she phoned home, Mrs. Gojuk was the voice of doom. "I know how they treat people out there. Like meat. Just like hunks of meat. They'll throw you to the dogs."

"You don't know anything, Mom."

"I know that people are the same everywhere, honey. As soon as they smell blood, they're on you like a pack of jackals."

"Is Daddy around?" she had asked, trying to get her mother off her philosophy harangue.

"Double shift. Getting in as much work as possible."

Theresa hung up, thinking to call later, when he would be home. But her agent had a film test for her, and the next day she got the call from Milos. Then she started getting calls from Cokesville reporters. Back in Pennsylvania, they couldn't see the radioactive ring around her.

IT WASN'T THAT Bruno Gojuk's prejudices were more odious than everyone else's. He just wanted to live with people who looked as much like him as possible. When a black family got too close for comfort, he packed up the family and moved several blocks away. Like everyone else.

"It's not up to me, Theresa," he'd explained. "The bank won't give them mortgages unless there's no whites in the neighborhood. That's a fact. That's just a fact. If we didn't move, they would have nowhere nice to live."

Bruno had picked up his lunch pail and headed for the Chevy in the carport. He stopped by the azalea bush to see if the neighbor's dog had peed on it again. The ends looked a little burnt. He went back into the basement and came out with a three-pound bag of rat poison. He sprinkled a little in a dish with some dog food and set it by the shrub, then got in his car and drove to work.

As soon as he was gone, Theresa retrieved the dish and emptied it into the garbage can. She washed the bowl and refilled it with dog food. Mrs. Wojic's little yellow dog bounded across the street, ate some food, and peed on the bush. "I wonder," she told the dog, "if they know just how lucky they are."

THERESA'S MOTHER WAS no longer on speaking terms with God and didn't attend the wake, which was just as well, because she couldn't handle crowds and the mob outside the funeral parlor filled the street. Theresa's brothers complained that it had turned into a circus and took Jason across the street to Kelly's Emerald Isle, leaving Theresa alone on the receiving line with her sister, Margaret.

"Don't you want a drink, Margaret? It's okay. I'll stay here with Daddy." Theresa was anxious to be rid of her sister's cowlike smile. She looked like she was auditioning for sainthood.

It also seemed unfair to submit Margaret to the endless line of people, when everyone had really come to see Theresa and Jason. They offered their condolences only after Theresa reminded them why they were there: not to gawk at her rumored implants, but to pay their last respects to Bruno. The widow next door, Mrs. Szewczak, even asked for an autograph. Mrs. Szewczak felt that her family and the Gojuks had a special bond, since both their boys had been blown up in Vietnam. Paul Szewczak and Steve Gojuk were mentioned in the same breath when anyone remembered to talk about them at all. The boys had enlisted together in a rush of youthful ignorance. One minute they were whole. The next they were pieces in the jungle, their buddies scrambling to find their mostly unrecognizable parts. Parts of Paul Szewczak, whom Theresa dated briefly when he was home on leave, came home in a flag-draped coffin. At least the Szewczaks had that. Her brother Steve had been guarding an ammo pile. The only thing the Army's graves identification unit delivered to the Gojuks was a tightly folded American flag.

Theresa wrote "Much love, Tess Randall" on a page of Mrs. Szewczak's autograph book.

"It's not right that a son go before the father," Mrs. Szewczak said, putting her autograph book back in her purse and shutting it tight. She was still preoccupied with the death of her son and husband. It probably didn't even register that she was at someone else's wake.

"Well, their suffering is over," Theresa said.

"Now I have no one," Mrs. Szewczak said.

Theresa said nothing.

Mrs. Szewczak wiped her eyes with an embroidered, neatly pressed handkerchief and moved on to examine the slab in the coffin. The sisters sat down on the mourners' chairs that lined the side of the wall, ignoring the rest of the people in line.

Margaret turned to her sister. "What did Daddy have to live for, anyway?" she asked. "They're tearing down the mill next month."

Theresa looked at Margaret in surprise. "Are you saying he's better off dead? We should be happy he's dead? Because of the mill? Jesus, what about Steve? You think he's better off dead, too?"

"You're not here. You don't know what it's like. What they're saying. What they're thinking." Margaret tapped her pocketbook, reassuring herself it was still there.

It had been a long time since Theresa had spoken with Margaret, and she was surprised at her gumption. She was normally such a mouse.

"Look around," Margaret continued. "The town is dead. What do we have to live for?"

"So you're saying if the mill goes, everyone should just roll over and die? My God, there's a whole world to live for. There's a whole world outside of these stinking mills. You know, once you get out of Cokesville, you can actually see the sunset. It's not a tired orange ball falling into a bowl of pea soup."

They sat in silence for a while. "That's easy for you to say," Margaret said finally. "You're not living here. Our world is shrinking. Disappearing. Soon it'll be as if we never existed." She sobbed into her tissue. Theresa got up and greeted a few more people, then sat down next to Margaret, exhausted.

Theresa was lucky. She was one of those people who looked good when she cried. Her face didn't get all red and splotchy like Margaret's, whose nose seemed to grow to twice its size. Theresa reached into her pocket and pulled out a brown plastic prescription bottle. She slipped a pill into her sister's hand.

"What's this?" Margaret stopped crying long enough to see what Theresa had given her.

"Just take it. It won't kill you."

"Is it a tranquilizer?" Margaret asked, interested.

"It's Halcyon."

"Do you take them?"

"On an emergency basis. There's no reason to suffer."

"Will I get addicted?"

"Jesus, just take it. There's no reason to suffer."

THE NIGHT AFTER Bruno's wake, Mrs. Gojuk and her daughters went through his drawers. He didn't have much. He had a Zen philosophy on possessions, even though Theresa was sure he didn't know what Zen was. The only magazines he ever read, which he threw away as soon as the new ones came, were *Popular Mechanics* and *Consumer Reports*, neither of which ventured into abstract thinking. But Zen he was. For example, he owned only two shirts. "One on my back, one in the wash," he had said. One belt, because he had only one middle, and one hat, for obvious reasons. He had a few more pairs of socks and underwear, although for years he washed those every night by hand, trying to get a rotation going; trying to pare down his worldly goods to what would fit in a single chest of drawers.

Beneath his underwear was a brown envelope filled with important papers: bank account, life insurance policy, title to the house. Some black-and-white pictures fell out, tiny prints. Mrs. Gojuk rummaged through them.

"They were Bruno's people," Mrs. Gojuk said. "That's his mother, Ilonka. Her brothers." Theresa looked at the picture. A group of tall sturdy blonds shored Ilonka up. "Your father took that picture." Mrs. Gojuk started to cry. Margaret shooed her from the room. "Go lie down, Ma. You're overwrought."

"Yes, go lie down," Theresa echoed absently as she turned each photograph over, looking for names. One was dated 1932. A beautiful script in blue-black ink from a fountain pen identified the men in the photo as Felix Gojuk and Theodore Cheslock: her and Annie Kusiak's grandfathers. Theodore, the larger man, had his arm around Felix's shoulders. They were standing in front of an ocean liner, dressed in Sunday three-piece suits. Two large suitcases were on the ground in front of them. They were radiating happiness. Was this the day they disembarked in America? Did they think they'd escaped? Theresa snorted. Some great escape: right to Cokesville, Pennsylvania.

"Who are they?" Margaret asked, putting Bruno's clothes into a paper bag for delivery to Goodwill.

"The short one is Grandpop."

"Should we chuck them?" Margaret asked.

"No, you can't chuck them!"

"I don't want them." Margaret picked the photos off the bed and put them in the wastepaper basket. "They're too depressing. If no one remembers who they are, what's the point?"

"Aren't you scared you're going to be like them?"

"And what? If I throw their pictures away, I won't?" Margaret laughed. She had taken the Halcyon. "What's wrong with our being like them, anyway? They're our family."

Theresa was suddenly anxious to get away. "I have to get back to L.A." She looked at her watch as if she would be leaving momentarily instead of tomorrow.

"No one's making you stay," Margaret said. "You're not trapped here."

"That's not what I meant," Theresa said.

Margaret looked at her sister coolly. "Of course not." Then she shrugged and took the bag of her father's clothes downstairs.

Theresa waited until she heard her sister open the garage door before she pulled the photos from the wastepaper basket. Most were nameless. If they were family, Theresa felt no love for them. If they had ever done heroic deeds, no one remembered. No one in Cokesville was that heroic, anyway, if you asked her opinion. They worked in mills that others built and battled ferociously to make the town their personal domain. No outsiders welcome. "You don't see bluebirds living with robins, do you?" her father said.

As she'd packed her bag for Hollywood, determined never to set foot in Cokesville again, Theresa answered, "It beats the hell out of me why anyone would *want* to live with you."

She fingered the photos. If she threw them away, no one would even remember these people. Would that be such a loss? Some things were better forgotten. But her father remembered. He, who never kept anything, must have kept them for a reason. That reason was now petrified in a one-hundred-and-seventy-five-pound steel ingot. She stuffed the photographs back in the envelope to take with her.

Theresa could hear Milos's wife, Jeanna, downstairs, opening the door to yet another neighbor. Jeanna thanked the woman for the *halupki*s and said that Theresa wasn't home right now. The disappointed woman left reluctantly. Jeanna cursed lightly and went to quiet her children, who were bored with death and wanted to be home with their friends. "One more day," Jeanna told them.

"Do you need some help with dinner?" Theresa yelled down the stairs.

All the noise in the kitchen stopped and Margaret shouted, "Just relax. We're under control."

Theresa could hear Margaret and Jeanna argue briefly about dinner and then go about setting the table. They laughed once, and Theresa strained to hear over what.

Jason, Milos, and Gregory, her other brother, came home from the bar, sounding very drunk. They were laughing and thumping each other on the back. Jason stumbled up the stairs and found her sitting on the bed in the dark. He sat down next to her. The smell of whiskey and smoke almost choked her.

"Your brothers are something else," he said, kissing her cheek.

"Tomorrow they'll laugh at you," Theresa said. "That's what guys like my brothers and father do for sport. They make fun of . . . people."

Jason straightened up, then relaxed again.

"I'm used to it," he said.

Theresa sighed. "I'm sorry, I'm just upset. It's been a long day."

They sat silently for a while.

"Your brothers told me some stuff about your old man. He was one tough cookie."

"My father?" Theresa asked. "He was just a working stiff. With blinders on. He couldn't see anything more than two feet in front of him."

"It's different when you're a man." Jason took the envelope from her hand. "What do you have?"

Theresa turned on the light and spread the photos on the bed. "Do you think any of these people look like me?" She touched her face, tracing the shape to see if it matched any in the fading prints.

Jason squinted at the pictures, then at her. "In certain angles. I don't know. You kind of look like this lady here."

He pointed at one and Theresa picked it up. The woman was dressed in black. She was standing in front of a simple wooden house, squinting against the sun, and it made her look mean. She flipped it over. Nothing was written on the back. Was she a relative? Was her meanness something that traveled through the genes to make its appearance in Theresa when she least expected it?

She had married Jason only because he was black. Maybe it already had.

"This woman? Do you think?" She looked at the picture, then in the mirror over the dresser. If she furrowed her brows and puckered her lips, it was a pretty close call.

Margaret called up the stairs that it was time to eat. The box springs in the other room squealed as her mother got up, and Theresa heard her make her tentative way down the stairs. She tore the photo of the woman into little pieces, then ripped them again, making them disappear.

Mrs. Szewczak and the Rescue Dog

1976

MRS. SZEWCZAK KNEW her toes would fall off if Rescue Dog didn't find her soon. She stomped around the deserted bus stop trying to get feeling back into her feet. Her boots were brand new, but already, only two hours in the snow, they were soaked through. She started to compose an angry letter to the shoe company in her head, but felt too woozy to continue. The soft white snowbanks looked inviting, and she tried not to stare at them. She'd heard that sitting down was the worst thing to do if you were stranded in a snowstorm, so she kept walking from one end of the little hut to the other.

"Keep moving or die," she said aloud, "just like a shark."

This struck her as funny, and she began to laugh. She laughed for a long time, then realized she sounded crazy and stopped. Everything was quiet and the snow piled up. A jeep wouldn't be able to get through soon. Where was the Rescue Dog emergency squad?

She wished now that she had a key to the office, but she hadn't wanted that kind of responsibility. What if she forgot to lock it and something happened? She didn't want them to blame her. The owner and his assistant, the only two other employees in the Investstock Assurance Company's small office, had left hours before to go on a sales call, leaving Mrs. Szewczak alone to enter insurance claims into the ledger book, oblivious to the silent storm. The steady copying was like meditating. She'd grown to love it and didn't mind the half-mile walk to the bus stop. But today the remote location frightened her. She would just have to sit tight until Rescue Dog made the rounds of the bus stops looking for stranded people.

Her husband, John, hadn't approved of her working. He had made a big thing out of not asking her what she did or how much money she made. He never even asked her where her office was. After she started, they had had a big fight about it.

"Why do you want to work?" he had said. "Your job is right here. In this house."

"That's right," she'd said. "In this house. Cooped up all day in this house, cleaning and cooking. For what?"

"It's your job. That's for what. I go out and make money, and you take care of the house and me and—" He had hung his head, groping for the reason.

"And what, John? You're not here anymore. You might as well have died with him. Paul isn't here anymore. Paul isn't here anymore."

"Don't say that!" John had slammed the table with his fist.

"You have to say it."

"Don't say it!"

"Say it, say it, say it!"

Mrs. Szewczak shook herself. She was talking to the bus stop sign, not John. She brushed off the white powder that had accumulated on her coat and hat and went back under the shelter. She and

John didn't talk about anything after that. They lived like boarders. Pass the peas. Pass the bread.

Then, last year, John died, too. Out of habit, she never talked about that, either. She kept the obituary, yellow and brittle, in her wallet, next to Tess Randall's autograph. Now and then she read the obituary to herself. She never read it aloud, scared to wake herself from the dream she had entered.

She heard a motor in the distance and peered out. She couldn't see clearly. It was probably a jeep; nothing else would be able to get through roads like these. Whatever it was, it needed a muffler.

A huge green Pontiac snaked into view. The Pisaros, who lived across the street from her, used to have a car like that. Even though she knew they'd sold it, she hoped it was Mr. Pisaro. She stood in the middle of the road and waved frantically.

The Pontiac lumbered up the incline to the bus stop and swayed to a stop right in front of her. The driver rolled down his window, and Mrs. Szewczak saw, her joy giving way to apprehension, that it was a black man. He wore an army fatigue jacket with the name tag still attached over his left breast pocket: "Charone." He had a neatly trimmed beard, giving him a distinguished look. Another man, skinny, with long, bony fingers wrapped around a homemade cigarette, slouched in the passenger seat, his features shadowed by an oversized red, green, and black knit hat. Smoke curled out of the car. She paused a moment, seduced by the unfamiliar aroma, before addressing the men.

"Are you Rescue Dog?" she asked tentatively.

"What?" Charone asked. He squinted at her through the snowflakes, which hit him on the cheeks and nose, immediately melting. "Nah, we're going to the store."

"I'm waiting for Rescue Dog," Mrs. Szewczak said cautiously, "to take me home."

"I didn't see Rescue Dog or anybody else on the road."

Charone took the small cigarette from the other man. He inhaled deeply and held his breath. His eyes got huge and white from the effort.

"If you're not Rescue Dog, what are you doing out?" she asked.

Charone exhaled suddenly and the unusual smell rushed out to Mrs. Szewczak. "My old lady needs Pampers for the baby."

She stepped back instinctively. She had never seen it, smelled it, but she knew they were smoking marijuana.

"Look, lady, I don't think anybody's coming to get you. We'll take you home as soon as we get the Pampers."

"Maybe you could just take me to a phone booth so I can call my husband," she said. She didn't want these men to think nobody cared where she was. With an intake of icy breath, she realized that no one would miss her. She had spun a cocoon around her misery, allowing no one inside. If she didn't show up, no one would notice for days.

"Doesn't he know where you are?"

Mrs. Szewczak didn't say anything.

"I think there's a phone booth at the Kmart where we're going," Charone said. "We'll take you there."

The Kmart was at least five miles away.

"I think there's a 7-Eleven that's a little closer," she said.

"Nah. They're too expensive."

She kicked her heels against the ground and couldn't feel them. That was a bad sign. The next stage was turning blue. They might rob her, she thought. Her boss always paid her cash: she had sixty dollars on her now. People murdered for less. In New York some men had robbed and murdered a man who had only ten dollars on him. Then they dumped him in a garbage can. Maybe they would dump her in the woods after they got her money.

The skinny man in the passenger seat roused himself. "Hey, mama, you comin' or not?"

Mrs. Szewczak opened the back door. She moved some baby toys and a rumpled blanket, sat behind the driver to see his face in the rearview mirror. Inside the car wasn't much warmer than out, and Mrs. Szewczak shivered, thinking about her feet. The Pontiac fishtailed down the other side of the incline and moved on.

It was getting dark and hard to see anything past the road, only woods. She wanted to remove her boots to check on her feet, but didn't want to be caught off guard if one of them tried something.

"You really have good traction," she said. "You must have some great snow tires."

"Yeah. We also got a trunkload of bricks."

Charone looked at her in the rearview mirror. His expression never changed and he didn't volunteer any more information about the bricks.

Mrs. Szewczak thought she might die here, tonight. She fidgeted in her seat, then relaxed into the idea. It would be as easy as lying down in a snowbank. No one would blame her. These men were on drugs, and although they seemed relatively peaceful, she'd read a lot about the side effects of drugs. Normal men did strange, unpredictable things while high. Going on rampages for a fix. But she'd seen the plump bag the skinny man delicately tapped to fill a rolling paper. They seemed to have plenty to keep them happy. Of course, do people who do drugs ever have enough? She didn't know. If she was going to die tonight, it was more likely she was going to freeze to death.

"It's freezing in here," she said.

"Yeah. The heater don't work."

The 7-Eleven was on the left. The huge sign lit up the only car in the parking lot. It looked like the lights in the store were still on. She wanted to tell them to stop and she'd pay for the Pampers, but that would bring attention to her purse. She clutched her bag closer and they drove on.

Mrs. Szewczak had no idea where they were, and she felt fuzzy from the smoke. She was sure they should have reached the Kmart by now. Maybe they were lost. Probably that marijuana made them lose their sense of direction.

Suddenly Charone turned off the road and came to an abrupt stop. Mrs. Szewczak strained to see where they were. It was a deserted parking lot.

"Shee-it," Charone said, getting out of the car. "It's closed."

The other man followed him, his too-long jeans dragging through the snow, picking up white powder that would later turn to ice against his wiry legs. Mrs. Szewczak got out and tested her feet. They were still numb. Maybe she was going to die from the ground up, slowly freezing until she was a block of ice. The three of them went up to the dark store and peered inside. Not even the emergency lights were lit.

"Is the phone out here somewhere?" she asked. She would call Rescue Dog. They would come and get her, and that would be that. She would be safe.

Charone pointed into the darkened foyer. The phone was right next to the cigarette machines. He pulled on the doors, but they were locked.

"Shee-it."

Mrs. Szewczak looked mournfully at the locked door and thought about the trunk full of bricks.

"I have to call," she said.

"I know, I know." Charone pulled his beard thoughtfully.

"Couldn't we . . . do . . . something?"

"Nothing we can do. It's locked up."

"I guess," she said, disappointed that they didn't mention the bricks. "The 7-Eleven was open."

"Yeah. We'll go there."

In the ten minutes they'd spent at the Kmart, the sky had become completely dark. And even with their load of bricks, it took almost forty-five minutes to drive slowly back to the 7-Eleven. Finally, the sign came into view, and they inched into the parking lot, their tires spinning. The lights were off and the car that had been there was gone.

"Shee-it," Charone said.

"What are we going to do?"

"I don't think we can go any farther." Charone leaned back in his seat. "The roads are too bad."

Mrs. Szewczak got out of the car to examine the deserted store and ran back excitedly. "There's a phone in there."

The passenger was rolling another small cigarette. "That doesn't do us any good, mama."

"I saw some Pampers in there, too."

"What are you trying to say, mama?" He meticulously finished the ends of the cigarette and put it in his mouth. He looked back at Mrs. Szewczak with red rodent eyes. He put a match to it, sucking in his already spare cheeks.

"We have a trunkload of bricks," she said, impatient that they didn't make the connection themselves. "We could break a window and get inside."

The two men laughed loudly, the passenger coughing. He opened a window, gulping air. Finally, his coughing fit subsided.

"You crazy, mama," he said at last. "That's looting, and they shoot looters."

"No one's going to come out in this weather just to shoot someone for trying to make a phone call."

"Riiight."

They started laughing again.

"I have to get home."

"We'll take you home. We said we would. Cool your jets."

"We can't go any farther. You said so yourself."

"Then we'll just have to wait until someone finds us."

"When will that be? No one's out here. No one's going to come out here till the storm's over. I should have waited in the bus stop for Rescue Dog."

Charone took the joint from his friend and contemplated the situation. "I didn't see any other cars, did you? How come you're out in this shit, anyway? Doesn't your husband know where you are to come and look for you?"

"He'll be here," she said quietly.

For the first time, she prayed there wasn't an afterlife. She wanted no possibility that John could look down from his celestial perch, with his closed, angry face, and say, "I told you not to work. Look where it's gotten you. You would've been safe at home. I told you not to leave the house. You should be home, where I can protect you." She still couldn't feel her feet and bent over to pull off her boots. "I think I have frostbite."

"What?" Charone turned the light on and faced her. "Put your feet up here."

She pulled off her socks. Her feet were very red. She started to massage them vigorously.

"Wait! Don't do that!" Charone yelled at her. "That's the worst thing you could do."

"How do you know?"

"I was a medic in Nam."

"Yeah, he was." The other man nodded and dragged on the cigarette.

"That couldn't have taught you much about frostbite."

"I know more than you." Charone poked at her feet. "Do you feel that?"

"No."

He jumped out of the car and got in the backseat with her. "Where's that damned blanket?"

Mrs. Szewczak pulled it out from under her.

"Your socks are soaked. Here." He lowered her feet from the front seat and wrapped them in the blanket, then set them on his lap. Mrs. Szewczak felt awkward. Besides her doctor, John had been the only person in her adult life to touch her. For the second time that evening, Mrs. Szewczak prayed for the dissolution of heaven, so John couldn't spy on her. He would have another coronary if he saw her in the backseat of this beat-up car, her feet ensconced in the lap of this large stranger. It felt comfortable, too, she admitted, ashamed of the thought. And warm.

"My son was in the Marines. In Vietnam," she said.

"Yeah?" he said, interested. "What unit?"

"I don't know. I mean, I have it written down, but I can never remember it. Those military addresses are so confusing. I wrote to him almost three times a week." She sighed heavily and closed her eyes.

"When did he come back?" he asked.

"He came home on leave once, instead of going to Japan. You know, he wanted to see us. Then he went back there and he stepped on a mine." Mrs. Szewczak said that matter-of-factly, as if it weren't the first time she had ever said it aloud. When she closed her eyes she could see Paul, whole one minute, exploding the next. They'd collected only little bits of him that they found in bushes, scraped off other soldiers. They couldn't find everything, though. Bits of him were still there. Stuck on things. That was the thought that choked her awake at night. The vow of silence John had imposed on her kept the room still, but her soul screamed the horror. Every night her dreams were a fresh assault. "I guess you've seen a lot like that over there."

Charone didn't answer, just looked out the window.

"He wanted to go. Could hardly wait till he was eighteen," she said. "We didn't want him to. He's our only child. Was our only child. But he had to do it, he said."

"Yeah." Charone absently stroked her feet and gazed out the window.

The passenger passed the joint to the backseat toward Mrs. Szewczak. She shook her head, but Charone took it.

"I guess everybody did drugs over there," she said. "That's what I've read."

"Yeah, just about."

"Maybe Paul was on drugs when he stepped on the mine." She didn't know why she was saying these things to Charone. She never even said them to John. But it was something that Mrs. Szewczak had thought about for years. Maybe dope had made him careless.

Charone gave the joint back to the other man without dragging on it and looked for a while at Mrs. Szewczak. "Nah. He wasn't there long enough to get into that."

"Maybe it would have hurt less if he was on dope."

Charone looked at her intently. "Don't worry, lady. He probably never knew what hit him."

That somehow made her feel better. Maybe Paul never knew what hit him. The thought of him in the kind of pain a blast like that would cause was almost too much to bear. Every molecule of him tearing apart. It was good to think he never felt it, that he just sort of evaporated.

"I have to tell John," she said, squirming. "My husband."

She wondered if John could see what was happening to her, hear what Charone had said. Would that comfort him? Not that she blamed him for anything, but she knew that if you clasp living things too tightly, you might keep them close, but you also suffocate them. They would run away at the first chance to get some air. She knew that Paul had joined the Marines to escape his father. That's why she and John stopped talking, because if they talked about anything at all, the reason Paul joined the Marines would come up. And some things were just too terrible to say aloud.

She thought again about the situation at hand. "What are you doing with those bricks in your trunk?" she asked.

"I got a job finishing a garage for this guy."

"Are you a carpenter?"

"I used to work in the mill. Before it closed."

Mrs. Szewczak thought that Paul would be Charone's age if he were alive. Charone looked almost thirty. That startled her. Paul had been eighteen for so long in her mind, she rarely allowed herself to think of him growing older. He would have been married to some lovely girl. Maybe Theresa Gojuk. They dated briefly when he came home on leave before going overseas. Maybe Janet, the girl he dated in high school. Mrs. Szewczak had seen Janet a few years ago with her children, two beautiful little boys. Janet was very sweet to her, but Mrs. Szewczak couldn't take her eyes off those children. She cooed over them until they got embarrassed and Janet, smiling, pulled them away, back into their lives. They would have been her grandchildren. For the first time she wondered if she could have done anything to stop Paul from joining the Marines. She had never intervened between her husband and her son. She didn't want them to blame her for their anger, for their inability to communicate with each other. And now, she thought, she had lost her whole future. She was blameless, but alone. She would gladly trade blame for those grandchildren.

"I'm doing odd jobs," Charone was saying. "I want my kid to have things."

"How old is he?"

"Four months. Little Desmond is four months old." He pulled out his wallet and showed her a snapshot of a woman holding a bundle.

"Is that your wife?"

"That's Cynthia."

"You can't see much of Desmond."

"He's only a couple of days old there."

"Your mother must be so proud. Being a grandmother."

"Yeah, well, she already had twenty-five grandchildren. She died a couple of years ago."

"Oh, I'm so sorry."

"Yeah. She would've liked old Desmond. He's a special kid." He looked at the snapshot again before putting it back in his wallet. "I let my older kid get away. But I'm not letting Desmond get away."

He clenched his fists in a gesture that was familiar to Mrs. Szewczak, because John always did it. She didn't know what shape Charone's grip would make on Desmond's heart, but it scared her. She wanted to take Charone's hands in hers, pry open his hold on Desmond. But, of course, she couldn't. She had no rights with this man, this stranger.

"Jeez, it's getting colder in here." Charone looked at his watch, then peered in the blanket at her feet. "I think we'd better do something. Those don't look so good."

Charone got out of the backseat and took the keys from the ignition. His skinny friend was out of the car in a second, following him to the back of the car. Mrs. Szewczak could hear them arguing, but couldn't make out the words.

Finally, Charone unlocked the trunk, got out an armful of bricks, and walked up to the entrance. He took aim. The first brick broke the glass in the door and set off a blood-chilling alarm. He threw the remaining bricks ferociously at the glass that still hung from the frame. He ran back to the car. "Quick, what's your phone number?"

She told him, knowing that no one would be there to take the call. He ran back to the store. His friend joined him. They were a long time on the phone, and she could see them dialing and redialing her number, trying to get John to pick up.

They were coming back when a snowplow whirred up the road.

A police four-wheel-drive vehicle was right behind it. Its red lights were flashing. They had chains on their tires, but it was still astounding how quickly they made it to the store. It was miles to the police station. The snowplow cleared a path into the parking lot, then turned around and went back up the road.

Two policemen jumped out of the vehicle. They had their guns pulled and yelled for the two men to lean against the car to be frisked. One cop pulled a little plastic bag out of the passenger's pocket. He said something, jerking his head toward the Pontiac. The cop shoved the man's shoulder, pushing him down.

Presently one of the officers shined a flashlight in the car and opened the back door.

"You have some identification, ma'am?"

"Yes, yes." She fumbled in her wallet, scattering some cards on the floor of the car.

"Oh!" As she handed him her license, a piece of John's obituary broke off and landed at the policeman's feet in the snow. Mrs. Szewczak tried to tell the policeman to pick it up, but it was too late. It had already disintegrated. She stared at the pulp, horrified. In seconds even that was buried.

"Ma'am?"

Mrs. Szewczak shook herself awake to the present. "I asked them to do it, you know?" she said. "It was my fault. I made them do it."

The policeman guided the beam of his flashlight to her driver's license. "Get out of the car, please."

"I have to get my boots on," she said, reaching around the floor. "I think I have frostbite. That man, Mr. Charone, was helping me. Please, it's all my fault. Everything. I'm to blame."

The policeman looked first at her feet, then at her face. "Just stay where you are. We'll get you an ambulance."

The policeman wrote something on a little pad and went back to the squad car. The two men were still leaning against the car, snow piling up on them, but the cops seemed oblivious to the disappearing figures. Mrs. Szewczak watched them, as if her vigilance could keep them intact. But the darkness and the snow played tricks on her and she found their lines breaking up.

An ambulance finally pulled up to the Pontiac. The attendants got her out of the backseat and slipped her onto a stretcher. The sign on the side of the ambulance said RESCUE DOG. The attendants strapped her arms down, so she couldn't wave goodbye, but she bobbed her head around to see her rescuers, the two men leaning against the police car.

"I have to tell Mr. Charone about Desmond," she said desperately to the medic. "I have to tell him something very important."

"We have to get you to the hospital," the medic said. "You can tell him later."

They turned her around and pushed her toward the ambulance.

She called to them. "My John is dead, too."

Charone looked up, but she couldn't tell if he heard her.

"John is dead," she said, crying into the blizzard.

Her words fought to get through the snowflakes, but instead became entangled with them, blowing with them as they twirled up and over the dismal landscape before they landed on places unseen and unknown.

"I couldn't tell you before. I didn't mean to lie."

She called it as loud as she could, but they were already in the back of the squad car and didn't hear her.

Do Not Revive

1980

THE LETTER ADDRESSED to "Mrs. A. Kusiak" was from Tommy G. I tore the envelope into bits so Sam wouldn't see the return address, which was Greenville State Prison. Not that I was hiding anything. I wasn't. I never knew a convict before I met Tommy G. I didn't even know what he had done until the family of his victim found out he was in a halfway house and suddenly his picture was in the paper and everyone was signing petitions to get him off the street and back in the slammer where he belonged. Sam wouldn't have objected to my pen pal on moral grounds. He just wouldn't have seen the point of any friendship that couldn't be justified logically. And what possible justification could I have had for a friendship with a convict, whom, in all honesty and despite our correspondence, I barely knew? Sam would've sneered at me for wasting my time.

SAM SAID our marriage was illegal. He prided himself on logic, on his devotion to the truth, even if the truth led him to an unpleasant conclusion about himself.

"What do you mean?" I asked. "Illegal? Do you want a divorce? You're forty-three, you just bought a red car. Is this a midlife thing? If you want a divorce, why don't you just ask for one?"

Sam frowned, annoyed that his predictability would be seen as something other than a virtue. He was sensitive, too, to how he looked in the new red Miata. I didn't actually tell him, but—under the pretense of celebratory bonhomie—I took a photo of him in it. Since he was six feet two inches, his shoulders stuck way up over the seat. He looked like a wooden kid's toy, the ones with a round head on a cylinder in a plastic car; not like the dashing rogue about town he imagined himself to be. He was too vain to see the humor, even though later I felt bad and told him the car enhanced his appeal. But the damage was done. I had shown him how I saw him, and it was too late to take it back.

Plus the damned car set us back almost thirty Gs. We weren't poor, but thirty Gs is thirty Gs. If we had a kid, I told him, that would put him through one and a half years of college. I was trying to give his cliché some relative worth.

"Of course I don't want a divorce, Annie. Okay, maybe illegal is the wrong word. But why should society protect a childless couple? For tax benefits? That's immoral." Sam was a tax attorney and sifted everything through that dreary grid.

"How would you know who doesn't want children and who is just unlucky? And then what? You shouldn't get tax benefits until you actually have kids? What if you're trying to save so you don't bring them into poverty? Anyway," I said, almost believing myself, getting sucked into the quicksand of logic, "then divorce is immoral if you have children."

"Right."

"Really, I mean it."

"I do, too."

"But only until the kids are grown."

"What if they come back?"

We grew silent. Neither of us cared that much about children. We only used them as a focal point for the arguments that seemed, increasingly, what our marriage was all about.

WE WERE in the hospital room of Sam's father, Owen Bledsoe, whose lungs were filling up with fluid, whose bones were as tender as a cooked turkey's, and whose ninety-two-year-old skin was metamorphosing into purple oozing patches. The nurses turned him to relieve the stress on the worst stretches of skin, only to have new ones appear overnight. Soon, I thought—but didn't tell Sam—we'd have to stand the old man on his head, that being the only clear expanse on his body. Outside. Inside, he was as empty as a dried gourd. Seeds of his old self rattled noisily. Only Sam and his twin sister, Sandy, were able to understand his disjointed sentences, isolated words mostly, and place them on the larger canvas of his life, like pieces of an all-white jigsaw puzzle. When they were with him, he wasn't a collection of dried-up organs with a coconut head. He was once again the preeminent mathematician on the East Coast, the man who had changed forever the way we look at integers, as Sam and Sandy reminded anyone who forgot.

As we had no children, I wondered who would do that for us. Who will make sense of our lives when we are no longer able to do it for ourselves? Of course, neither of us was the preeminent anything on the East Coast, or anywhere else, so what did it matter? And then again, if you can't make sense of your life yourself, why would anyone else bother to do it for you?

"I don't think she's going to show up today," I said.

"We'll give it a few more minutes. She always comes through."

We were waiting for Sandy, who was still sleeping when we left the house that morning, and I really doubted that she would come to the hospital. She had flown in last night from New York. Her plane had arrived at ten o'clock, and we stayed up until two, talking. She hadn't brought her husband, Clark, or her two children. She thought it was premature.

"If he doesn't remember them, it would devastate them," Sandy had said of her children and why they weren't there to see their grandfather. "It's cruel for children to see someone they love in a decline, like Pop. I'd rather that they remember him as he once was."

"Well, this is the way he is now," I had said last night. "Do you pick the perfect time in someone's life and only know them then? Anyway, it's not as if he's dead. He's just different."

I didn't have to look to know that they were silently giving each other "the look" that said an outsider couldn't possibly understand the subtleties of their family. Besides being the children of a famous, beloved man—which I clearly couldn't understand, being the daughter of an ordinary Polish steelworker—their bond went back to the womb, bound in twining umbilical cords, glued with sticky embryonic fluid. Try getting past the doorman in that club.

"We don't want to frighten the children," Sam said, trying to be reasonable. "They have the rest of their lives to see the scary parts of life."

"How do you know what frightens children?" I asked.

"The doctor wants to know if we want him revived," Sam said, ignoring me.

"What do you mean, revived?" Sandy asked.

"If his heart should fail, do we want them to go to extreme measures to revive him?"

"There's nothing wrong with his heart," Sandy said. "I know he's ninety-two, but there's nothing wrong with his heart."

"Well, no, not right now. But say something happens. Do we want him revived?"

"Jesus, how can we make a decision like that? I hate that. What do they think? Do they think something's going to go wrong with his heart?"

"Well, no," Sam said. "They don't think so, but they need to know what the family wants in case something does. Go wrong."

"Didn't he make a living will or anything? Mom did. She didn't want to live a second past her time."

They nodded, satisfied that their mother had had the good sense not to live a second past her time. That's what they expected from their logical little family.

"I'm sure Pop doesn't want to live a second beyond his time, either," Sandy said.

"I'm sure," Sam said. "No rational person would want to live in the condition he's in."

Sandy pulled out her Filofax and wrote something in it.

Probably a note to pull the plug on Pop's remaining fluids as soon as it was seemly to do so, I thought. "What are you writing?" I asked.

Sandy looked at me, surprised. "Just a note to myself," she said, putting the Filofax back in her big black tote and snapping it shut.

"Is this settled, then, or what?" I asked.

"Is what settled?" Sam asked.

"You know. You're going to tell the doctors not to revive him."

"Yes, it's settled."

"Have either of you ever heard him say he didn't want to live in this condition? I mean, I never heard the guy ever say he wanted to die. Under any circumstances. Even when he had that hernia, and those things are painful as hell. And he let it go to the last minute. The pain must have been unbearable. He never said he wanted to die. Remember?"

I'd made a point of getting up so they couldn't stare at me and make me change my mind about what I wanted to say. "He doesn't even think he's ninety-two. He thinks he's sixty-five. I think he would like to live at all costs." I plumped the pillows on the sofa several times. "I don't think he ever wants to die."

Sandy laughed. "None of us wants to die."

"You just said your mother did."

Sandy looked at Sam for support.

"None of us wants to live like that. Like he is, either," Sam said.

"Well, that's you. Everyone's different."

The truth was that I didn't like Owen much and wouldn't care when he finally croaked. He'd never liked me, and although his senility didn't let him remember that, I did. Before we were married, he told Sam I wouldn't be a social asset, which, given my pedigree, was certainly true. In the hospital, though, he smiled, grateful for any kindness I chose to bestow on him, like giving him water from a Styrofoam hospital cup. Which is bare minimum kindness, so I didn't feel as if I wasn't acting true to my convictions. But he never said he wanted to be dead. And that was the point. People who want to be dead someday say that. When Owen goes, it will be totally against his will.

"A month ago, he was still making dirty comments to the nurses," I said. "He told one that if she was his wife, she wasn't doing enough for him. Can you imagine?" I laughed, but the siblings looked at each other, alarmed. "He thinks they're all coming on to him. I think someone who is making dirty remarks wants to live. Sex is about life, after all."

"Your imagination has completely run amok," Sam said. "Why don't you try putting some of it into your writing. You might get somewhere with it."

He looked at me defiantly, but I didn't want to start that fight.

"We'll talk about it in the morning," Sandy said. "I don't think there's a big hurry or anything. He's in bad shape, but I don't think he's going right this instant."

So we waited in Owen's room for Sandy to talk about it, and at three o'clock, just as she was arriving, I told them I had to leave. I had a class to teach. But really, I had to get out of that room, where the scions of logic were waiting to bring Owen's life to a tidy end.

IN HIS LETTER, Tommy G said he was glad the prison had such a good library. He was reading more and watching television less. I could see the difference in his writing. His spelling had improved. His grammar was correct most of the time. He apologized for the lack of content, but wrote, "Things don't change a lot in here."

On the back of the envelope was a stamped message that said: "Contents may not have been evaluated. The Department of Corrections is not responsible for the substance or content of the enclosed material."

WHEN SAM AND I WEREN'T arguing about children, we argued about my writing.

"You're supposedly a writer," Sam said. "But all you do is take potshots at everything. Everyone. It's boring as hell."

"What do you mean, I'm not a writer?" I asked. "I *teach* writing, for God's sake!"

"You teach *English.* To pampered prep-school brats. Big difference."

"I wrote that play."

"It was about tax lawyers!"

I laughed. "Well, it was funny. You gotta admit, tax lawyers . . ."

"It was just a collection of cheap shots at me and my family," Sam said. "Why don't you write about your own goddamned family?"

"Unfortunately," I said, "you *are* my goddamned family."

"Well, here's an original idea," Sam said. "You can change that anytime you please."

I TOOK my frustrations to the community gardens and rented a fifteen-by-twenty-foot plot. That's where I met Tommy G last year. He was always around, especially in the evening, when the gardens were mostly deserted. He looked like a fifty-year-old James Dean, wearing a snug T-shirt with a pack of Marlboros rolled up in his sleeve. His brown hair was combed back, the defeated pompadour brushing his forehead. It occurred to me when I first saw him that he was frozen in time, which it turned out he was. He had been in jail for twenty-five years, then moved to a halfway house, across from the gardens. Even after I found out he'd been in jail, I didn't think much about him except to be thankful he was there. A lot of crime was reported that summer in the reeds by the river and I was happy for the male presence. I was aware of his whereabouts in the gardens like a green blip on a radar screen.

Sometimes he would shoo me home when the sun was setting and I was lost in my weeding. "Your man will be worried," he'd say. He always admonished me for working too hard. "Your man should be down here, doing that," he said when I was hauling bricks to build an apron under the hawthorn tree. He nudged me away from the wheelbarrow and took over. "Where is he?"

Where is he?

He started bringing a thermos of coffee and an extra paper cup for me. It was instant coffee with lots of sugar. I couldn't fall asleep the nights after I worked in the garden because of that brew. We talked about me, mostly. I told him about Sam, probably more than I should have. I told him I wanted children, but even though I was twenty-seven and should be having them now, I couldn't with a man who was scared of the unknown. I told him I always wanted to grow peas, but I didn't, because I never knew if I was going to be in the same place long enough to harvest them. We talked about my teaching English to rich kids who weren't much different than kids I knew in Cokesville. We agreed that a lot of life was just luck.

Tommy told me he wasn't very good in school and that's why he volunteered for the army, for Vietnam. He thought if he were smarter, his life might have turned out differently. But he didn't want to tell me what he did in Vietnam or why he had been in jail.

"It would make you ugly to know those things," he said. "Whatever you put in your head is what you become."

He kept a respectful distance, talking over the fence, watching me. I thought then that he was a little in love with me. Now I think he was wondering how much I knew about him. The truth is, at that point I didn't know anything. I knew he had been in jail, but I didn't know for what until the end of the summer when the family of his victim found out he had been released to a halfway house. They got their story in the newspapers and had petitions signed demanding that the governor reverse his release order.

I showed Sam the article in the paper about Tommy G. "What do you think about that?" I asked him.

He scanned the article and shoved the newspaper back at me. "They should fry the sonofabitch."

"We don't have the death penalty."

"What possible use could there be in keeping scum like that alive? He brutally kills a sixty-year-old woman for cigarette money." His face looked pained. "On Christmas Day, no less. What kind of a monster is that?"

"He was on drugs. He was a deranged Vietnam vet. He went over there and killed and killed until he thought he was God. No one told him he stopped being God when he was discharged."

"How do you know so much about it?"

I closed my eyes, trying to remember. Maybe I made it up. Maybe I needed a way to explain the fact that the person who did this undeniably horrible thing was, to my mind, a good man. "It's just a feeling I get."

"We should reinstitute the death penalty. What logical reason could there be for keeping him alive?"

OWEN'S HOSPITAL ROOM was overloaded with cards and flowers. Almost all were from his former students and people whose work he enabled by setting the ground rules for integers. There was barely room for his three faithful visitors: Sam, Sandy, and me.

"Who would have thought people loved integers so much?" I asked, flipping through the cards.

"Numbers are every bit as creative as your stories," Sam said. "Of course people love them."

One of my major grudges against Sam and his family was their delusion that mathematicians and engineers were as creative as artists, and that art was just something you cut from the bottom line of school budgets. As if all knowledge were accessible through charts and graphs.

"Well," I said, "no one is really concerned about Owen the man. They are all mourning Owen the mathematician."

"What's the difference?"

"He isn't dead yet, for one thing."

The green squiggles on the monitor indicated that Owen, man or mathematician, had the vital signs of a young horse, even though his mind and casing were rotting around key organs.

"I have to go home this evening," Sandy said. "The children are out of control. Clark can't handle them."

"What about your father?" I asked.

"Sam's here. And you." She looked at her brother for approval.

"You don't think Owen would like to see his grandchildren?" I asked.

"I don't think he would even know them. He hasn't spoken a word in weeks."

"His lines indicate he knows all too well who's here."

"Well, everyone's talking about him as if he's dead." Sandy searched nervously in her black tote.

"Are you dead, Owen?" I asked the old man loudly, as if he were deaf. "Move your big toe if you're dead. See?" I said, triumphantly. "He's not dead."

"You don't have to joke about it, Annie. He's my father."

I got up and walked around to the front of his bed. His chart was hanging off the edge. It had a little yellow sticky on it, which I peeled off and waved around on my thumb. " 'Level Two Care'?" I asked. "What's that?"

Sam and Sandy exchanged their look. "We told the doctors to take him off life support."

I couldn't believe how cool they were about killing their own father. "When? Are they waiting for you to leave or what? Is there a ceremony?" Even though I never liked the guy, I wanted to throw my body over the plugs so they couldn't get their hands on them.

"This could go on forever," Sam said. "There's no reason to let him suffer if we can help it."

"He's only suffering," Sandy said. She finally found what she was looking for in her tote: her airplane ticket. She sighed and examined the time. "I've really got to get to the airport, Sam."

"You don't have to stay here," he said to me. He went over to his father and lightly touched his head. "Dad, there's an article in the new *Scientific American* that mentions your work. They're using it as a basis for extracting fuel from plants. Very exciting stuff."

Sam gathered up his coat and followed Sandy out of the room. Neither of them looked back at me.

I fought my revulsion and pulled the visitor's chair close to Owen. A tube for oxygen was jammed up his nose, and his mouth was wide open, the loose skin flapping with each exhale. Nobody had bothered to insert his teeth. His gums and tongue were still pink, but flat, dry.

"Are you suffering, Owen? Do you want a drink?"

I put the straw into his mouth. Before I could even tease him with a few drops, his gums clamped down and he sucked up all the water in the carafe. I refilled the container and put it back on the table. After rearranging his get-well cards and flowers, I picked up my coat, turning to leave.

"Thank you, Annie," he said.

Startled, I looked at the old man's face. His eyes were still closed. I went over and tweaked his big toe.

"Goodbye, Owen."

A BLIZZARD IN THE NIGHT had closed most of the roads, but the interstate was still open. Sam said I was crazy for going out in such foul weather. What could be so important that I had to defy the treacherous road conditions? The answer had no words, really, so I just left.

Greenville State Prison was two hours from Springfield and I had no idea when visiting hours were. I just drove. On the interstate, which was cleared off, a state trooper pulled me over, asking me what I was doing out.

"It's an emergency, Officer," I lied, struggling to define the nature of the emergency, even to myself. But I felt it. My heart was pounding and my breathing was shallow. The trooper looked at me closely, obviously thinking me in no state to drive, but finding nothing specific to pin his suspicions on, he waved me on. I skidded back onto the highway, plowing toward Greenville.

The prison was easy to find. It was harder to find Tommy G. The guard who signed me in asked several times for the name of the inmate I wanted to see. Was I expected? Was I sure this was the one

I wanted to see? Was I family? Didn't I know that visiting hours didn't start until three? Finally, he ushered me to a paneled waiting room. Old *Newsweek* magazines were piled on a side table, but I couldn't concentrate to read. After a few hours the room started filling up with women, mostly. They were all dressed as if they were going out on dates—high heels, skimpy dresses—not as if they were in a middle of a snowstorm. At exactly three o'clock a guard opened the door and the women stampeded out. I got up, too, but the guard told me to sit back down. "Someone will be with you in a minute," he said.

Finally, a big man in a suit came out and, taking my elbow, guided me behind huge steel doors and down the hall to his office.

"You're not from the newspapers, are you, miss?" he asked.

"Of course not. I'm just a friend of his."

"He never gets any visitors."

"Doesn't he?"

"You've never been here before? You're a friend?"

"Well, friend, yes. I mean, we write. Letters. I knew him before. I don't know him personally that well." It felt like a betrayal, saying that. Didn't know him as well as I knew Sam or Sandy, really? I didn't want to say I understood him, and we had a friendship based on instant coffee and sympathy taken on cool summer evenings under a hawthorn tree. I didn't want to say I knew the heart of a murderer, because what did that make me? "We write every now and then."

The man indicated that I should sit down. He did the same, waiting for me to arrange myself before he leaned forward. "He's not here. He's in the hospital. He tried to hang himself with a garbage bag in the kitchen on Christmas Day. One of those thirty-nine-gallon size."

"My God!"

"He fractured his wrist breaking his fall. Some other damage, too. Not too serious, but enough to keep him out of action."

"I see."

"He'll be okay. He does this every Christmas."

"*Does* he?"

"I thought you were a friend." He got up. The conversation was over.

I WAITED a few months to write to Tommy G. I didn't tell him that I went to see him, that I knew about his hospital stay. I did, however, tell him that the doctors pulled the plug on Owen, and guess what? Nothing happened. He didn't die. He stayed exactly the same. I go to see him now and then, even though I technically have no obligation to do so because I am no longer in the family. Sam left me a few days after my jaunt in the blizzard. He said he couldn't live with a woman whose passions overruled her intellect. That was in January. The woman he moved in with had their child in March.

IN APRIL, I got another letter from Tommy G. He had read about the torrential rains in Springfield and was concerned about the gardens flooding.

He has only two more years of time, although he doubts he'll settle in Springfield. When his parole is over, he'll move to California. He doesn't think he can pick up where he left off here. Too many things have changed. Too many things have stayed the same.

One night under the hawthorn tree, he told me that there were times in his life when nobody knew his name. When there wasn't a person on the planet who could call him anything but "Buddy." Even though we'll never see each other again, he asks me to keep writing to him. "You don't have to say much. I just want to know you're okay."

He reminds me that the best part of gardening is turning over the soil in the spring, when everything starts over again.

Last Call

1982

HELEN GOJUK IS forty-nine years old and dying of an anonymous cause. That she is dying there can be no doubt. Her unmarried daughter, Margaret, has called everyone, putting them on alert, chatting with them about the intimate details of her incapacity. Margaret has even moved her things into her mother's bedroom, while Mrs. Gojuk is stuck on a rented hospital bed in the dining room, where she lies like a queen bee: oiled, fed, changed, unable to perform even the simplest tasks to ensure her own survival. Father Novakowski, who she thought was a confederate and from whom she expected more encouragement, visits daily, praying with her to accept God's will. She has seen him fingering the holy-oil vial in his pocket like a loaded pistol, anxious for it to be pressed into service. She's dying, all right. Everyone says so.

"You're not dying, Ma," Margaret says, turning her over to change the sheets. "There's nothing wrong with you."

"Then why can't I move? Eh? Why can't I move?"

The cause of her ailment is unknown, because she will not submit to the probes and tests that would give a name to her suffering.

Not that she has anything against the scientific community. She doesn't. As far as Mrs. Gojuk is concerned, they are benign but misdirected people. After all, how can naming an ailment make it go away? How will a picture, on sonar or X-ray, make it easier for her to climb the stairs or pass the night in peace and comfort? It will do nothing, as amusing as it might be for those doing the naming and looking.

No, for the abysmal state of her affairs, Mrs. Gojuk doesn't blame science, which she knows has no power to cure or kill. She blames God.

"God has brought me to this." Mrs. Gojuk clutches the metal bars of her bed as Margaret wipes her bottom and fits her with a new diaper. Humiliated, she turns her face away from her daughter. "It's up to God to get me out."

"God has nothing to do with it," Margaret says. "God is too big to be concerned with you. He operates on a planetary level. Famine, nuclear war. That's His arena."

"Where did you get that idea? That God is cold and indifferent to His creations?"

"Where did you get the idea that God is so petty?"

Margaret zooms into the kitchen to wash her hands and rushes back into the dining room to turn on the television and program the VCR. She rearranges the hat that Father Novakowski gave her mother. It's a novelty hat, a beer can on top with a clear pink straw wrapping around her head, ending at her mouth. It's the only way Mrs. Gojuk can get water while her daughter is at the office.

"I gotta run," Margaret says. She pats her purse and coat, making sure she has everything.

"Hmm." Mrs. Gojuk is glad that Margaret has a job. She can be left alone with the television, without her daughter's banal commentary.

"Are you okay? Do you want me to call Mrs. Szymakowski to look in on you?"

"Why? So she can see me like this? She'll come, anyway." She pouted. "Are you taping it?"

"Yes."

Margaret hesitates before she wraps her mother's hand around the remote control and leaves.

Mrs. Gojuk barely notices the door closing. She is focused on the television. The talk show will be over in a few minutes. Then *Generations*, the daytime soap opera starring Theresa, comes on. Theresa's evening sitcom, *Seattle*, has been canceled and she has taken this job as a stopgap just to stay in the business. Her next step will be through the trapdoor, unless she manages to get a role in a decent movie. Everyone says she has no talent and that she wouldn't be anything at all if she weren't so beautiful. But isn't beauty more important than talent? And, Mrs. Gojuk thinks, not one part of Theresa isn't beautiful, as anyone who watches daytime TV can verify. Some women make catty remarks about Theresa baring all on daytime television, but Mrs. Gojuk knows they are jealous. If they had half of Theresa's looks, they would be in Hollywood with their drawers down and backing into a lens every chance they got. But it wasn't only Theresa's body that was mesmerizing. It was her face, her manner. She was so lovely Mrs. Gojuk sometimes couldn't believe she'd had a hand in her creation. She sighed with admiration. And her soul? Her soul was as perfect as her body. When Margaret told Theresa about their mother's plight, what did she do? Did she do something ordinary like recommend another doctor or hospital? No, she did not. Right away, she sent her mother two tickets to Lourdes, the place of miracles. A miracle. Only Theresa understood that her condition didn't require pills or surgery. Her condition demanded that God take notice of what he had wrought and fix it. Her condition demanded a miracle.

Finally, the theme song comes on and Theresa's picture fills the thirteen-inch screen. In today's episode, Theresa's lover turns out to be an Egyptian spy. Theresa must decide whether to be loyal to her lover or to her country. Mrs. Gojuk cries, moved by her Theresa's dilemma. Someone is knocking on the front door, but instead of hollering for them to come in, Mrs. Gojuk turns the sound up all the way and concentrates on the show.

ARPAD AND ESTHER ZAARY LIVED three row houses down from the Gojuks. They were Hungarian and went to St. Elizabeth's Church. Their two children had grown up and moved away ten years earlier. Arpad was a chipper, whittling the bumps and imperfections off the cold molded steel with a jackhammer. Because you couldn't do your job with your hard hat and goggles on, being a chipper was one of the dirtiest and most dangerous jobs in the plant. But the chippers took pride in the danger, and the fact that they were chippers was the first thing out of their mouths when you met them.

So it wasn't a surprise when Arpad killed himself shortly after he lost his job. Arpad's was the fifth suicide in as many months after the steel plant shut down. The sixth, if you count Bruno Gojuk, who'd jumped into a pot of liquid steel seven years ago, when the plant had begun to shrink. Which Margaret, for her mother's benefit, didn't count. Between them, it had been an accident.

But still. Five or six. It was becoming almost routine for the fifty-five-year-old men of Cokesville Forge to look at their newly idle fingers, start fiddling with this or that, until they finally found their way to the hunting rifle in the garage. When the wife went to Mass, it was easy to brood that the new economy had no place for them. Easier still, when brooding turned to despair as black as steel, to place the barrel of the rifle in their mouth and a toe on the trigger.

The widows were charged with altering the final destination of their husbands' souls with novenas, a nine-day round of prayers, and arguing with the priest about their men's right to be buried in holy ground after they had betrayed the faith.

"I wish my father would have the imagination to take the plunge," Lynn Murphy told Margaret over drinks at Lynn's going-away dinner. "Sweet Jesus, that man is a total loss. My mother should just kill him. It's beyond me why she sticks around."

It was just the two of them. Lynn, a labor-relations lawyer, was moving to Boston, seeing how there was no longer any labor in Cokesville to mediate, litigate, or otherwise ameliorate. More important, she was going to find a husband before it was too late. God knows there weren't any men worth marrying in Cokesville. The marriageable ones had left, one way or another.

Although she could never admit it aloud, Margaret admired the men who did away with themselves so tidily. It was a manly act. A flip of the bird to a fate that had dealt them so cruelly out of the game. Father Novakowski, the parish priest, had warned her against the contagion of despair. But it had nothing to do with despair. It was just the opposite. Men were creatures of action. They didn't hang around waiting for their fate to be decided. They decided it themselves. Like her father had.

She pitied Lynn Murphy, whose father had only enough gumption to spend his pension check on Pabst and quick pick tickets. His 1972 Plymouth was a fixture in the 7-Eleven parking lot, doors open, belongings tumbling out. His drunken, unlucky presence lent dignity to his more decisively self-destructive brethren.

Margaret looked at her hands uncomfortably. "He's your father. You don't mean that, Lynn."

"Don't I?" She stared at Margaret, then shrugged. "Come with me to Boston, Margaret. What's to keep you here? You're the one who's always saying this town is dying."

"It is dying," Margaret interjected, as if she were contradicting her friend.

"No. Dead already. Somebody should play taps."

"My mom . . ." Margaret said.

"Bring her!" Lynn said.

Margaret raised her glass. "Here's to you in Boston."

"To us in Boston," Lynn said.

They knocked back their drinks, and Lynn looked at her watch. "One more. Then I got to get going. I have interviews at ten o'clock tomorrow." She motioned for the waiter. "I never knew anyone who hated this town more than you. And yet you stay. You must have some wonderful memories." She looked at her friend suddenly, as if to catch her at something.

Margaret laughed. "Someone has to turn out the lights. That's all. I just want to turn out the lights."

IT WASN'T a surprise that Arpad Zaary killed himself. What was surprising was how he killed himself. Days before the event, his wife, Esther, fearing his depression, had put his hunting rifle in the back of the Mercury station wagon, covered it with an army blanket, and driven to the woods behind the reservoir. She threw it into the smoking coal seam, a smoldering gash in the earth. She wiped her hands briskly, squinted around for witnesses, which she hadn't considered until that moment, then stumbled back to the car, trembling at her daring. Taking his hunting rifle, his prize possession, and pitching it into a crevice was an act of defiance if there ever was one. She had never defied Arpad in the thirty-five years of their marriage.

She hadn't counted on him having enough cunning to find another way to self-destruct. The other men had used their hunting rifles. When she disposed of that, she figured she had disposed of the problem.

That night, for the first time since the suicides began, Esther slept peacefully and didn't bolt awake when she realized she was alone in the bed. She lay still and listened. She knew that Arpad was in the garage, and if he was looking for his rifle, he wasn't going to find it. She waited awhile for him to return and question her, practicing responses to his accusations. But he didn't come back. She tiptoed into the rec room over the garage trying to make sense of the noises downstairs. He was working on the '53 Buick. She could hear the engine. The thought that he was doing something so ordinary, so harmless, made her smile. She turned on the television and lay down on the floor, waiting for him to return, and died, breathing the odorless carbon monoxide through the floorboards as he was dying in the car below.

MRS. GOJUK LISTENS as Margaret and Father Novakowski sit in the kitchen discussing her pilgrimage to Lourdes. She turns down the volume on the television to hear them.

"It's out of the question, she can't go anywhere," Father Novakowski says.

"What's the difference? Boston, Cokesville?" Margaret answers. "We won't know anybody there, and we can start over."

"She's incontinent."

"I'll hire a nurse to accompany us."

"On your salary?"

"Well, you'll be working, too."

"I don't know what I can do."

Mrs. Gojuk strains to hear her daughter's reply, but she is speaking too softly. The priest answers, but his voice is lower, too. Ever since she received the tickets from Theresa, she's been obsessed with going to Lourdes. It's a holy place. God is guaranteed to be there. Why are they talking about Boston?

Margaret and the priest murmur for a while, then there is no sound at all. Mrs. Gojuk turns off the television in order to concentrate. The kitchen chairs scrape the floor as they get up, and Margaret sees the priest to the door, where they linger for a while, speaking in their new low voices.

"Good night, Mike," Margaret says, before closing the door noiselessly and appearing in the room. Her face is flushed and her hair, usually tied carelessly in a cloth-covered elastic, is even more disheveled.

Mrs. Gojuk regards her daughter coldly. "You call the priest 'Mike' now?"

Margaret doesn't answer, tucks her errant locks back into their constraint.

"He's not much of a priest, anyway," Mrs. Gojuk says, reluctant to give her the benefit of attracting a man worth having, but unsure of how to denigrate the masculine value of a celibate, who, after all, shouldn't be valued for his masculinity. She rolls the videotape again and freezes on a close-up of Theresa. "Has he ever met Theresa, I wonder."

Margaret takes the remote from her mother and runs the tape. She shrugs. "Has she been home since he came to St. Cunegunde's? Omigod! Is that Manny Gonzalez?" She presses the pause button and peers into the screen. "Omigod! It is. What's he doing on the show kissing Theresa?"

"It is not Manny Gonzalez. Where did you get such a stupid idea? That's her Egyptian lover. Look at the credits." Mrs. Gojuk doesn't have to look at the TV to know it isn't Manny. Manny is a Puerto Rican who went to high school with the girls. He had an awful crush on Theresa and used to walk up and down in front of the house hoping to get a peek at her. "It's not Manny Gonzalez at all.

Why do you say such stupid things?" Mrs. Gojuk knows Margaret is jealous of Theresa.

Margaret throws her head back and laughs. "Manny Gonzalez passing himself off as an Egyptian. I got to call her right away." She wraps her mother's hand around the remote and runs upstairs.

"Don't ruin it for her," Mrs. Gojuk yells after her. "You always want to ruin it for her."

"If it's Manny, she already knows it, for God's sake. How am I ruining it?"

"Just don't make it worse for her than it already is."

"Let's see," Margaret shouts down the stairs. "She's gorgeous; she's out of this town and on TV. How can what I say make it worse?"

NO RULE DEMANDED that Margaret attend every funeral at St. Cunegunde's, but she did. She sat in the back, so as not to attract attention, which everyone noticed and commented on approvingly.

She wasn't so bold as to attend the wakes. Those, she figured, were family affairs. But anything that happened in the church belonged to God. And if it belonged to God, she could claim part of it.

Sometimes she would only stay until Father Novakowski gave the prayers, then she would slip quietly out the side door. That was all she had come to hear, anyway. She attended daily Mass and confessed daily for the same reason: to be close to Father Novakowski.

"Bless me, Father, for I have sinned." Margaret knelt and whispered urgently into the dark screen of the confessional. She leaned in, eyes closed, as though it were less of a sin to want a priest in that dark wooden box, where absolution was instantly available. She could get her desires forgiven on the spot.

Father Novakowski let out a sigh, and Margaret saw him shield his face with his hand before reciting his prayer. When he was finished, Margaret began.

"I have a pie," she said. "You could come over and have a piece of pie with me. Peach. No one would think anything's wrong with that."

"Margaret, no!"

"It's only pie, for God's sake. I'm not asking you to break your vows. Which you already broke when we made love, so I don't see what the big deal is."

"Margaret, please!"

They stared at each other through the screen.

"When?" she asked. "When are you going to decide?"

"I'm praying on it, Margaret. There's a lot at stake here. My vocation. My vows. This isn't a decision to be made lightly."

Margaret sank back on her heels. What about her life? He said he loved her. Didn't that mean that he loved her more than he loved God? If he belonged so completely to God, he would never have succumbed.

"I thought you loved me," she said.

"I do, Margaret. I do."

"Say it. Say the words!"

"Not here. Not now. Bow your head and say an act of contrition. I will, too."

He mumbled the words with her and quickly closed the door between them, shutting out the light.

MRS. GOJUK STOPPED speaking to God when her son Steve died in Vietnam after a grenade hit the ammo pile he was guarding. The lieutenant from the Army's graves identification unit stalled her request to see the body, finally admitting that there wasn't much to see. It would be ghoulish to view what was left, he had said.

But God could put it back together, refashion Steve from his scant remains. It was a lot more than He had to work with in the Garden of Eden, where He made Eve from a single rib. He could do it again. Wasn't He all-powerful? That's what His front people claimed. She smiled through two wakes and a funeral mass, brushing off condolences, confident that God would fix Steve. He would make him whole.

But the last of Steve was lowered into the ground in a coppery box and no God appeared. Mrs. Gojuk couldn't believe it. He could do anything He wanted, yet He chose to stay away.

Steve was the first, but not the only one, of course. There was Steve's friend Paul Szewczak and his cousin Johnny Pisareck. The casualty list grew each day. Mrs. Gojuk railed against a God who ignored her pleas to save her loved ones, to leave them with her just a little longer. When she cursed Him, He took another, until she finally kept her rage to herself, keeping her diminished circle intact by seeming to submit to His power.

She thought she had reached a treaty with God when her husband, Bruno, was killed in an accident at the plant only a week before he was to retire. After he fell into the vat of bubbling steel, nothing was left, not even a nose or a toe or something to work with. As was customary, the company delivered the one-hundred-and-seventy-five-pound ingot, which is what they said Bruno weighed. But it wasn't even his real weight.

She refused to go to his funeral, refused to partake in any service that would glorify the will of God when God was pointedly ignoring her. What did she have to do to get His attention?

And then this.

First her feet refused to walk in the direction her brain specifically requested. She found herself going to strange places, reaching for unwanted items with arms that disobeyed her clear commands.

Finally, they stopped working altogether. Fluids spurted from every bodily orifice, keeping her indoors. Margaret had to mop her up. For a few days, even her speech was gibberish, her tongue and palate struggling to make contact.

"What is it, Mom?" Margaret asked, wiping the sweat from her mother's brow. She had, by this time, rented the hospital bed to which Mrs. Gojuk was confined. "Relax. It'll come. You have yourself all tied up in knots. Just try to calm down."

Mrs. Gojuk grunted, unable to express her rage, her unhappiness.

"Do you need something, Mom? Are you hungry? Thirsty?" Margaret turned her and reached down, checking her diaper; she was dry. "What's the matter?" She held her mother's nearly lifeless hand.

Only Mrs. Gojuk's index finger had life and will. She poked her fingernail into her daughter's hand, hard.

"Ouch! Hey, what are you doing?"

Mrs. Gojuk scrunched her eyes shut and willed her tongue to find its place behind her teeth, forced words to form. "Theresa," she said.

"Theresa? What's the matter with Theresa?"

"Tell her," Mrs. Gojuk said. She sighed with the effort of talking and collapsed her tense body into the mattress.

Margaret dropped her mother's hand. She straightened things in the already tidy room, adjusted the Venetian blinds to make sure light didn't hit her mother's eyes at the wrong angle.

"Tell her," Mrs. Gojuk commanded, loudly this time.

Margaret continued with her busywork, not looking at her mother.

"Tell Theresa to come. Tell Theresa," Mrs. Gojuk demanded. The words were getting clearer, easier.

Margaret stopped. "She knows, all right? She knows, she knows, she knows. She knows, and look, she still isn't coming. Okay? She knows and nothing's changed. What do you think? Do you think she's God? She sent you some stupid tickets to Lourdes. Which you can't use. She doesn't even know you can't get on a stupid plane. Okay? She knows you're paralyzed. What do you think? Do you think she can cure you? She's not God, Mom. I don't care if she's on TV. I don't care if she's the most beautiful woman on the face of the earth, she can't cure you. She's not God."

"Tell Theresa," Mrs. Gojuk said, feeling stronger.

Margaret left the room. "She's not God."

FATHER NOVAKOWSKI FLUNG the stole around his neck and pulled a chair up next to Mrs. Gojuk's rented hospital bed.

"Do you want me to hear your confession?" he asked.

Mrs. Gojuk turned her head away from him. She was annoyed that he had come when *Generations* was just starting. She felt obliged to turn it off.

"Whatever you've done, I've heard worse," the priest said.

She laughed. "What do you think I could be doing here? I can move one finger and my head." She rolled her head on the pillow to demonstrate.

"The biggest sins, we commit up here." Father Novakowski pointed to his own head.

Mrs. Gojuk wasn't about to talk to this hypocrite about sin. Wasn't he sleeping with Margaret? A man who vowed chastity was going around sleeping with women. What did he see in Margaret, anyway? It perplexed her. Margaret was a solid person, pleasant in a bland way. But she reeked of the ordinary. Mrs. Gojuk couldn't see men risking things for her affection. Theresa, of course, she could see. Men had given up beloved wives and families for her. But Mrs.

Gojuk didn't hold it against them. They couldn't resist. Theresa was like a magnet, attracting everyone, including married men with lives to lose. Including her own mother.

"Have you ever seen my other daughter?" Mrs. Gojuk asked.

"The actress?"

Mrs. Gojuk snorted, as if "actress" were too limiting a word for Theresa. Wait till he saw. She pressed her finger on the play button of the remote. "Get out of the way," she commanded, "my remote doesn't go through bodies."

Father Novakowski moved his chair to the foot of the bed. Mrs. Gojuk pressed again. The picture came on with a crackle of light. Theresa was almost naked, making love to her Egyptian inamorato. It sounded like there was a microphone inside her throat.

They watched, mesmerized. Mrs. Gojuk looked over at the priest and was pleased to see him blushing.

"Please, Mrs. Gojuk," he said.

"She's beautiful, isn't she?"

Father Novakowski lifted his eyebrows and shrugged. "It's hard to tell on television. You can't see her soul. You can only see her body."

"Soul?"

"She's playing a part. You can't really see what she looks like."

She scowled at him, displeased that he seemed immune to Theresa's charms. "I suppose you think Margaret has a beautiful soul?"

"Mrs. Gojuk, have you ever considered that Margaret has rearranged her whole life for you? She is, right now, trying to move you and her to Boston, where you can have a richer life."

"Boston! Where would she get such an idea? Why would I go to Boston? Believe me, she's only thinking of herself." Mrs. Gojuk closed her eyes. "You want to know what a good soul is? Theresa's soul is good. She sent me those tickets to Lourdes. She understands. She knows. She has a beautiful soul."

Father Novakowski took off his stole and shoved it in his pocket. "You can't go to Lourdes," he said. "It'll kill you."

"You think my Theresa would give me something that would kill me?" Mrs. Gojuk said.

"Margaret is only looking out for your best interests. She's never left your side through all your losses, all your moaning and complaining." The priest took his vial of holy oil out of his pocket, looked at it absently, and pointed the cork toward her. "You yearn after a daughter who's forgotten you and take for granted a daughter who loves you. Frankly, I don't know why she does."

Mrs. Gojuk ignored him and looked at the television. The naked couple was interrupted by a hooded, masked figure bursting through the door, waving a machine gun. He made a speech about loyalty and patriotism, then proceeded to spray them with bullets from the weapon he had anchored on his hip. Theresa and her Egyptian flopped over the side of the bed, dead. Mrs. Gojuk stared at the tube in disbelief.

"I'll see you later." The priest glanced at the television and, not seeing anything of significance, left the room.

All remaining feeling left Mrs. Gojuk's head and finger. She couldn't even press the button to rewind and examine this atrocity. They'd killed off her Theresa. This time God had gone too far. Despair snaked through her soul and wrapped around her heart, choking it so all that was left of her was vocal cords. She let out a scream that resounded throughout the house, called back the priest.

Margaret, working quietly at her desk three miles away, stood up suddenly and told her supervisor that she would have to leave right away. Her mother needed her.

THIS TIME the doctors were sure of their diagnosis: Mrs. Gojuk was in a coma.

"We don't really know what causes them," she heard the doctor tell Margaret. "She can be in it for an hour or for years. We have no way of knowing what's going on with her."

She'd lost what little movement she had in her fingers and head, and she couldn't see, but she hadn't lost consciousness. She knew she was in the hospital. She could plainly hear every word they were saying about her. She heard the doctors make their grim pronouncement, and—no surprise to her—she didn't hear them offer a solution. Margaret warned people that her mother could probably hear everything, so the interesting conversations were held in the hall, out of her range.

Father Novakowski came in once, but Margaret pulled him out to the hall. Margaret obviously didn't think there was anything else that the priest could do. He had already given her Last Rites at the house. When her scream had brought him back in and he saw no signs of life in her, he got right to work, praying and anointing. He had sped through the prayers for the dead, finishing before the ambulance came. He apparently thought nothing more was expected of him, because now he didn't even say hello to her. God's official emissary had deserted her.

No one said anything to her. She was left alone with the moaning and stench of the woman in the next bed.

"Shut up!" she screamed silently.

But the woman moaned, and no one offered either of them relief.

Mrs. Gojuk envied that woman her pain. At least she had something to hang on to, to focus on. Mrs. Gojuk felt as if she had fallen into a dark cave, without the markers to tell her where her feet should go and where her head belonged. She had no way of knowing what time it was, or even what day. Each minute seemed like a year as she examined the seconds in that minute, waiting for her salvation. She knew she had missed her flight to Lourdes. Margaret had probably already cashed in the tickets and would use the money to move to Boston. They had killed off Theresa, and her trip to Lourdes was canceled. Those two thoughts echoed back and forth against the walls of her cave. Eventually, though, even they got weaker.

She felt like she was floating in a black, cold void. Maybe she was already dead. Maybe she was dead and in hell. Maybe hell was being alone and not knowing if it was ever going to end. She used to believe that God would rescue her. But Margaret was right. God was too busy with the big issues to be concerned with her. He was occupied with flashier news, like earthquakes, floods.

Of course, He did pay attention to some people, those He anointed. His favorites. Like Moses, the Disciples. She just wasn't one of His favorites. That was the fact of the matter and she had to face facts. No charm she possessed, no tantrum she could throw, would make Him prefer her to His favorites.

"Forgive me," she said silently. "You can't help who you love." She thought she might be crying, but couldn't feel if tears were actually falling down her cheeks. "You can't help who you love."

She heard someone come in and waited expectantly while they fixed the curtains, then came over and combed her hair.

"You have a visitor," the nurse said, hardly containing the excitement in her voice. "Tess Randall is in the hall waiting to see you. I'm a big fan of hers. She's so beautiful." The nurse finished primping her. "I can see where she gets her looks," she said.

Mrs. Gojuk warmed herself on this insight.

The nurse rubbed something on her lips, and Mrs. Gojuk realized it was lipstick. She had feeling in her lips. Her toes felt full of pins and needles, as if awakening from sleep. The sensation crawled up her legs, then her torso, spreading to her arms and fingers and finally up to the rest of her face, where she was able to open her eyes.

"Oh my," Mrs. Gojuk said.

The first thing she saw was her beautiful daughter, Tess Randall, standing in the doorway.

"Mother!"

Mrs. Gojuk smiled. "Theresa."

"THE MEN HERE are fabulous!" Lynn said to Margaret on the telephone. She had been in Boston for a month and already had dates with three men. "They are so sophisticated. They actually go to operas and aren't even gay."

Margaret had never been to an opera herself and wouldn't recognize the names of any but the most famous. Couldn't hum the tunes from even the most familiar.

"I've been to *Così fan tutte* three times so far. I couldn't let any of them know that I'd just seen it," Lynn said. "Still, it was so different from a Cokesville date to the Pocono Playhouse to see Celeste Holm."

"I thought Celeste Holm was dead," Margaret said.

"Is she? I hadn't heard that. Anyway, it's just an example." Lynn let out her breath sharply. "What have you been up to?"

"I don't know. I'm back at work. Nothing much."

"You could do all that here in Boston," Lynn said.

There was a long silence. Margaret could feel the distance pulling at their friendship, which wasn't, she realized now, based on much more than the fact that, at twenty-nine, they were two of the oldest unmarried women in Cokesville. Without that to connect them, the educational and cultural gaps between them were as wide as a canyon.

"Your father came to the funeral," Margaret said. She could hear Lynn light a cigarette on the other end. "We talked a little."

"Did you have a nice conversation?" Lynn asked.

"He was drunk."

"Big surprise."

Margaret heard a knock on the door and peeped through the living-room curtains. She smiled. It was Father Novakowski.

"I gotta go, Lynn. Call me this weekend."

"I can't. I've been invited to Martha's Vineyard. This one is great. He's never had his heart broken, so I don't have to deal with all that. I'm telling you, Margaret, you gotta come to Boston. You'll never get married in Cokesville."

"Call me next week. Have a good time." She looked out past the curtain again to make sure the priest was still there.

"Look in on my mother, will you, Margaret? She's pretty much alone now that I'm gone."

"Hmmhmmm," Margaret said, clicking the receiver and opening the front door.

MARGARET REMEMBERED her promise to visit Lynn's mother when she stopped by the 7-Eleven for a quart of milk and saw old man Murphy's Pontiac taking up two parking places. She walked up to the car to say hello, so she would be able to tell Lynn later that she had, and noticed an awful smell, like an outhouse, coming from the open door.

"Mr. Murphy?" She put her hand over her nose and peered inside.

He didn't answer. The front of the car was filled with empty Four Roses bottles and quick pick tickets. He had soiled his pants and vomited down the front of his shirt.

"Jesus Christ," Margaret said. She noticed that his chest was heaving, so he wasn't dead. She turned to leave, gagging on the smell, forgetting why she had even come to the store, calling Mrs. Murphy from the pay phone to come and get her husband.

IN THE CONFESSIONAL, Margaret held her breath until the little door that separated them opened. The beloved silhouette appeared different.

"Mike?" she said.

A strange voice answered her. "Do you want to tell me your confession?"

"Where is Father Novakowski?"

"He went on retreat. I'm Father Karak."

"Retreat?"

"Do you want to tell me your confession?" Father Karak asked.

"Is he coming back?" Margaret whispered.

"I don't know. I'll be here until he does."

Father Karak bowed his head to hear her confession and began his prayer. Margaret ran from the confessional and into the street, the bright morning light cutting her eyes.

"EVEN YOUR BROTHER says you should come to Boston. He's here. I'm here," Lynn said.

"You're seeing Milos?" Margaret asked, surprised.

"Not 'seeing' seeing. I just run into him every now and then. We know a lot of the same people. I didn't know he and Jeanna were divorced."

"They were here for Mom's funeral. They acted normal. He never told me they were having problems."

Margaret was sitting on the front step of her house waiting for the mailman. She had gotten the portable phone so she could talk to Lynn while she waited for another letter from Mike Novakowski. They were formal letters, filled with the bare essentials of his spiritual journey on this retreat. She reread them, looking for emotion behind the chiseled lines. Once, in frustration, she even shook the letter, hoping something like love would fall out. It didn't, of course. She tied the pristine missives in a ribbon and slept with them under her pillow, imagining the better part of him would be transported to her through dreams.

"Where do you see Milos?" Margaret asked.

"Well, once at Skinner's, a bar where the financial crowd goes after work," Lynn said.

"But neither of you are financial people."

"There's no law that says we can't go to Skinner's if we don't work in a bank, for God's sake. What's wrong with you? You gotta get out of that town. Nothing's going to happen for you there."

Margaret could see the mailman turn the corner and go into the Herbinko house. She felt a surge of happiness and wanted to run up to him and demand her letter. It was difficult to stay on the step and feign nonchalance, but part of the fun was the sweet torture of delayed gratification, seeing how long she could last before tearing it open. She would put the letter in her pocket and make herself wait for ten minutes before reading it. Surely Mike was going through much more, wrestling with his soul, with God. It would be like a test of her worthiness, making herself wait for ten minutes.

"Are you seeing anybody new?" she asked. "I mean, besides my married brother. What about that guy who took you to Martha's Vineyard?" The mailman had gone next door to the Szewczaks'. Margaret forced herself to breathe in and out like a regular person.

"It didn't work out. Why is it they think if you're not twenty, you're only good for sex, not for marriage? I would think it would be the other way around."

"Go figure."

The mailman came up the walk. He fished in his bag, pulled out a stack, and handed it to her.

Margaret flipped through the envelopes—bills, a card from Theresa—and saw the one she wanted. Black ink on thick cream-colored stationery. When she'd first received one, so grim and formal, she thought it was a death notice, until she saw the return address. But it cheered her now. She let it disappear back inside the bundle, clamping the edges of the larger envelopes together so it wouldn't slip out.

"What do you think, Margaret?" Lynn asked.

"About what?"

She sighed. "Never mind. I'll call you next week."

"What about Sunday?"

"No, I've been invited to the Berkshires by this guy. He's part of the lawyer orchestra in Boston and they're playing in Tanglewood."

"Is he married?"

"He plays the oboe. Really, Margaret, you should think about Boston. Don't you want to get married and have children?"

"Yeah, but not to just anybody. I'd at least want to have something in common with him."

"What can you have in common with a man?"

EVERY SATURDAY MORNING Margaret put flowers on her parents' graves. Her father, Bruno, was buried in the church cemetery with a Catholic service, despite the ambiguity surrounding his death. Only he knew what was in his heart as he fell from the catwalk that circled the vat. And since only he could know what label his death deserved, the Church finally had given him the benefit of the doubt and admitted him to its inner circle.

Although her mother had been more vocal in her despair, she hadn't acted on it, and so had died in a state of Catholic grace. She had been sick, had gotten better, then had slipped away when no one was looking. Even Margaret, who had loved her mother dearly, had become so involved in her own problems that she had stopped noticing her. Now she wondered if her mother had died because no one saw her. Is it possible to cease to exist because no one is paying attention to you? If you become invisible, are you already dead?

Margaret used to comb her hair and put on makeup before she went to the cemetery. She stopped when she realized no one saw her there except widows, and there was no need to fix up for them. Margaret noticed this change in herself about the same time she noticed that she no longer ran for the phone, because the only person who called her was Lynn, who would tell her that so far no husband candidates were working out. She no longer waited on the step for the mailman, because she had finally received an emotional letter from Father Novakowski, who had come off retreat and, yes, was leaving the priesthood, but he was not coming home to her. He had met a woman there, a nun, who was also giving up her vows. They were, Mike said, on the same spiritual journey. He prayed for Margaret to understand.

Arpad and Esther Zaary had no children in Cokesville to put flowers on their graves, so for a while she did. And then she just stopped. And soon she was walking over their plot on her way to her parents' graves without thinking about them at all. She got sick that June and couldn't tend her parents' graves, and by the end of the summer, she still hadn't gone to visit them. After all, they were dead and couldn't see her anyway.

Mrs. Herbinko's Birthday Party

1986

"FOR GOD'S SAKE, hurry. Loosen her girdle."

"The hooks are rusted, they won't come loose."

"There's the ambulance now. It's okay, Mother, the doctor is here." Gloria Marzak absently stroked her mother's face and wiped the drool from the corner of her mouth.

Latonia Herbinko blinked at the mayhem around her and wondered why it was taking so long to die.

The emergency squad ran into the room, their equipment knocking paper plates half filled with birthday cake and ice cream off the table. One medic took her pulse while the other shined a bright light in her eyes and peered in.

"What's her name?"

"Mrs. Herbinko. Latonia. We think she had another stroke."

"Latonia, can you hear me?"

Mrs. Herbinko closed her eyes against the light. No one had called her Latonia since Ignatz died.

"She can't talk. She's had three strokes already, you know."

"Get the oxygen over here, she's fading." The medic pushed on her chest.

Mrs. Herbinko looked up at the medics brandishing hoses in her face and at her middle-aged daughters—Gloria, Joan, and Linda—wringing their hands. All she wanted was to be free of her cumbersome body and reunited with her husband, Ignatz, who had died in a mine disaster forty years ago. That was all she'd thought about and prayed for ever since. She couldn't understand why these people were prolonging her agony.

"Leave me alone," she said simply.

"Mother!"

"She talked. Mom, what did you say? Say it again!" Gloria, her eldest, shook her frantically. Mrs. Herbinko tried to shrink away, but her body couldn't respond.

"Oh my God," Linda, her youngest, sobbed. "After all these years, oh, Mom."

Mrs. Herbinko wished someone would take off her ridiculous party hat. They had been subjecting her to these birthday parties ever since her first stroke left her powerless to protest. The ignominy of dying while wearing the hat was more than she could bear.

"We're losing her," one of the medics yelled. "Give me that syringe." He jabbed her indelicately in the chest.

The injection thrust Mrs. Herbinko to the ceiling, where she looked down on the scene below. Her daughters were hysterical and the medics were shaking their heads.

"But she talked," Joan was saying.

"That happens sometimes, right before . . ." The medic turned off his valves.

Mrs. Herbinko didn't hear anymore. She felt so light. The chaos beneath her was getting dimmer and smaller. She saw Father Pavlek come into the house. No one bothered to remove her hat.

The air around her was blue and cold. She let herself get sucked into the stream that carried her away.

This is great, she thought. She wiggled a little to let the cool air circulate around her body, and she drifted until she came across a slightly pudgy middle-aged man who had a strange orangish-red glow about him.

"Hello, hello," he said.

"Hello. Who are you?" Mrs. Herbinko asked.

"Raoul."

"Raoul, I'm Mrs. Herbinko." She noted with some annoyance that her speech was still garbled, but Raoul didn't seem to have any difficulty understanding her.

"What's that glow?" she asked.

"We all get it," he said noncommittally.

He didn't seem inclined to conversation, but this was all so new that Mrs. Herbinko felt she should ask some questions. "I really thought my speech would be better."

"Did you? What's wrong with it?"

"And my arm, look! It still doesn't work." She held it up with the other arm, dismayed.

"I don't think you'll have to use it."

"I thought we were all supposed to be in a perfected state here. Like when we were sixteen." She said this a little critically.

"Hmm. I know what you mean. I thought I would drop a few years. And a few pounds." He laughed and rubbed his belly delightedly. "Who you were at sixteen is not the person you've become. Anyway, where would you draw the line? Are you your most perfect when you are exactly sixteen years old, or are you more perfect when you are sixteen and a half? There are so many variables, and not enough time, really, to work out the details."

Mrs. Herbinko could see the logic, but was disappointed nonetheless. She didn't want Ignatz to see her like this, after forty years and four strokes. He had a roving eye and was so easily distracted. She always imagined they would be like they were on their wedding night. "I wouldn't think that would be such a problem for . . . well, you know, for Him." She looked nervous. "I am in the right place, aren't I?"

"Oh yes, you're here, all right. Most folks go into a holding pattern for a while, but I guess with your strokes you didn't have much opportunity to misbehave."

"Hmm." She settled in next to him, adjusting to her new surroundings. She could hang in the air without actually sitting, and she was able to get around without her wheelchair, even though her left side was still paralyzed. "Do I have to have an interview or anything?"

"Oh no. You're here. You're in."

"Well," she said, looking around. "What do I do now?"

"Do? You can do whatever you like."

"May I see somebody?"

"Of course." His warm glow deepened. "If they're here, that is."

"Yes, I'm sure he is. Ignatz Herbinko. He fooled around a little bit, but I've prayed for him for the last forty years, that we would be united here. How can I find out if he's here?"

"We have to look at the Plenary Indulgence Statistical File." He led her effortlessly through the atmosphere to a pond filled with golden letters, like a magical alphabet soup.

"You know, nothing here is as I would have thought. Don't you know him? I'm surprised you don't know everyone without this sort of thing."

"Afraid not." He bent his head low over the pond.

To her astonishment, words were forming out of the disarray.

"Goodness, you've said enough novenas to get a hundred and fifty souls in, but you've only credited Ignatz Herbinko's account. Look, here it all is. Your first novena did it, actually."

Mrs. Herbinko was feeling awkward now that the anticipated

moment was approaching. He left a young woman and would now see a worn-out old lady. "What if he doesn't recognize me?"

"Oh, he'll recognize you."

They zoomed through the cold air at an exhilarating pace. "He's been looking over you all this time. It's the rule. Kind of like saving someone's life down below, but in reverse. He's responsible for you."

"But wait! Will he have aged? Will I know him?"

"Here we are." Raoul stopped suddenly. The only person in sight was a small older man. He was entirely bald. When he saw them approach, his glow became almost blinding, so Mrs. Herbinko couldn't see his face.

"Ignatz Herbinko, I have Latonia Herbinko here," Raoul cried out, pleased with his part in this reunion.

"Latonia!"

She squinted into his brilliance. She couldn't see his features clearly, but they weren't exactly as she remembered them.

The man took both her hands in his own. "Latonia, you made it."

If her memory of Ignatz's appearance was foggy, her memory of his touch was clear. This man's hands on her were too gentle. Ignatz's were rough, a little cruel even.

"This isn't my husband."

"Of course it is," Raoul said.

"I know my husband," Mrs. Herbinko said, flustered by her own impatience.

"Sir," Raoul said officiously, "what is your name?"

"Ignatz Herbinko."

"See," Raoul said triumphantly, turning to Mrs. Herbinko as if the matter were settled.

"Well, it's not the Ignatz Herbinko I was married to."

"Nevertheless. The Plenary Indulgence Statistical File indicated this is the man you prayed for."

"How do you know who I prayed for? Doesn't *He* know who I prayed for?"

"Really, Mrs. Herbinko, there must be thousands of Ignatz Herbinkos. You have to be specific. How are we supposed to know which one you meant? Remember when we looked in the Plenary Indulgence Statistical File? How many Ignatz Herbinkos were there?"

"I saw only one."

"You're right, actually." Raoul looked perplexed.

"There is only one," the latest Ignatz Herbinko said. "Your husband was born Ignatz Cyzbynko, and that's how he's registered up here. When he went to America, immigration officials couldn't spell it and made him Herbinko."

"Who are you?" Mrs. Herbinko asked crossly.

"Ignatz Herbinko."

"Oh yes. Well, how do you know so much about us? I certainly don't know you." She narrowed her eyes.

"I know all about you," he said meekly. "I've been your guardian for the last forty years. Since you got me up here and all. The rule, remember?"

"Some guardian. I've had four strokes and I've been treated like a child. Ignatz would have never have let that happen to me," she said.

"It seemed like it was in your best interest. You were such a lusty thing." His eyes shone a little, remembering her before her strokes. "I'm sure you would've gotten into some serious trouble if you were able, and you wouldn't be here now."

"That wasn't for you to decide," Mrs. Herbinko said.

"You were so pretty. I wanted to make sure I would see you up here."

"That's very selfish. I wasted forty years of my life. I could have been having fun."

"You'll have a lot longer to have fun up here," Ignatz said.

"Well, it doesn't seem like much fun so far. I can't find my husband because of some sort of bureaucratic snafu, and nothing makes any sense. At least down there they shoved birthday cake in my mouth every now and then."

Indeed, some crumbs still quivered on her upper lip. Ignatz Herbinko saw them, too, and tenderly brushed them off.

"I'm terribly sorry you're not happy," he said.

"It's not your fault, I guess, although nothing is going according to plan."

She was finding it increasingly hard to stay angry. Mrs. Herbinko noticed him for the first time. Actually, he was nice, even if he had ruined everything. That tremendous glow certainly helped his appearance, as did the way he looked at her. Her Ignatz never looked at her that way, at least not for very long. He was afraid he would miss some other woman if he looked too long at her.

Ignatz Herbinko took her hand. "I'd like to show you around. It takes some getting used to up here."

"Well, I guess so. I have so many questions. What happened to Raoul?"

"Look! You're starting to glow. It's beautiful."

"So I am. What a wonderful shade!"

They admired her color for a while. Then Ignatz Herbinko reached over and carefully pulled off Mrs. Herbinko's birthday party hat.

The Great Wall

1986

THERESA GOJUK'S BROTHER Milos was in the newly remodeled reception area of the Eifel Corporation, in Boston, Massachusetts. He was a quality-assurance engineer, pretending to read the personnel file of Ms. Mohandes, the candidate he was interviewing for the open engineering position. Ms. Mohandes, who appeared to be Indian, was wearing the uniform of the new working class: a blue skirted suit that flopped around her lanky body and a white bow-tied collar that brought attention to the dark down on her cheeks. She was standing right in front of him, waiting to be invited into the office. But Milos was waiting for a polite moment to tell her he had to go to the bathroom. His prostate was basically shot, and he knew he wouldn't make it through an hour interview. He hitched his pants up over his belly, then froze in alarm when he noticed he had on one blue sock and one brown. Quickly he sucked in his gut to release the pants and let the cuffs fall back around the tops of his wing tips before Ms. Mohandes noticed, too.

"I just have to go to the men's room, Ms. Mo . . . Mo . . ." His tongue rolled around the foreign configuration of letters that formed her last name on the green personnel file. A green file from personnel was code for "Go," as in "Hire this person, she's a qualified minority." The Eifel Corporation had a vigorous affirmative-action program largely because of the bad publicity that resulted when Bud Wright was fired for telling racist jokes to Glenda Wills, who, as it came out in the trial, was a black woman. But who knew? Milos certainly wouldn't have guessed she was black. Nobody thought so, and they discussed this marvel endlessly at lunch and during furtive asides in the men's room.

"Mohandes." The dark woman smiled and held out a slender hand for him to shake, which he did, but very gently, so he wouldn't hurt her. Small women like Ms. Mohandes made his muscles tense trying to avoid flailing out and inadvertently hurting them. Nothing major, just little bonks and elbow pokes, things like that. That's why Jeanna left him finally. She said it was Freudian, that he wanted to hurt her, and why couldn't he see it? But he didn't want to hurt her. He loved her and was just big and clumsy and took up too much room. But still, one day Jeanna decided he had become the enemy. And such a dangerous, alert enemy, he thought, he couldn't even manage to wear two blue socks.

"Mohandes. Yes." He motioned for her to have a seat and he went down the hall with Ms. Mohandes's file clamped under his arm to the men's room and lined up at the urinals next to Bill Applegate.

"See the game last night?" Applegate asked.

"Fell asleep in the third quarter." Milos winced as the stream of urine tried to make it through his swollen prostate, which felt like it was on fire, thanks in small part to the spicy takeout chicken he had eaten for dinner and in large part to the beer he drank to wash it down.

"Not the same since Bird retired," Applegate said.

"Yeah," Milos said.

"Since Bird is gone," Applegate continued, "what do you got? Pinkney? Dee Brown? Bird was like a god. When Bird, McHale, and Parish came out on the floor, they were like gods! Gods! It's just not the same."

"Yeah," Milos said. He felt bad when Bird retired, but the truth was that the fun had gone out of basketball when Reggie Lewis died of an apparent overdose, not when Bird retired. Reggie played small forward for Northeastern before being drafted in the first round by the Celtics. Local kid makes good. His downfall broke Milos's heart. But he couldn't tell Applegate that he missed a black kid more than a six-foot-nine-inch white god. He couldn't tell any of his friends that. But he couldn't tell his friends a lot of things. He couldn't tell them, for instance, that the list of things that gave him pleasure, like beer and basketball and takeout chicken—even sex, for God's sake—was, through some horrible alchemy, turning into the litany of things that gave him pain. He couldn't tell them he was becoming a worthless old coot who couldn't match a pair of socks and who took up too much room on the planet, and that people like Ms. Mohandes were queuing up behind him to nudge him off.

They walked out of the men's room into the hall. Applegate pointed to the green folder under Milos's arm. "I interviewed one of those yesterday." He snorted, and Milos was relieved not to hear any pity. "What I don't understand," Applegate said, "what I really don't understand, is how those people can all afford to go to MIT, but they can't afford to eat. MIT, for God's sake! But they have their hands out for foreign aid and welfare and everything else they can think of to get from us."

He slapped Milos on the back and walked him down the hallway, as if Milos were a gladiator preparing for battle instead of an obsolete engineer going to interview the woman who would, in all probability, replace him.

Ms. Mohandes sat primly on the sofa by the receptionist, her feet crossed at her ankles, looking at a piece of paper, probably her résumé, Milos thought. She glanced up hopefully when she heard them coming.

"Is that her?" Applegate whispered.

Milos nodded.

"Arf!" Applegate barked in a low voice. Milos stiffened; he was sure that Ms. Mohandes had heard him. She wasn't pretty and she was very skinny, and Milos felt bad for her because of that.

"Ms. Mo . . . Mo . . ."

"Mohandes," the young woman said.

Milos looked at her for a long moment, and Ms. Mohandes waited until he had his fill. She was used to that look that men gave her. They would stare at her until they got comfortable with her ugliness. Usually, comfort would turn to friendship. She was a likable, smart person, after all. Occasionally, though—and more often than prettier women would believe—comfort would turn to lust, as it had with her husband, Irmil. That thought gave her confidence, and she smiled at Milos, who seemed flustered by the smile and motioned for her to go into the office.

Ms. Mohandes sat down and looked around for a picture of children or a wife, something to use to make conversation, but the office was bare except for a framed poster of the Great Wall of China. Ms. Mohandes felt her heart beat with a little panic, trying to relate the Great Wall to an American. Most of them were proud of the fact that they didn't even know where the Great Wall of China was, and her personnel recruiter had told her it was especially important for an ethnic woman like herself to try to connect with her interviewer. She waited until he looked up from her folder before she took a deep breath and spoke. "Do you know," she asked, "what Nixon said when he was at the Great Wall of China?"

"Nixon?" Milos asked. He looked as if he was recalling something painful.

"Richard Nixon." Ms. Mohandes shifted her eyes to the poster, willing Milos to follow suit.

They stared at the poster for a moment. "He said"—Ms. Mohandes paused—"he said, 'This is indeed a great wall!' "

Milos was silent for a minute as he continued looking at the poster. Then he said, "You're certainly qualified for this position, Ms. Mohandes."

Ms. Mohandes was embarrassed that he ignored her comment about Richard Nixon, who was President almost fourteen years earlier, in 1972. Despite his age, maybe Milos didn't know much about Nixon. She was always shocked that she knew more about American history than most Americans, who had a slash-and-burn attitude about the past. But at least he'd got her name right. That was something, wasn't it?

"In fact," he said, "this is an entry-level position. You're probably overqualified."

Heat rushed to Ms. Mohandes's face. There was always a reason to keep her out. How could she refute it if someone said she was overqualified? She started to speak and Milos held up his hand to stop her.

"I'm going to recommend you," he said.

"Thank you," she said. It was the fastest interview she had ever heard of, and she would replay it endlessly later, trying to figure out what had sold him on her.

Milos got up and indicated she could leave. She noticed for the first time that Milos's shirt looked like it wasn't ironed, that he just took it out of the dryer and hung it up. That made her sad. He was probably divorced. That's why he didn't have pictures of his family around.

"This is a very good office," she said, gathering up her briefcase and walking out, trying to rearrange her posture to show she was grateful and worthy to be given a chance to prove herself.

"It's not my office," he said. "It's just where we interview people."

Ms. Mohandes hung her head, ashamed that she didn't know, or somehow guess, that such a thing as an interview office existed. It was probably rude, too, she realized now, to have mentioned Richard Nixon. He was disgraced, after all. Maybe Americans were sensitive about that.

"I am very happy I will work with you," she said, trying to atone for her offenses.

Milos walked her to the elevators and handed her her green personnel folder. "Take this back to human resources."

He held the door with his foot, and what she thought was the beginning of a smile crossed his face, but evaporated. He looked like he wanted to say something important, but all he said before the door closed was, "You know, I voted for Nixon."

Writing Lesson

1990

My mother climbed on the roof of her house a month ago to repair some loose shingles. It had been a wet September, and she was worried that the leak would get worse if it wasn't repaired right away. She was a strong woman who had operated a forklift alongside men in the steel mills. And she was an impatient woman who wouldn't wait for my father to do it. She took the extension ladder from the garage, propped it against the house, clenched some nails in her teeth, and clambered up.

I didn't see her do this. I was in Sausalito, California. No one saw her. Which is just as well, because in my imagination she fell gracefully: holding her hammer, smug with satisfaction that she'd managed to nail down the loose shingles before her baggy work pants caught the breeze, puffed out like a parachute, and transported her gently to earth.

Which isn't how it happened, of course. She slipped on the wet roof and plummeted like a hundred-and-forty-five-pound sack of potatoes, puncturing her kidneys and breaking her neck. Somewhere in the three days I was home for her funeral, I must have asked my dad to visit me in Sausalito, and somewhere in those three days he must have agreed, because he's here now, helping me turn a walk-in closet into a writing nook.

"She didn't leave you any money, Annie," he says.

"I don't need money," I say. I know my mother hoarded money, but I can't imagine her parting with it in death any more than in life. I picture the undertaker padding her casket with sacks of money, like sandbags, to cushion her entry into the next life.

My father twists the pliers and removes the pin from the closet door hinge. "She didn't want to give you anything until you made something of yourself."

"She doesn't think I've made anything of myself? I'm a teacher."

I'd moved from Los Angeles to Sausalito five years ago with Artie, a computer programmer, because he was normal. I was trying to be normal. We talked about having a family, but I never got rid of my diaphragm. He left last year, and I had to take a job teaching high school English.

My father hands me the pliers and pins, then lifts the door off. "What do you need this office for, anyway? You can correct your papers right there on the kitchen table."

I got a press pass from the *San Francisco Examiner* for the Romance Writers' Conference at the San Francisco Sheraton. I have to write a feature for them in exchange for the credentials. Then I can attend any of the classes I want. Today was the first day of the weekend conference, and in one of the seminars I looked in on, the moderator said it was important to have an area that was dedicated just to writing. The only spare room I have in my five-hundred-square-foot condo is the closet. The wardrobes for my different lives—screenplay writer, gardener, teacher, idle housewife—are piled up on the sofa like an archaeological dig.

"I'm writing. I need a place to write."

"There's not a lot of money in writing, is there?" he asks.

"I don't need the money," I say again. "I'm not doing it for the money."

"If you were going to make it as a writer, it would have happened already, don't you think?"

"You sound just like Mom. What did she think I should make of myself, anyway?"

"She didn't say."

IT WAS A LIE to tell my dad that I didn't need money. Who wants to admit they're broke at thirty-seven? My teaching job just keeps me out of bankruptcy. The down payment on my condo wiped me out. All my credit cards are maxed out: I paid my mortgage with them for the last four months. When I read in the newspapers that the romance writers were meeting in San Francisco, it was like the sun breaking through the clouds of my financial despair.

"I can write romances," I told Theresa on the phone. "Why didn't I think of that before? Everybody reads romances. More people read romances than the Bible."

"Aren't you supposed to write about what you know?" Theresa asked.

"My parents had a good romance," I said. "My mother could do anything. Dad worshipped her."

"I thought your parents fought a lot," she said.

"Well, I can write about unhappy romances, then. When you think about it, most people aren't happy. That's just life."

"Your life maybe," Theresa said. "Nobody wants to read about your crummy romances."

"Okay, Mrs. Pierce. Or is it Mrs. Seligman this month? I forget which husband you're on. Maybe you can give me some pointers on a good romance," I said.

"You don't have to be mean," Theresa said.

VERA COLEMAN WAS the keynote speaker at the romance writers' convention. Vera, the bestselling romance writer in the history of the planet, churned out four books a year, each one selling more than a million copies, and the auditorium is packed to hear her advice to fledgling writers. I arrive early and hold up the press badge dangling from my neck to push my way up front. The hostess steps to the podium, gushes an introduction, and everyone stands, clapping and yelling to welcome Vera, who turns out to be a six-foot-four *man* wearing cowboy boots, a ten-gallon hat, and a string tie. He gets a wolf whistle when he smiles and, patting the air with his outstretched hands, quiets the crowd.

"Is this a joke?" I ask the dumpy woman with horn-rimmed glasses next to me.

She puts her finger to her lips.

I turn the other way to an expensively dressed woman with a complex coif. "What can a man know about romance?" I ask her. "Jeez, I haven't even figured it out."

She shrugs and smiles. "I have three grandchildren," she says. "What's to figure out?"

WHEN I COME HOME, my father is running wire into my closet so I can have a light over my desk.

"I hope I'm not disturbing the neighbors," he says. "I've been hammering a lot."

"They're never here. They go to school." Two Chinese American women live downstairs. I never see them, but I always smell their cooking—heavy peanut oil permeates the hallway.

"This apartment is too small," he says. "You should get a bigger apartment with an extra bedroom."

"I like the view."

"It has a nice view," he agrees.

We can see Alcatraz prison across the Bay from my deck. San Francisco is beyond it.

"When are you going back to Cokesville?" I ask.

"Do you want me to leave?"

"Don't you have to go back to work?" My dad has been working in the copy center at Staples ever since the steel mill closed down.

"I get a couple of weeks for bereavement." He puts down the spool of wire. "I thought I would look for David while I'm out here."

I watch him unscrew a fixture, scared that Mom's death had made him lose his mind. My brother David went to Vietnam and we never heard from him again. My father points across the Bay to San Francisco.

"I think he may have stayed out here after he was discharged," he says.

I look across the Bay, my heart suddenly beating fast.

"David's alive?"

"We got a letter from him. From San Francisco." He opens the book he had been reading and pulls out a worn airmail letter.

I grab it from him. The return address is 2435 Prado Street.

"It's postmarked twenty years ago," I say. I want to open the letter, but my hands are shaking. I put it down so I don't shred it. "He can't be there anymore."

"Your mother decided we shouldn't answer him, because he deserted his wife and kid. But now," he says, "she's dead."

THE SEMINAR THAT I ATTEND the next day is "Writing a Good Sex Scene." Theresa had been particularly derisive of the sex scenes in my screenplays. "Haven't you ever had sex?" she had asked.

"Your sex scenes are so twisted. For one thing, everybody talks too much. They end up arguing and not doing anything." Apparently I'm not the only one who can use some pointers. The auditorium is standing room only, and I bully my way to a seat, waving my press pass. Most of the women look like middle-aged librarians—my future self, I think ruefully—notebooks on their laps and pencils poised. I turn to the woman beside me wearing reading glasses and balancing a paper cup of coffee and a copybook on her lap. Her name tag reads *Connie Sears.*

I put out my hand. "Annie Kusiak."

"Were you in the plot seminar this morning?" she asks.

"No."

"What have you written?" she asks. She looks like she's trying to place me.

"Written? Well, nothing like this yet. Although I'm going to try." I show her my press badge. "I'm a journalist. I do feature pieces for the *Examiner.*"

She hands me a business card. "This year I wrote *Something Borrowed.* It's up for the Heart of Glass Award." I realize she wants me to include her in my article.

The woman in front of me passes back a sheaf of papers. I take one and hand the pile to Connie Sears. It's a breakdown of the different romance categories and the type of sex permitted in each one: above the belt, below the belt, before marriage, before marriage only if engaged, during marriage if your husband is unfaithful, during marriage when your spouse is incarcerated for insider trading.

"The most important thing to remember," the lecturer is saying, "is that there are no memorable sex scenes in literature. It's all in the buildup. No one ever quotes a sex scene. The important thing is to get in, do your business, and get out."

I point to Connie Sears's name tag. "My mother's name is Connie."

"Connie Sears is the name I write under."

"And remember," the lecturer concludes, "once your characters start to make out, it's all action. No conversation in bed."

MY FATHER isn't around when I get home. I wonder if he's gone to San Francisco to look for David. I grab a beer from the refrigerator and go out to the deck. The smell of eucalyptus trees wafts down from the hills. I sit, put my feet up on the rail, and look out at Alcatraz. I hear female laughter from the condo downstairs, which is odd, because I never hear anyone there during the day. Then suddenly I hear a man laughing with them. It's my father. I strain to hear what they're saying, but I can't make it out. I put my beer down and run down the stairs. The door is open into their living room. My father's feet poke around the front of the television set. The two Chinese women are kneeling beside him, laughing. They rise when I come in.

"Hi, there." I try to smile and stick my hand out for them to shake. Their hands dart in and out of mine like white boneless fish. "Hey, Dad, is everything okay?" I ask.

"I'm fine, Annie. I'm hooking up their VCR. These things are tricky as hell."

My mother always did that kind of stuff around the house. It's funny to see my dad trying to do it. I pick up the instruction manual, which is lying on the box. "There's a picture right here." I show it to the women, as if their English isn't good. "It's easy."

"Yeah," my father says, "I saw that. But this one is different. The ports are different."

My neighbors laugh, a tinkling sound that I find really irritating.

"I hope you're not going to take too much longer. Theresa is flying up from L.A. to have dinner with us tonight. Remember?"

"Why don't you go ahead without me? Lin and Liu invited me to eat with them. I don't want to impose on you all the time."

"Theresa is coming down specifically to see you," I say, "because she couldn't make it to the funeral. She'll be disappointed."

My father comes out from behind the television set and stands up, his hands on his hips. "No, she won't be."

Lin sees me to the door.

"We will take good care of your father," Lin says. "Don't worry."

She closes the door behind me.

I MEET THERESA at an Italian restaurant in North Beach. The waiter spends a little too much time explaining the specials, and I know he recognizes her. He finally hands us oversized menus and leaves.

"That guy recognized you," I say.

"If I had a thousand dollars for everyone who recognized me . . ." Theresa says. She sounds pleased, though. She's forty years old and is in the stage of her career where people say she looks familiar but they don't know from where. She had a hit a couple of years ago in the movie *Stand-Down*, the first big project financed by her production company. She played a Marine colonel being court-martialed for disobeying a direct order. Now she pulls back on her face with both hands. "Do you think it's time?" she asks.

"You look weird," I say. "Do you know how they do that? I saw the operation on television. They cut your face off and lay it on the table next to you."

"I may have to, anyway," Theresa says. "For professional reasons."

For professional reasons, I think, I may have to gain twenty pounds and and start wearing sensible shoes.

"I hate to admit it," Theresa says, "but my mother had it right. You're like a piece of meat in this business."

"I know how I'm going to write the romance novel," I say. "I have the plot. The guy goes to war. His wife has a baby while he's gone. He's in intelligence and he falls in love with a prisoner he's interrogating. He gets her pregnant and she has the baby. But when he comes back after the war to tell his wife he's leaving her, at the sight of his three-year-old daughter, he falls back in love with his wife."

"What does he do with the other woman and her kid?"

"I haven't figured that part out yet."

Theresa makes dough balls out of a roll and drops them on the table.

"My father thinks David is alive," I say suddenly.

"Your David?"

"My parents got a letter from him when he was discharged. It was from here."

The waiter takes our order, smiling at Theresa.

"What a bastard," she says.

Memories of my brother have taken on a life of their own, as they do for all dead people. Over the years he's grown colossal, my memories piling up like offerings until he'd become so big I couldn't see him anymore. And now I find out that this *god* I'd created has judged me so insignificant that I didn't even warrant a phone call to tell me he's alive.

"He really is a bastard," I say.

THERESA HAS a meeting the next day in San Francisco with some potential backers for her next project, so I drop her at her hotel and drive over to Prado Street, which is in the Marina district. It's a frame house, nicely kept up. I turn off the ignition and pull out David's letter. I read it by the streetlight. "Dear Mom and Dad," it says. "I hope you are well. I am back in the States. Being over there has changed me and it would only make you unhappy if you saw me now. Before I come back to Cokesville, I need some time to cool off, get some perspective on my life. I'm looking for a job and will write as soon as I get set up. Your son, David."

The windows on the second floor are lit up, and for a long time I watch them. One by one, the lights go out, then suddenly the front door opens. It's a man with a large garbage bag. I hold my breath. My heart is beating so hard I'm almost blind. The man strolls down the walk with the garbage bag until he is at the curb, close to my car. He drops the trash on the sidewalk and lights a cigarette, looking up at the sky. He can't see anything, of course; it's foggy as usual, but he continues looking up as if he's waiting for something to appear. When he finally turns around, I see his face: It's not David. I wait until he finishes his cigarette and goes back into the house. Then I turn the key and drive back to Sausalito.

WHEN I COME IN, my father is still awake, reading a Robertson Davies novel. He holds up the book to let me see the title. "I never heard of him. This is good."

"Yeah," I say.

"You know, Lin downstairs is studying for her master's in American literature. She can help you with your writing. She said she would."

"Robertson Davies is Canadian, not American," I say.

I sit down on the chair across from him and put my head back, staring at the ceiling. "You loved Mom, didn't you, Dad?"

I can hear the page turn.

"Of course I did."

Pieces of Paper

1994

JACK'S NIECE IS getting christened, but instead of thinking about the beauty of the service, the child's soul, Monica Kusiak Slepchuk is thinking that she wore the wrong thing. She knows she wore the wrong thing. She is humiliated to see variations of navy blue and straw hats on every woman but her. After much thought and consultation with her boyfriend, Jack, who is now loitering near the back of St. James Cathedral in his own blue suit, she had finally settled on vintage Chanel, a pillbox hat with veil à la Jackie, and the highest heels she owned. Festive enough for a celebration, she decided. In her Catholic family, a christening is a bon voyage party. Bottles of holy water launch life's crossing. Everyone cries, not only for the joy this child will know, but also because they can't resist pulling back the curtain to glimpse the inevitable bitter end.

This Episcopalian service—so close in words, so distant in spirit—confuses her. Only dry eyes in the house. She wants to sneak out the back door with Jack and have a smoke, but she can't, because she's holding the child over the baptismal font. The minister pours water down the baby's head. The baby screams as the devil scrapes his horns leaving her soul. She becomes a child of God named Matilda. Everyone smiles. Monica brings Matilda close and dries her. She has one golden lock on an otherwise bald head. Monica wraps it around her pinkie, like a curler. Matilda's first curler. For years, everything will be a first. She feels excited for her. Everything still to come. As her godmother, Monica feels entitled to guide her, tell her the score. But she's only twenty-five. Not only does she not know the score, but before she met Jack she was playing a different game. This new game has a rule book, but half the fun is not letting new players see it, and she stumbles through the innings like a blindfolded outfielder.

She looks down at Matilda's blond curl, the lace dress that has been dry-cleaned for the tenth time. She has everything. Monica knows she has nothing the baby needs, but it doesn't matter. Matilda is one of the lucky ones whose life will have answers; unlike Monica, who was bequeathed only questions.

"Have a good trip, kid," Monica whispers in her ear.

Matilda falls asleep. Her mother, Jack's sister Georgia, thrusts her arms out nervously, not trusting a person who wears vintage clothing to hold a child.

Monica gives her up the way people always do, as if the person receiving the baby needs special instructions.

"Watch her head," she says.

The minister, dressed in his cassock, follows the party to the exit. He touches Monica's elbow in a friendly way. "Good job," he says.

"You, too."

Everyone is nodding at her, so she thinks that maybe what she wore is okay. She licks her crimson lips and smiles, knowing she's all wrong. Finally, Jack steps out from behind a pillar, grinning like the Joker.

She grabs the lapel of his traitorous navy suit. "Get me the hell out of here," she says, dragging him outside the cathedral. They squint into the noon sun and lean against the old stone. Monica breathes heavily, as if she had just escaped a rolling boulder.

"Nice talk for a godmother." He looks both ways, as if they're being stalked, but the truth is that everybody has pretty much forgotten about them. They are hailing cabs downtown to the reception without a backward glance. Monica wonders if he notices that, too. That in choosing her, he has chosen to be forgotten. But of course he notices. He's not blind. Sometimes she just wonders how much he minds.

THE RECEPTION IS being held at a "club" of the type Monica didn't even know existed in New York before she met Jack. It's an unmarked house in the middle of the city, filled with living rooms, working fireplaces, leather chairs, cigars. Codgers in cutaway coats carry Scotch in good crystal on old silver trays. Most of the time women aren't allowed in the club, or are allowed only in certain rooms, like the one they're in now. People stand near anything that will hold their drinks and plates of canapés. Even though it's her christening, Matilda is not here. Only one child, in a proper dark blue tog, plays on the Oriental rug.

"I have to say hello to Uncle John," Jack says, leaving Monica at the entrance of the giant room to pay respects to his namesake and trust-fund replenisher.

Monica raises an arm to him, imploring him not to desert her, but he's gone, lost in the sea of navy. She uses her raised arm to grab somebody else's Scotch from the silver tray gliding by like a magic carpet.

"Thanks," she says.

The old man nods and heads back to the bar to get another, while she downs the one in her hand. Two women in blond bobs swim over like eels. They are Georgia's former roommates, Holly and Leigh from Wellesley. Holly used to date Jack. Maybe both of them did. Everyone wants to marry him still, even though he and Monica have been living together for more than a year. Where they come from, living together doesn't count for anything. Only getting your name on a bridal registry counts.

"What an interesting hat," Leigh says.

"It was my mother's," Monica lies, trying to give her hat a pedigree. She looks around for the silver tray.

"God, that's so thrifty," Holly says, tittering. "My father would love you."

"I just like it. I could've bought a new one," Monica says, and feels stupid immediately.

Holly lifts her bobbed head, and a waiter appears bearing three more drinks. Even though Monica is wearing ultra-high heels, Holly and Leigh seem taller than six feet. They fix their attention on her fingernails.

"I wish I could wear nail polish that color," Holly says, "but you have to have really long fingernails."

"You just have to eat your Jell-O," Monica says absently.

It's hard not to pay attention when women like Holly and Leigh speak, even though Monica does her best to ignore them, as Jack tells her to do. You're so much more real than they are, he says, more honest. But Monica doesn't believe him. They're educated, they're beautiful. Newspapers take pictures of their parties. But more than that, they seem to know all the rules in the book. Jack claims there is no such book, but that's just because he's got it memorized.

Monica is saved by the little girl who is sitting on the carpet, drawing. She has serious orange hair and teeth that will one day make an orthodontist happy. But nevertheless she commands respect. Monica's, at least. She plants herself in front of the trio and holds a piece of paper up to her face like a hymnal. The sheet is practically obliterated in lime green crayon.

"I have a program for this party," she says.

Leigh and Holly tousle her unlovely hair and wander away, bored.

"It needs a program," Monica says.

"First I need to get everyone's attention. Attention! Attention!" the little girl cries.

No one but Monica listens, but apparently that's enough of an audience, because she continues on.

"First we will have a ballet," she says.

"Do you do ballet?" Monica asks her. All girls in this milieu have toe shoes, she's pretty sure.

"I used to do ballet, but now I do gymnastics."

Through with childish things. "So who's going to do the ballet?" Monica asks.

"They're coming," she says, looking down at her scribbling. She holds the paper on her knee and makes a green check on it, as if reminded of an important task still to be completed.

She's so sure that a ballet troupe will come marching into this exclusive Manhattan club that Monica looks to the door to see if they've arrived. No. No dancers yet.

"What's your name?"

"Lyle Ewing van Faasen." She says it as if she were reciting a prayer. "But my daddy calls me . . ."

"Muffy?"

"Lyle."

MONICA MET Jack at the planetarium in New York City last year. She was there to track down a primal memory, of her and her real father, David Kusiak, looking at the Milky Way. Monica's father is tall, handsome, knows everything. He points out the vast possibilities in the universe. Look at the evidence of this potential, he says. You can't even see where it ends. Or begins. Somewhere up there, he says, a star was born the same time you were. Your star. All you have to do is find it, claim it. Monica was small, maybe four, wearing a straw hat with a black ribbon. How could she not believe him? His hand was so strong, gentle. And look at all those stars! Like confetti. One of them was hers.

But that memory is an impostor, because Monica never knew her father. They never looked at anything together. She never held his hand as she does in this memory. She's held only his photograph, a dog-eared portrait of a Marine who is now younger than she is.

Monica doesn't know where these false memories come from. Her mother, Beatrice, says Monica went to the planetarium with Henry, her second husband, the man who claims to be her father, the man she is supposed to call "father" under pain of forfeiting the privilege of being anybody's daughter. Henry took you to the planetarium, her mother says, that's what you remember. But it's not Henry. Her mother's husband is short and bald, and instead of knowing everything, like her real father, knows nothing at all. He doesn't think there's a star with her name on it. He only thinks there may possibly be a job out there with her name on it, and he wishes Monica would find it soon, so she won't come back and live with them.

Monica retraced her steps, going to the planetarium, hoping to see her real father waiting there for her. Instead, she saw Jack standing in his spot. He would look up at the Milky Way, then scribble in a palm-sized notebook. Monica stared at him so intently, wishing him away, that he had to turn.

"Are you okay?" he asked.

"What are you writing?" she asked, realizing she had no right to actually get him to move; realizing that he was quite handsome, and her heart was about to do a somersault.

He showed her. He was renaming the constellations. It was time, he said. The old names were completely irrelevant. No one knew

Pegasus or Orion anymore. No wonder no one knew anything about the stars, confusing configurations with names that meant nothing to anyone. He renamed one constellation Mick Jagger's Belt. Another was Prince and Sting. Wouldn't you want to know which stars composed Mick Jagger's belt? Or Prince and Sting?

"Are you allowed to do this?" she asked.

"I'm doing it," he said, with the confidence of his class, the confidence that Monica has since learned to worship and resent. "It's a done deal."

"Don't you need permission or something? From somebody?"

"Don't be silly." He looked at her for the first time. "What's your name?"

"Monica."

"Monica, what a pretty moniker." He searched the sky and suddenly jabbed his pencil heavenward. "There."

"There what?"

"That one's Monica."

JACK'S MOTHER, Hettie, chides her for not mingling.

"This is a good time to get to know the family, dear," she says, "and our friends. Everyone's anxious to talk to you."

Monica can't decide whether Hettie is so out of touch with reality that she doesn't see that everyone here has already said what they wanted to say, which is "Keep out," or is she just hoping that her son hasn't latched onto a total loser? Hoping that her protection will transform her? It was at her insistence that Georgia asked Monica to be Matilda's godmother.

Hettie hooks her arm through Monica's, and together they inch through the room. Monica looks around for Lyle Ewing van Faasen, but she's disappeared with her program notes. Monica's on her own, without a script.

"And do you know Jack's fiancée, Monica Slepchuk?" Hettie is saying to a gaggle of society dragons. "She's a performance artist. A real independent."

"I performed in college," one of the women says. "I danced." She holds her drink up and shimmies her hips.

"So you're Jack's fiancée?"

Fiancée? She had told Jack that she never wanted to get married, that an artist couldn't have a normal relationship. Didn't he take her seriously?

"What exactly does that mean, 'performance artist'?" one of the women asks. "Are you an actress?"

"I act up. Act out," she says, stealing some psycho jargon.

"I see."

Monica reaches into the beaded bag tied around her wrist, takes out a few complimentary tickets to her show, and passes them around.

"I don't know where this is," one of them says, squinting at the theater's address.

"Is everyone clothed?" another asks.

"It's just me," Monica answers. "I'm a one-woman show."

"Just you? What exactly do you do?"

Monica wants to say, I stick it to people just like you. I stick it to people like my fake father, Henry. I stick it to everyone. I'm a raging porcupine onstage, waving my tail, shooting darts. But it seems too hostile in this subdued atmosphere of oiled mahogany, throats cracking from too much Scotch and tobacco. The oxygen is so thin here, it has even managed to subdue Monica, the perpetual bad girl.

So she says, "I juggle."

WHEN MONICA WAS sixteen, she had run away from home and shown up at Tess Randall's door in Hollywood to become an actress.

Her mother, Beatrice, had said that Aunt Tess had started her own production company, and Monica thought that would guarantee her entrée into showbiz.

"I could do background stuff," Monica had told her. "In crowds."

"Does your mother even know you're here?" Tess asked.

"Mom said you left when you were sixteen."

"Eighteen."

"To go into acting."

"There was more to it than that," Tess said.

"Please let me stay! I can't go back there. Death, death, death. That's all they talk about. The place reeks of decay. You know what I got for my sixteenth birthday?" Monica had asked. "I can't even say it, it's so disgusting."

"Say it," Theresa said.

"A cemetery plot. A cemetery plot! Actually, our family has an entire row, like a street, can you imagine? Like a street with houses of dead people. I got a double, so that my future husband, that lucky guy, can be right next to me forever. It's too creepy to even think about. My mom said that it cost a thousand dollars a plot now, but if I waited until I died, it would cost double, so she got two for me. For my sixteenth birthday, I get a cemetery plot."

"So, does your Aunt Annie have one, too?" Tess asked.

"Yeah, it's right next to the one that was supposed to be for my dad." Now she supposed she would have to share eternity with Henry Slepchuk instead of her father. "Just try me," Monica had said. "If I'm not good, tell me to get lost. I just want a chance."

"If you aren't any good, you'll be stuck out here," Tess said.

"It's better than being buried alive in Cokesville."

A MONTH AGO, Jack tried to help her find her father's grave in Arlington National Cemetery; find his name on the granite memorial in Washington. But they could find neither. The reason being, the Marine sergeant from the Bureau of Veteran Affairs in Arlington told them, that he didn't die over there. He went there, yes. But he came back. Got an honorable discharge, and then poof. He disappeared. Re-upped for the invisible army of homeless, wacko, drugged-out alkie vets.

"Could be anywhere," the sergeant said. "Even, you know . . ." He cocked his head toward the ground.

He gave Monica a copy of her father's discharge form, his medals and citations. She held his thin pedigree.

"Don't get your hopes up," the sergeant said.

"I'm sorry," Jack said when they were out of the building. He tried to put an arm around her, but she brushed him off.

"Where was your father?" she asked angrily. "How come he didn't go Vietnam? How come Henry didn't go? Was my father the only one too dumb and too damned poor to get the hell out of it?"

JACK FINALLY finds her.

"Uncle John invited us to go sailing with him this weekend," he says.

"He doesn't even like me. Why don't you just go?"

"What do you mean, he doesn't like you? He loves you, Monica. Everyone loves you. You're gorgeous. How could he not?" He kisses her lightly on the cheek and smiles his goofy smile at her. "I love you."

"I have a show in the Village."

"Oh, that."

He looks away, distracted. He isn't exactly ashamed of what she does, but after the novelty of her performance art wore off, he just got bored. It's too personal, he said. It made him uncomfortable. One of the rules in his invisible rule book is that you don't show emotions in public. Performance art is pure emotion. Plus, he thought it was childish. Why don't you just live, he said, instead of playing at living onstage?

"I have an idea. Why don't we get married, then go sailing," he says.

He says it jokingly, but it's an old topic with them.

"We're fine the way we are."

"You're already living with me. You could live with me and get all the rights and privileges thereof."

"At least two women in this room are hot to marry you. I'll point them out if you'd like."

"It's not like I'm insulting you here. We have the magic. I just want to make the magic real. I'm asking you to start a real life with me, as a real grown-up couple."

"My life is real. A marriage license isn't going to change that. You can tear it up anytime, and then what do you have?"

"You're just being dramatic," Jack says.

"I'm an actress. I'm supposed to be dramatic."

"You were in one movie, which, by the way, never even got distributed. I'm not saying it was your fault, but that's the truth."

The world feels wobbly. Monica grabs the back of the sofa for support and looks to see if Jack is okay. But he doesn't seem to notice the strange planetary condition. He's looking for a waiter with drinks. He raises a finger.

"It's not like I'm insulting you," he says.

AFTER HER FIRST MOVIE with Tess's production company, Monica hoped she would get the lead in the next because she had a contract. But Tess had sent her packing instead.

"You can't carry a film," Tess had told her.

"It wasn't my fault about that movie," Monica had said.

"I'm not saying it was your fault. But the fact is that we need a bigger name to fill the seats."

"Maybe if I had more time to prepare," Monica said. "If you would help me."

"There's no use talking about it," Tess said. "We already cast it."

"But I have a contract," Monica said.

"You should get on with your life."

"This is my life. It's the life I want."

"If that's true," Tess said, "you'll find a way to make it happen."

UNCLE JOHN, a tall man with a hooked nose and a red scalp, finds her.

"Are you having a good time, dear?" he asks.

"Excellent," Monica says. "Tasty Scotch." She's now on her fourth or fifth.

"Now that you and Jack are getting married, I have to tell you," he says, leaning in close. "We're damned proud of you."

"What do you mean?"

"Pulling yourself up by your own bootstraps. Making something of yourself. Coming up from nowhere and making something of yourself. Look at you."

He massages the back of her neck, but she squirms away. She feels the heat rising from her neck. She can't seem to focus.

"From what nowhere do you mean?"

"You know, Polish family and all."

His lack of embarrassment astounds her.

"My family isn't Polish. We're American."

He stops the waiter and hijacks two more drinks. He bows slightly and hands her one, which she accepts.

"Now that you and Jack are getting married, he's agreed to work for me. Put all that education to work at something productive. Make Hettie happy. You, too. Pretty soon you'll have children"—he pointedly eyes her abdomen—"and you won't want him around the house. We men just get underfoot."

He chuckles at his wisdom. "Hey, I have to tell you a Polish joke. Now that you're in the family. You'll like this one." He smiles at her conspiratorially.

She glares at him.

"A Polish gentleman told me this," he says, "one of the most successful entrepreneurs in Hartford. He controls all the garbage collection in Hartford."

"Excuse me," she says, "I have to pee."

WHEN JACK AND MONICA came back from Arlington, she asked her mother why she hadn't told her her father was still alive. Her mother said she didn't know he was. She thought he was probably dead by now. She'd heard he wasn't in good shape when he was discharged. He never came home, she said. He never even called. Not even to see you, she said, looking at her as if Monica were no better than she. His daughter couldn't pull him home, either. Another weak attraction. She managed to get a divorce but had no place to send the papers. She pulled the divorce papers out of a box of his belongings that she dragged from the attic.

"You can have these if you want," she said. "I should have given them to you before." She looked relieved, freed of her burden.

Monica rifled through the box. Besides the divorce papers there were school things. Report cards—he wasn't a great student. And letters of citation for sports—he was a very good athlete. A few letters from him to her mom. From the war.

"Don't you want these?" She held up the bundle of letters.

Her mother folded her hands. "That was so long ago."

"Aren't you even curious to know where he is? If he's alive? What he's doing?"

"I have a new life now," she said.

MONICA FEELS a small pressure on the back of her leg. It's Lyle Ewing van Faasen.

"This party isn't going very well," Lyle says.

"I agree."

They survey the room, dissatisfied with the party's progress. Lyle still holds her iridescent program notes.

She lights up as if she has just thought of something. "I know," she says. She puts her glass of soda on an end table, out of harm's way, and starts tearing the page into one-inch strips.

"Do you know what we do now?"

"No."

"We spray them with this." She retrieves a sample bottle of perfumed spray out of her plastic purse. "Here, help me spray."

They split up the strips and spray like mad. The room starts to smell like vanilla, a little-girl smell. Expertly, Lyle lays the strips on the back of a sofa to dry.

"When those are done, we tear them up and throw them around the room," she says gleefully. "Do you know what we call this game?"

"Pieces of Paper?"

Lyle looks stunned.

"Yes. That's right. You're the first person to ever guess it. And I've played this game a lot. You must be very smart. What's the matter?" She sits beside Monica on the carpet. "It's only a game. Please don't cry. It's only a game."

She tears some of the strips into bits and lets them float through her fingers like confetti.

"See? It's only paper."

Now You Don't

1994

I MET THERESA GOJUK for a drink in the Denver airport. We'd heard the news that the fire burning in the coal seam under Cokesville had finally reached the gas main and "Kaboom!" as Theresa said dramatically, spilling her red wine on the dove gray carpet of the terminal lounge where we had agreed to meet.

I'd been treading water in Sausalito, and Theresa saved me. She'd introduced me to a Texas oilman, Bryce Taylor, and I married him and managed to metamorphose into a Lone Star cowgirl. My hair got big. My boots got pointy. My chili rings five bells. The only writing I do is at night after Bryce is asleep, and that's a series of paperback romances. It pays, as Theresa says, "in the tens of dollars." But I don't need the money. Thanks to Bryce, I don't need anything. I tell myself I am perfectly happy and that I was writing only to adopt a different skin, because the one I inherited in Cokesville was a poor fit. It was what Theresa and I had in common: we both wanted a different skin. She went to Hollywood to find one. I ended up in Texas. So, Texas is good. I feel like I disappeared into a foreign country where I speak the language. When I look into the mirror, I know who I am: somebody who doesn't live in Cokesville, Pennsylvania.

When Theresa heard the news of the explosion, she was on the phone instantly, at the same time I was calling her, arranging for a meeting at an emotional, if not quite physical, halfway point between Los Angeles and Dallas. Neither of us wanted to go to the other's home, so we agreed to meet in the Denver airport.

"I feel like I have to huddle with my own kind," she said on the phone.

"What the hell kind is that?"

She hung up without answering, and I caught the first available flight to Denver.

I was already at the bar when I saw her sashay toward me. She looked beautiful. To the casual observer, still the ingenue. Only her eyes betrayed the weariness of a person whose success depended on "ratings" that never quite reached the big red bubble at the top of the clap-o-meter. As she came closer, I saw that she had the look that semi-famous people get, that searching of faces for happy recognition that only sometimes comes.

"Read this," she said, slapping an open newspaper on the counter without saying hello. "They love me in France."

"Well, France," I said. "Now there's an endorsement." Calling up my high school French, I perused the article in *Le Monde.* It was true, she seemed to be some sort of slut goddess over there. A Yankee Brigitte Bardot. "Congratulations. You have the respect of the people with the loosest morals on the planet." I read on, then looked up at her, surprised. "They found out about Matthew?"

"It wasn't like it was a big secret or anything." She scooped up the paper and shoved it into her bag. "He's probably roaming Europe with his enchilada looking for sanctuary."

Matthew had appeared at Theresa's house four years ago, when he was twenty, at the same time I was visiting her from Texas. He had gone through the adoption agency and found out Theresa Gojuk was his mother. No one had to tell me who the father was. Matthew was the spitting image of Paul Szewczak, the neighbor boy who had died with Theresa's brother Steve in Vietnam. Paul came home on leave and knocked Theresa up. Then he went back to Vietnam and blew up. One of the messy pieces he left for others to identify was his son, Matthew. Theresa had assumed Matthew was safely out of her life until the day he appeared looking for "sanctuary," as he put it, on her Hollywood doorstep. At first, we thought he was in some sort of paramilitary organization, because of the way he spoke and his army surplus wardrobe. Then he told us he was in showbiz, too. In a few days, we found out the specifics.

"The bouts are staged," he said in Theresa's weight room, pumping up for his gig as a professional wrestler, the Nihilator. "But you still got to be in shape to take the falls."

He was a beautiful boy, and he looked so much like his father that I had to remind myself he wasn't the ghost who occasionally visited my dreams but a different person entirely. "He was serious, too," I told him. "Paul Szewczak. Your father."

"Was he?"

He wanted to know about his father, about his birth family. And Theresa surprised me by pulling out a brown envelope full of photos. He flipped over each one and solemnly read the description of who was in them and the dates.

"This is my dad?" he asked, holding up the Marine portrait of Paul.

Although that picture was the way we thought of him now, and probably always would, I wanted to tell Matthew that it wasn't fair to think of him as only a dead Marine.

"Pictures don't tell the whole story," I said.

"He didn't look like this?" Matthew asked.

"For a moment he did," I said.

"My mom here," Matthew motioned with his head toward Theresa, "says you're a writer. Have you written anything about my dad?"

"I write bodice rippers, honey." I laughed indifferently.

Theresa shoveled the pictures back in the envelope and handed them to Matthew. "You might as well keep them," she told him. "I had them long enough."

Theresa, despite what the critics said, was a good actress. She didn't reveal anything more than the old bones of her relationship with Paul, and Matthew failed to breathe life into the names on his birth certificate. He was soon edgy and spent most of his get-acquainted visit in the weight room. He gave us free tickets to the wrestling show. We watched him take his first fall, then left.

He came back with me to Texas. I don't know why I invited him. My skimpy maternal instincts were exhausted on Bryce's two grown children, but I was curious about Matthew. What would the spawn of Cokesville be like if they never experienced Cokesville? The answer seemed to be a taciturn professional wrestler named the Nihilator.

We frustrated each other quickly. Matthew wanted to drag me back emotionally to the one place I never wanted to visit: Cokesville. And I wanted him to answer for all the people who had left my life without saying goodbye.

Soon, Matthew found a Mexican girl with a four-year-old daughter. Then he found Jesus. Then he disappeared. The mention in *Le Monde* is a surprise. He's developing a cult following in France as an actor in martial-arts movies.

Mrs. Szewczak, Matthew's grandmother, died last year. Theresa never told her that she had a grandson and a Mexican granddaughter-in-law who had a ready-made family.

"It would've killed her," Theresa had said.

"Which part?" I asked her. "The part that she had Mexican in-laws or the fact that she could've had a smaller dose of loneliness?"

"Don't judge me, Annie. It's hard enough."

The nearest heir the state could find—a second cousin living in Tucson—had auctioned off Mrs. Szewczak's house and belongings when she died. Theresa's sister, Margaret, who didn't know she and Mrs. Szewczak shared a relative, sent me and Theresa Polaroids to see if we wanted anything: a dower chest from the old country full of embroidered linens for which Ukrainian women were famous and an autograph book filled with greetings from people who darted in and out of Mrs. Szewczak's life like hummingbirds. I told Margaret I would buy the autograph book if it went for less than twenty dollars.

And now, in the airport lounge in Denver, Theresa and I split a bottle of red wine and then we split another. We never talk about the past. It's a rule with us. No looking back, or we'll turn into pillars of salt. We make blow-up jokes about Cokesville, and speculate that now that everyone is scattered, we can't go home, even if we wanted to, to see everyone at one time. We say we are glad. There's no one in that awful town we ever wanted to see in the first place. We stop ourselves before we get maudlin, before we ask, "Whatever became of Mrs. Herbinko? Whatever became of Father Novakowski?"

We do say that it's kind of weird being from a town that no longer exists. That even if we wanted to see where we came from, we couldn't, because it's just not there. We're like rabbits that were pulled from a magician's hat, coming out of nowhere for the show. Disappearing before anyone thinks to miss us.

Theresa looks at her watch, pretending she can focus on it to see the time. She has to get back to L.A. for a photo shoot of Hollywood doyennes for *Vanity Fair*. She's pissed because the booze will destroy her skin.

"Oh hell, it won't be the first time," she says. "We're a bunch of geezer babes, anyway."

Her career has revived since she formed her own production company five years ago. Now everyone takes her seriously; if not for her acting, certainly for her ability to make projects happen. Her portrayal of a sultry Southern matriarch on a made-for-TV movie won actual critical acclaim. And, at forty-four, she's perfect for grandma parts. Hollywood's version of grandma, anyway. She doesn't look like any *babba* I've ever known.

"Don't get me wrong," I tell her, "but you make an *excellent* old lady."

She laughs. "You know who I channel for old ladies? Mrs. Szilborski! With her stupid can of Mace." Theresa does a perfect imitation of Mrs. Szilborski. "How scary is that?"

I see her to her plane. "Maybe Christmas this year," I say, awash in wino sociability. "Bryce and the kids, you know. It feels like home. It's kind of nice."

"Maybe." Theresa gives me a funny smile. "Yeah. Why not?"

She doesn't have to remind me that Bryce and the kids are borrowed. They originally belonged to someone else, like everything in my life. Like the house I'm living in, like the chili recipe I stole from a friend's kitchen. Like the plots for romance novels I borrow from other women's lives, because my own stories end so unsatisfactorily. My worst fantasy is Bryce's ex-wife coming to the door. "I've come for Bryce," she'll say. And I'll hurry to pack my bags and say to her, "I'm sorry. I know I don't belong here. It's just that I had no place to go. Could you just tell me, where am I supposed to go?"

Theresa glides into the corridor to board the plane without looking back. I wave anyway. Now that we've lost our one connection to the earth, we're like balloons that some child has carelessly released. No longer part of a bunch, we float upward, farther and farther away from everything recognizable. Even each other. Soon no one will see us and it will be as if we never existed. Whatever became of Annie Kusiak? Theresa Gojuk?

Margaret bought me Mrs. Szewczak's autograph book for fifty cents. When I read it, trying to piece together a life told in hasty good wishes—including mine—I realized I couldn't, for the life of me, even remember what she looked like.

My flight to Dallas isn't for another hour and I browse in the gift shop. I pick up a Denver Broncos T-shirt and think of a neighbor in Cokesville who would like it. But surely she isn't there anymore. She was evacuated long before the blast. Everyone is gone. I thought they would be there forever, if I needed them. They would stay put. Instead, I had lost them. The thought stuns me, and I suddenly want to write down everything I can remember about the people in Cokesville, so they can live just a little bit longer. I hug myself, rocking back and forth on the balls of my feet. The shop girl comes over to me.

"Are you okay, ma'am?" she asks.

I nod, handing her the T-shirt.

She looks at me quizzically. "Do you need anything? I'm right here if you do."

I shake my head and leave the shop, ambling over to the gate for the flight to Dallas. Some of the people waiting wear cowboy hats and boots. The men tip their Stetsons when I pass. The women smile. They're perfectly nice people, these Texans, I think. At least they aren't from Cokesville. And I look at them, trying to find the difference. Wondering if they can see mine. Wondering if I've waited too long to write my way back home.

I stare at one woman, and she shifts uncomfortably, eventually changing her seat so her back is toward me.

They announce our flight and I give my boarding pass to the steward.

One of the other passengers says to him, "I hear there's thunderstorms all the way in. Is it going to be a rough ride?"

"We fly above all that," the steward says.

"You can't get entirely above a thunderstorm," the passenger persists. "They always say that, and it's always a rough ride."

Then he turns to me and touches the brim of his hat, smiling politely. "You live in Dallas?"

I nod.

"Just a couple of hours," he says. "It'll be good to be home."

Epilogue: Excellent Sperm

1994

AT TWENTY-FIVE, Nikolai Leonidovich Minarekov was miserable. Shrouded in misery. The most miserable person on earth. Is anyone more miserable than a young man who has lost the gift of youth, which is optimism despite persistent rumors that things will turn out badly? Is anyone more miserable than an artist who has seen the bedrock of his inspiration dynamited out of existence? Because even if that bedrock was evil itself—and it was—it had allowed Nick a firm ground on which to stretch his artistic muscles. Without it, he flailed, grasping at frail twigs and roots to break his tumble into creative limbo.

Nick, of course, blamed his fickle countrymen for his fall from grace. Without warning, the prevailing wind in his country had shifted from Marx to Keynes, blowing him off course. One day children wore red kerchiefs around their necks, saluting statues of Lenin; the next day they wore silk power ties in imitation of Wall Street warriors, who had suddenly become Russia's idols. How could he be expected to sift through reality to find a kernel of truth, if truth was as changeable as a tie?

And truth was the issue for Nick, because Nick was a poet. His keen poetic vision bore through the bankruptcy of Communism, exposing it in iambic pentameter, in dueling couplets. He had uncovered the truth, and his compatriots rewarded him. At twenty-two, he had been a hero, idolized. But in his short, brilliant career, he had watched in horror as his slim volumes—coveted during the repressive regime, passed around furtively like dirty postcards—were dismissed as irrelevant when free markets overpowered black markets. He was out of favor. No longer needed. He had fulfilled his function and was tossed aside. But more than that, his poems were no longer considered art. How could that be? Wasn't he an artist? And as an artist, wasn't everything he produced art? The politics didn't matter. If the molecules of his body lined up to produce an artist, it only followed that anything that configuration produced was art.

He submitted a few poems to a Moscow periodical, criticizing his countrymen for not recognizing his predicament, but needless to say, the work was poorly received. That is to say, ignored. An artist can suffer being maligned, hated, adored, or mocked, but never ignored. His existence became unbearable.

During the year prior, he had received letters supporting his work from from a Jewish organization in America (he wasn't Jewish, though the organization claimed irrefutable bloodlines). They would sponsor his immigration, if he so desired, and he finally had to admit that yes, he so desired. And quickly, more quickly than was flattering, Russia released him to Boston, Massachusetts, where he had been for eight months, with the immediate problem of finding something to do with his life that he was passionate about, because Lynn Murphy, the woman he was living with, said he could not stay with her unless he got a job he was passionate about. If he couldn't write poetry—which he couldn't; he was simply dried up—he had to find a profession he was passionate about.

"I don't care what you do," she said, "as long it's something you're passionate about. I can't be with someone who's not passionate. Why don't you try law school?"

Lynn had been a labor lawyer in Cokesville, Pennsylvania, something that he could understand. But in Boston, she was practicing real-estate law. Nick would go through her briefcase to see what it was about real-estate law that excited her so, trying to see why she became passionate about foreclosing on people who had lost their jobs and could no longer afford the mortgage. She worked long hours, arguing her cases aloud to herself even after he had fallen asleep. She made a pocketful of money, but her work and its rewards left him cold. The only passion he felt was when they were in bed, where he was the engine and she was his caboose.

"Caboose," he said, "I can go to law school, sure, but law is not, I think, sincere profession."

"That's a little insulting," Lynn the Caboose said. "It's also ungrateful. The law is paying the bills around here."

"The bills, yeah," Nick said, stroking her back. "It's okay for you, but for me, I don't think so."

Lynn turned around and pulled the sheets up over her breasts. "I don't know what it's like in Russia, but in America, no one's pure. Everyone hustles. And artists are the biggest hustlers of all. They're not concerned with the truth any more than lawyers are. Have you ever read Michael Crichton? Danielle Steel? They're the biggest authors in our country, and even they wouldn't maintain they actually deal with truth. What is the truth, anyway? It's what everyone thinks it is. Truth is relative. If a jury finds a man innocent, he's innocent in our society, regardless of whether or not he actually committed a crime. If a CEO can convince the stock market that his company is on the rise, the stock rises and makes the CEO rich, whether or not the company was good in the first place. So truth is irrelevant."

"Only lawyer would say truth is irrelevant."

Lynn kissed his cheek. "Honey, you're just not used to it yet, because you never had any. But money is the yardstick, the payoff. In a democracy, it's the only way to judge a man's worth. What else are you going to measure? Good intentions?"

"Money, bah," Nick said as he lay back on his arms, staring at the ceiling.

"What kind of weird attitude is that?" Lynn asked. "The artists I know are crazy for money. We pay big money for art in this country. Don't get me wrong, they're devoted to art, too, but artists want to live well like everyone else. They want to spend summers on Martha's Vineyard and winters in Aspen. Don't you want to live well?"

Nick made a sour face. "Yes, I want to live well. I want poetry in my life. I want magic. I want truth. Not truth of stock market and law. That truth leaves no room for poetry. I want truth of magic and company of people who want same things."

"Look around," Lynn said. "Don't you like this house? Don't you like it that I can buy you nice clothes and we can afford a nice car? And that we can get away whenever we want? Don't you like that?"

Nick got lost in gloomy speculation on the truth, how his devotion to the truth was keeping him from pleasing his lover, keeping him frying burgers and onion rings at a fast-food restaurant, which he thought was at least an honest, straightforward way to make a living. Making people food: what could be more sincere than that? In Russia, no one bothers to ask what you do for money. You work all day, with a boss you despise, and then drink with friends later. Life is the same for everyone.

Lynn wouldn't tell her friends that Nick worked at a fast-food restaurant. She told them he was applying to graduate school. She was shamed by his lack of ambition.

"If you're looking for poetry, what possible difference does it make what you do for a living?" she said. "You don't have a problem working at that grease pit. You think a burger joint is a more sincere place than a law office? You find poetry in fast food?"

Nick flipped the sheet back, admiring her. "You have breasts like beautiful golden arches."

Lynn sighed and said, "You'll see, darling. You'll find out. No one can escape. Not even a Russian poet."

She got up and went into the shower, while Nick pulled his work uniform out of the closet. Even the weirdly cut trousers and shirt couldn't camouflage his superb build. He swelled his chest, trying to burst the button. Almost. He smiled to himself. Then he frowned. He had to find something in this money-hungry country to be passionate about.

WHEN NICK WAS in Russia, he was passionate about everything, mostly his desire to leave Russia. Who could live in such a crazy place? Craziness all around and nothing to eat. And it didn't matter what economic system was in vogue, there was still nothing to eat. He was passionate about that. His friends got sick of his bellyaching and told him if he was so hungry, to go to America. Like him, his friends were university-educated schoolteachers making the equivalent of a dollar a week under capitalism, while the uneducated invented ways to turn crooked schemes into buckets of rubles. They were ruining his country. He was passionate about that. He was sure he didn't want to live in a place where schemers and self-promoting scoundrels ruled.

America had to be better. Sure, he had read about the decadent West all his life, but he knew *Pravda* was less than absolute truth;

Tass was less news bureau than news filter. A lot wasn't getting through. So he had kept an open mind. When he made the decision to come to America, he was optimistic. He would see for himself. But America stunned him.

"What do you do?" Americans asked at the parties to which he was immediately invited because Marcia Bloom, the administrator of the Hillel organization at Boston University, wanted to make sure he met the right Americans. "What do you do?"

"I write poetry," he said.

He couldn't be that big a poet or they would have heard of him. His volumes would be collecting dust on an eye-level shelf in their bookcase right now.

"Do you write under another name?" they would ask hopefully. But when Nick answered no, they would ask again, "What do you do?"

Of course, he soon found out they meant "What do you do to accrue vast sums of money?" because if he didn't have vast sums of money, what was he doing at this party? And while he found it a peculiar question, a rude question, an intrusion into his personal life, he found they wouldn't leave him alone until they unearthed the secret font of his money.

"What do you do?" they asked. "You must do something." They seemed concerned that he might not be contributing to the gross national product.

When he felt their attention drifting (and he needed their attention more than money), he found the wit to answer, "I want to be capitalist."

"Ahh," they answered, charmed with a concept they could grab on to. A Russian who wanted to be a capitalist! He was one of us. He might not be making money now, but he was on his way. In fact, Nick found the current of capitalism almost impossible to resist. He became a vocal, enthusiastic—if not actually producing—

capitalist. People made a point of introducing him to established capitalists, who patted him on the back and gave him avuncular advice. Nick soon found that the thing he had in common with American capitalists was the same thing he had in common with Russian capitalists: they liked to drink. He made the transition from vodka to Scotch while ignoring the pointers for success that middle-aged men in navy blazers dispensed as liberally as their libations.

He had met Lynn at one of these parties. She was older than Nick by ten years. He thought she was attractive in an American way: good teeth, obviously affluent. A little skinny, Nick thought. The age thing didn't bother him too much, because she really liked sex; she would go after him with a ferociousness that he mistook for a huge libido, until he understood that sex was a stress reliever after a tough day at work. But still. He could tell by the way her eyes starred up when she looked at him that she didn't see him. She was blinded by something. At first Nick thought it was his handsomeness. In Russia, he had often been compared to Boris Pasternak. He could say that without vanity, because it was true, since he was, in fact, distantly related to him, and so the resemblance was more than coincidental. But it wasn't his handsomeness alone that appealed to Lynn. Since she had moved to Boston from Cokesville, on a mission to find her elusive other half, she had grown weary and almost despairing. If she couldn't find her other half ready-made, perhaps, she thought when she met Nick, she could mold one.

"You'll go to graduate school, find a decent profession, and that will be that," she said, happy with her raw clay. He was husband material, albeit different than she had imagined. But isn't that how it often happened? She would mold him, be his Pygmalion. Send him off to grad school—an economics degree from a Communist university was absurd, didn't he think?—get him producing money, and then together they would produce babies. They would be a veritable factory, with smoke coming out of the chimney. The alarm clock was clanging in her head. She was thirty-five years old, for Pete's sake. She was a little worried about her ability to have healthy children at her age, but she would get scrupulous prenatal care. She would stop drinking immediately to give her eggs a chance to regroup.

"And of course, you'll have to get checked out physically," she said. "Sooner rather than later, I think."

"Physically?"

"Make sure you can have babies. Chernobyl was right down the street, for God's sake."

"I was very far from Chernobyl. I lived in Moscow."

"Still, the prevailing winds." She used her Filofax the way women of another generation used hope chests. She made a list of what it would take to make Nick a husband. She tapped her pencil, thinking. "I know. Dr. MacMillan."

So Nick found himself in Dr. MacMillan's waiting room, exchanging covert glances with the receptionist, a lush blonde who pretended to fill out paperwork whenever he looked up from his magazine and noticed that she was looking at him. Once, he caught her eye, and she smiled. He looked away, disturbed at her frankness, disturbed that he found her mesmerizing when he was here to find out if he would be a good husband for Lynn. He completed his medical and personal history and handed it to the receptionist.

She scanned it quickly and handed it back to him. "Fill in your profession."

Nick frowned and wrote "Poet" in the box.

She smiled when she read it. "What have you written?"

"Nothing lately," Nick admitted.

"You're an artist and you have lost your magic."

"Yes, yes. Is true!" he said, anxious to unburden himself. He peered deep into her blue eyes. She had ancient eyes, eyes that had seen life from start to finish, although the rest of her looked no more than twenty years old. "My magic hides like mouse from eagle. Like shy girl who has declared love to indifferent lover." He paused, amazed at her keen intuition. "How did you know?"

"It happens more often than you'd think," she said.

"But that's not why I come to doctor. I come to see if I have magic down here." He pointed to his crotch.

"Maybe that's where it's hiding. We get artists all the time who want to sell their sperm."

She smiled, and Nick looked away, embarrassed.

"I'd rather have an artist for a father than a banker. Wouldn't you?" she asked.

She went back to stamping papers, and Nick sat down. Finally, a nurse, a black woman in a pink smock, came out a side door, announced his name, and he went into an examining room.

"You're here for what?" she asked, not looking at him but at the medical history he'd completed in the waiting room.

"I'm going to be married," he said.

She looked at him critically. "You need a blood test?"

"The to-be-married test," he said, confident that such a thing existed.

She jiggled the keys to the syringe drawer. "You mean the blood test."

"My fiancée needs to know if I can make babies."

The nurse opened one of the cabinets, handed him a plastic cup.

"There's a bathroom across the hall. Put it on the table by the refrigerator when you're finished. You'll get the results in the mail in a week."

He hurried through his assignment. When he left, an older woman with gray hair was sitting at the receptionist's desk.

THE PROCESS OF FINDING a profession was going slowly. Nick didn't like the idea of the law. He was sure of that. He couldn't have passion for something that was so indifferent to the truth. He could have no passion especially for lawyers whose sole reason for being was to manipulate the truth to satisfy the highest bidder. Even though he had been a teacher in Russia, Lynn didn't want him to be a teacher, because it didn't pay enough. Passion wasn't the only requirement Lynn had for his profession. Also, he didn't like medicine. He could see poetry in beautiful bodies, but ugly bodies depressed him. He liked the aesthetic side of architecture, but he didn't like the engineering. And that's what it usually came down to: engineering, no real design. Just look at the buildings Americans surrounded themselves with: no better than the People's Architecture.

"I think you are still a Communist," Lynn said. "You wouldn't work at that burger place if you wanted to be a real American."

They were getting ready for a dinner party for some of Lynn's friends. Nick was slathering the salmon steaks with seasoned butter. She wrenched the plate of fish away from him.

"What are you trying to do? Give my friends heart attacks?"

"Bah. You Americans are so concerned with heart. You die like everyone. Except you die hungry. Rich country and everyone dies hungry." He waved his basting brush at her. "People every day line up for Big Bertha with bacon and cheese. You are, I think, hypocrite."

"Just because people eat that stuff is no reason to work there." Lynn put down the platter and looked as if she were going to cry. "If you loved me, you wouldn't work there. You would find something to do that made more money, something I can be proud of. We're going to get married, for God's sake. Why can't you find something to do that I can be proud of?" She pulled a tissue out of her pocket and wiped her eyes.

Nick sighed and wrapped her in his arms.

"What do you want, Caboose?" he asked. "Tell me what you want me to do. I am passionate about nothing but you. I do anything to make you happy."

"Is that true?"

He stroked her curly black hair, graying in a shock at the forehead, and smiled at her. "Yes, is true."

Her tears evaporated. She ran into the bedroom and came back with her briefcase. Her eyes shone with excitement as she opened it, pulled out a brochure, and handed it to Nick.

"I've been doing some research for you. Now, don't get mad when you see this. All artists are entrepreneurs, anyway. This would just make you better at the business side of being an artist. Promise not to get mad, okay? Just look at it."

The doorbell rang and Lynn tensed. "Now, remember, don't tell them about Big Bertha's. Just say you're looking into graduate school." She tapped the brochure, smiling. "You're just looking. Okay?"

Lynn ran to greet her guests, leaving Nick with the brochure. He examined it suspiciously. It was from the Boston University School of Management. He read it closely. If he attended this school, they would make him a Master of Business. He pictured himself learning all the different ways to trick people into parting with their money, and his heart sank. He was getting further and further from the truth, and deeper into the quagmire of the American way. It wasn't what he had in mind when he left his beloved—yes, he thought now, it was beloved—Russia. He thought of Lynn's pillow breasts, her enthusiasm for the good life, her enthusiasm for doing what it takes to live that life. He thought in Russia things were just as corrupt as in America. But in Russia he was much poorer and he was always hungry. Ah, so that was it. In Russia, he had reduced truth to the yearnings of his belly. But he had not written a poem since he moved in with Lynn, since he had acquired a comfortable existence. Was his muse drowning in Big Bertha's—with extra cheese—onion rings? The avalanche of paper and Styrofoam that customers left for others to throw away? Was his muse overpowered by the roar of the Saab 900 Aero that Lynn let him drive? Did that mean he was no longer a poet? No, he couldn't believe that. He had been an artist for as long as he could remember. He didn't know how to be anything else. He was an artist, and so everything that issued from him was art. Even his Big Bertha onion rings were art, because he made them. He thought of Lynn's disappointment in him. He decided to convince himself that if he became a Master of Business, that would be art, too. And Lynn said artists were entrepreneurs, anyway, so there was no conflict. He would become a Master of Business.

HE HAD just gotten home from Big Bertha's when the phone rang. A woman's voice was on the other end, tentative.

"Mr. Minarekov?"

Nick was used to getting phone calls at this time of day from telephone solicitors. They tried to sell him everything from lightbulbs to city bonds. When he had first moved in with Lynn, he had agreed on the phone to donate some money to the International Firefighters Brotherhood, and so had been put on the master—as Lynn put it—sucker list. He was now paying the price of being a master sucker.

"Mr. Minarekov?"

"Yes, yes, go on."

The woman cleared her throat. "You don't know me. I am a friend of Sybill Arbuckle." When he didn't register recognition, she said, "Dr. MacMillan's receptionist."

He straightened up. Her name was Sybill Arbuckle. She had flitted in and out of his daydreams since his doctor's appointment. "Is she okay?" he asked.

"Oh yes. She's fine. She's just fine," she said. "I saw her today at lunch," she added, as if to verify that Ms. Arbuckle was doing just fine.

"Fine."

"This is hard to say. Although I am rather at the end of my rope, so I'd better just come out and say it." She took a breath. "Sybill says that you have excellent sperm. There it is." She waited for a reaction, and when she got none, she laughed and said, "Sybill says you have excellent sperm. The count, the quality. None of the tails are broken off. None are sluggish. They're raring to go. You have excellent sperm, and I need some."

Nick paid attention to the woman for the first time since she mentioned Sybill. He found it interesting that someone wanted something other than money from him. Giving money wasn't art. Giving his sperm would be. "What is your name again?"

"I didn't tell you. I'd rather you didn't know. I'd rather it be as impersonal as possible."

"But you know my name."

"It couldn't be helped. Well, all right. Why don't you call me Janet? I don't want it to be so impersonal either, you know? Or I could have gone to a sperm bank. Sybill says you are a very nice person."

They were silent for a long time. Finally, Janet said quietly, "What do you think? I'll pay you, of course. If it works, I'll pay you whatever you want."

"No, no. Not for that," Nick said quickly.

"Of course, maybe you want to think about it. I kind of hit you with it out of the blue. It's all I've been thinking about for a year, so I know what I think about it. But you probably haven't considered it. We can just talk about it if you'd like."

She gave him her address and they made a date. "Nothing definite," she said. "We can just talk."

As it had been established that Nick had excellent sperm and was applying to become a Master of Business, the wedding plans proceeded. The letter from Dr. MacMillan confirming the prognosis and a copy of his application to join the fold of capitalism commingled in the Baccarat crystal bowl that held their incoming mail. Lynn had registered at three jewelry stores, intent, it seemed to Nick, on amassing the biggest Baccarat crystal collection in history.

"We don't have anybody on your side yet," Lynn said. "I've asked Margaret Gojuk to be my maid of honor, but I don't think she's even going to come."

Lynn was writing out a guest list. She had already come up with 150 nearest and dearest and was waiting for Nick to volunteer some names of his own. He was sure his parents wouldn't come. In Russia, marriage was not the huge deal it was in America. He would send them a photo.

"You must have some friends," Lynn said. "I know you don't spend all your time around here writing poetry."

Nick ignored the dig. "Put down Carmellia Brooks. Desmond Hall," he commanded.

Lynn did as she was told. "I never heard you talk about Desmond Hall. Is he from school?"

"Big Bertha's," Nick said.

Lynn put down her pen. "Nick, do you really think he would be comfortable at a wedding on Beacon Hill?"

"What? You don't like black men? Pushkin was black."

"It has nothing to do with that! I didn't know he was black. I just don't know what kind of people work at that place. Criminals, I would think."

"Maybe I cannot come. I must be criminal, too," Nick said.

Lynn slammed down the pad of paper. "You don't have to make a mockery of this."

"I wasn't making mockery, Caboose, come here." He pulled her onto his lap. "I just don't see how this marriage has anything to do with me. You are marrying the letter that says I have good sperm and the letter that will make me a Master of Business. Where am I? Where is Nikolai Leonidovich Minarekov, the artist?"

Lynn blinked away a tear and sniffed. "You can read a poem if you want."

"My poem are in Russian and condemn system that has already failed. I need to write new poem. I am drowning, Caboose, don't you see? I need to find new magic."

"Our marriage will be magic. You'll see." She got off his lap and pulled out her Filofax. "The caterer is going to be expensive, but what the hell, you only do this once. Right? Aren't you glad now that I have a good job as a big bad lawyer?" She made a face at him, dialed a number on her cell phone, and blew him a kiss. "You can read a poem. Americans don't like poems, but if it's in Russian, no one will understand anyway. Just one, though. And short. Okay?"

IN RUSSIA, Nick had never thought about personal morality. He and his friends were so busy policing the morals of government, and then the free enterprise that sprang up, that whatever an individual did to survive in that oppressive chaos was forgiven. Anyway, Russia was a puritanical society, in word if not in actual deed, so he had never acquired a vocabulary for the morality of human sexuality.

"You're even more handsome than Sybill told me," Janet said.

They were drinking espresso at a coffee shop. Nick examined his cup, embarrassed. He could not get used to the boldness of American women.

"She tells me you're a Russian poet," Janet said.

"Yes, yes. I'm Russian poet." Nick looked around uncomfortably. He didn't know how he was going to be able to give this Janet his sperm. She was older than forty and didn't appeal to him physically. She was too fat, for one thing, wearing a flowery, arty dress that emphasized her overabundant curves, making him think of a cabbage bin. And she wore too much expensive jewelry. So bourgeois. He could not picture himself getting it up and into this sparkly patch of cabbage.

"Do you have any children?" she asked.

"No, no children. But I can," he said, almost defiantly.

"Yes." She smiled. "I know. You have excellent sperm." She fiddled with her liquid silver necklace, assessing him. "I waited too long. You know? I waited for the perfect man, waited to be rich, waited for this and that. Now it's almost too late. Sybill tells me you're engaged."

He thought of Lynn. He had never actually asked her to marry him. She had told him they would, and when he didn't contradict her, she went ahead with plans.

"We live together. Yes, I guess," he said, "we will marry."

"Ah." She was quiet. "You look like an artist." She laughed. "Artists are generally good-looking. But you look familiar, too. Was your picture on a book of poems or something?"

He thought of the chapbooks that made the rounds in Moscow and St. Petersburg. But there were no pictures of him in them. Only his soul. Only his poems, which speak for themselves. She probably had him confused with somebody else. "Boris Pasternak is great-great-uncle," he said. "His picture is on lots of books. Maybe you think I am him."

She smiled benevolently. "Is Boris Pasternak a Russian writer?"

Nick scowled. He was growing increasingly convinced he wouldn't be able to give Janet his sperm.

"I have a check written out for you," Janet said. "If you agree to do it, I'll give it to you right now." She pulled a piece of paper out of her purse and slid it across the table to him.

He looked at the amount. He blinked. He made himself think of the "Girls of the Ivy League" in *Playboy* that Desmond shared with him during their breaks at Big Bertha. Finally, he felt stirrings where he thought none would come.

"Is it a deal?" Janet asked.

Nick laid his hand affectionately over her bejeweled one. "Yes, is deal."

THE JEWISH ORGANIZATION that sponsored Nick's immigration requested that he give a reading to the Boston University Hillel. They wanted to see what sense he made of this great big beautiful country of America. They wanted to see it in poems. New poems that they could take credit for.

"It's thrilling for us to see how others see America, see us," Marcia Bloom, the committee chairwoman, told him. "You've been here ten months, I'm sure you have a lot to show for it."

"Yes," Nick said.

"It will just be coffee and pastry. Nothing too elaborate. We're not fancy people."

"Yes," Nick said.

"Just as a favor to me, do you think you could give me a copy of what you've written? Like a sneak preview?" Marcia giggled.

"No!" Nick said, thundering. "No one sees poem before reading."

"That's fine," Marcia said. She was used to temperamental artists. "We'll pick you up." And, she added, because she knew that their bad tempers were inversely proportionate to the difficulty they were having with their art, "we don't want you to get away!"

NICK BECAME CONVINCED that the truth he had lost, the truth that had eluded him since he arrived in America, was inside him. It wasn't in his job or in the corrupt—yes, let's face it, America was corrupt to the bone—system under which Americans prospered so wonderfully, so materialistically. Their prosperity was so profound that it seemed ludicrous to him even to question the means by which that prosperity was achieved. "Looking the gift horse in the mouth," as Janet said. Americans were not even looking for truth anymore, if in fact they ever had, he thought. They were bored with that. Americans wanted interest compounded daily, hourly, by the second. That was the only thing that could capture their attention. Not the truth. The truth was boring, painful, took too long to unearth, and was, anyway, unprofitable. It was up to him. The truth was inside him, but he had lost the key to that compartment.

"You see?" he told Janet as they bathed in their fourth baby-making glow. "If I could just find that key."

Janet lay with her legs raised against the wall. She wanted to make sure that Nick's excellent sperm had every advantage, including gravity, in capturing an egg.

"My temperature was right today," she said. "I think this is it." She reached over and squeezed Nick's hand.

He kissed her absently.

"Thank you, Nick," Janet said. She blushed a little. "I'm going to miss you."

"I will too, little babushka. Do you think I make baby?"

Janet nodded her head. "I think so. I feel so happy. I don't feel like I usually do. I can't describe it." She laughed nervously and started to cry. "My hormones are all screwy. That's a good sign."

Nick pulled on his shirt and trousers, flexed his muscles in front of the mirror, trying to make a button pop. He saw Janet watching him and he clowned for her. Flexing and posing. He turned to her and she was sobbing.

"What's the matter, babushka? Did I do something to make you sad?"

"No, I'm not sad," she said, hiccupping between sobs. "I just realized why I feel different. I don't feel lonely."

THE WOMAN SIPPING espresso with Nick wore a straw hat with a big red rose.

"Sybill said you were handsome, but my, my!" the woman said. "You're not gay, are you?" She laughed. "You don't look Jewish."

The woman—"Call me Raquel"—talked loudly, and Nick looked around quickly, hoping that no one heard her. If anything, Raquel was less attractive than Janet. Fatter, older, a voice as annoying as ungreased gears. Her fingernails were like smooth glass on the turbulence of her skin, which was wrinkly and baggy from age. Or wear. She, too, wanted his sperm.

"I've read everything you've written," the woman said confidentially. "Your poems are very angry. Where does a young man get anger from? What happened to make you bitter?"

Nick looked at her wearily. She had confused him with somebody else. There was no way one of his chapbooks could have made the journey to America from Russian. "You read Russian?"

She laughed. "Good heavens, no! I just love English. I read your poems in translation. I wouldn't learn another language if you paid me a million dollars. And why would I? When English is the most perfect language in the world."

"Yes, English is good language," Nick admitted. "But some things you can say in Russian, you can't express in English. You don't have the words. If you don't have the words to capture them, the idea flies away. Like little bird." He sprayed his hands outward, then folded them in his lap.

"That's beautiful. You are a poet."

"Yes, I am poet." Nick crossed his arms defiantly. "Because I am poet, everything I do is poem."

"Everything?" Raquel reached in her purse and pulled out a check. She laid it on the table in front of him. "Is that enough? I don't think we have to discuss details. Sybill says you've already worked that out."

"Sybill says?"

"She's a lovely girl." Raquel put a bill on the table and led Nick out of the café. "How much do you get paid for one of your poems?"

NICK HAD NEVER CONSIDERED the perfect woman. When he was in Russia, he was too absorbed with the decaying corpse of his government to consider such frivolous matters. And then, being handsome, he never had to think about women at all. They were there. In his lap, as it were. You don't think about things that come easily. You put your effort into the things you cannot have.

He thought about the perfect woman now. He wanted to write about her. The words were forming inside him, but he couldn't get them to line up right.

"Are you doing homework?" Lynn poked her nose inside his study.

"Yes, yes, I do master business work," he said, lying, trying to cover his failing attempt at poetry.

She looked over his shoulder. "You shouldn't do it in Russian. Your English will never improve if you insist on thinking in Russian."

"I am Russian. I think in Russian! Okay?"

"I'm just worried that if you think about business school work in Russian you'll get horribly confused. I mean, Russians don't have the slightest idea what business is about. You probably don't have the vocabulary for the concepts. Is everything okay? You look ill." She put a hand on his forehead.

He swatted it away. "Please go away. I am very busy with this stuff."

"I told you to quit your job. It doesn't pay anything, anyway, for God's sake. It's just tiring you out when you should be concentrating on your studies. You're exhausted. You're not yourself anymore."

She took the paper away from him and began massaging his temples.

"There, doesn't that feel better? Doesn't that make you forget everything? We want to clear the passageway so that all that comes in is good American business sense. We're going to be so happy, darling. You'll see."

She clapped her hands suddenly.

"We got more Baccarat today. The Rogerinos sent us the iced-tea pitcher. And Tess Randall sent us twelve champagne flutes with a lovely note."

She started massaging again.

"The problem with you Europeans is that you think too much. You tie yourself up in knots with issues that we Americans resolved years ago. The answer is to not think but to just keep going. The meaning of life is to have a good life. There, doesn't that feel better? Doesn't that make you forget everything?"

Nick closed his eyes. He tried to imagine the perfect woman he had almost captured. But she had flown away. Like a little bird.

THE BASIS OF Nick's art was the premise that the thing that distinguishes humans from animals is that they can think. They can reflect on their humanity, on their life. Even if they were miserable, the fact that they knew they were miserable was enough to qualify them as a human being. For example, if a man sat in the dirt ripping the meat off a bone, his dog sitting next to him doing the same, who was miserable? Only man had imagination enough to see what could be, and so was miserable when he thought about what he had now. The dog was in canine heaven.

That idea was controversial in Communism, which regarded humans as organic but soulless spokes in a machine, unable to reflect on what life could be. This idea was what made him an underground hero. He had dusted off the neglected souls of his compatriots and revealed their sparkling potential for pain as well as pleasure.

But he was shocked to find it controversial in capitalism as well. Shocked to find that while capitalism didn't numb the soul with pain and drudgery, it expertly numbed the soul with pleasure. And pleasure of a base kind. Shopping. Video games. Sitcoms. All you can eat. Vicarious sex. A bizarre equation where fun equals a cathode-ray screen plus daily overindulgence.

It was easy to write poetry about the yearnings of the soul and the body that housed it—yearning is what poetry is all about, after all—but he was at a loss to describe a culture trapped in its body by too much fun. Where was the magic in that?

THE MANAGER OF Big Bertha's closed the place early to throw Nick a bachelor party, although women were allowed to stay if they didn't mind that the men had chipped in for the Budget Stripper. Nick made up a batch of big burgers with extra cheese and a platter of onion rings. One of the kids brought in some beer, another pulled out a boom box and a bag of weed from his locker.

"I don't know why you're doing it," the manager said, throwing a friendly arm around Nick. He was short and fat—needless to say, considering his vocation—and thoroughly admired beauty in the male sex, because, as he put it, "I wasn't always fat and bald, you know, and I seem to remember being much taller." He liked having Nick around as a reminder of how he used to look. "If I looked like you, I would still be catting around, know what I mean?"

The stripper came early and had an astounding appetite, considering that her livelihood depended on her figure. "I can eat anything I want," she said, scarfing down more than an average portion of burgers and fries with a nondiet beverage. "I just dance it off!" She wiggled her fanny in Nick's direction and, inspired by his slack-jawed admiration, began to strip.

She didn't need any music. She accompanied herself with a steady stream of chatter, aimed mostly at Nick. "I'm a student at Boston College," she said. "I'm studying women's literature." She swung her arms around and—presto—off came the shirt.

"Why just women?" Nick asked. "Why limit yourself?"

"Why not? We've beaten dead white male literature to death. There's nothing else to learn from that."

Bump, bump and Nick found himself holding the bra that she had deftly removed and flung into his hands. The bra was thickly padded. The stripper was, in reality, as small as a boy. He felt protective toward her because of that, and looked around to make sure that no one was making fun of her. No one, except the manager, was even paying attention. "Have you studied this dead white male literature?"

"I don't have to, to know it's bankrupt."

She finished stripping with a detachment that Nick found interesting but unarousing. That was probably why she was the Budget Stripper. He was left with almost all her clothing. Politely, he handed it back to her.

"I'll call you sometime," the stripper said.

"I'm getting married." He shrugged and smiled. "It's my party."

As Nick unlocked the door to let her out, an older, peevish, hungry-looking man tried to get past him.

"It's a private party," Nick said.

The old man peered into the party going on inside, hobbled away disgruntled. So Nick wasn't surprised when the sirens and bubble lights arrived a few minutes later and the police busted everyone for an impressive list of offenses, including underage drinking, alcohol on the premise without a license, and that bag of weed.

NICK CALLED Raquel to post his bail, not daring to tell Lynn. But she was waiting up when he came home at 3:00 a.m. Waiting for her jailbird. A soon-to-be-deported jailbird.

He waited for her tears. But she looked at him coldly. She had done her crying earlier.

"Who is Janet Springer?" she asked.

"Janet Springer?" He scratched his head. "Ah, Janet!" She had never told him her last name.

"Janet Springer. She called. She had her ultrasound and wanted you to know that everything is fine. It's going to be a boy."

She said every word calmly, with no emphasis. She waited for him to respond, and when he didn't, she threw a Baccarat glass against the wall.

"You're the father, aren't you?"

He was silent. This rage was new and interesting to him.

"Answer me, you stupid bastard!"

"*Da*, I'm father."

"All your talk of high morals. Magic. 'I'm looking for magic,' he says. Truth. 'I'm looking for truth,' he says. Bullshit! You're just looking to get laid. You're just looking for easy fun. Pleasure with no consequence. The life of pleasure and indolence. You know what

Janet Springer is looking for? We had a nice little chat. You know what she's looking for? She's looking for child support. What do you think about that?"

Nick frowned. "She said no child support."

"Not money, you idiot! She wants you to be a part of his life," Lynn shrieked. "She wants you to take him to baseball games and . . . I don't know what else she said. What do you think of that? Nothing in life is free, buster."

The wedding was called off, naturally. Although Lynn searched for ways to salvage Nick, in the end she had to admit that you can't change someone. No matter how much she wanted Nick to be her Master of Business, the sergeant at arms for her middle-class bourgeois lifestyle, the father of her postponed children, it wasn't going to happen. He was a wild card, and she needed an ace. They both cried, missing the future that was no longer theirs. They drank, threw each piece of her Baccarat crystal against the wall, drunkenly admiring the way the morning sun reflected off the shattered glass. She let him kiss her on the caboose—once only—then kicked him out.

Which, it turned out, was where he wanted to be.

He moved in with Desmond, his buddy from Big Bertha's, who was squatting in a boarded-up storefront in Mattapan. They had no phone and no mailbox—the better to avoid those warrants for deportation. There was no electricity, and he had to go across the street to the gas station to use the bathroom, the door of which they kept jimmied open so that they could have access even when the station was closed. They lived on the money that Nick had earned making babies and talked of saving up to get a better place. But neither of them checked the listings in the paper.

BIG BERTHA'S WAS ALLOWED to reopen under new management, and Nick got his old job back. It would be easier, the new manager said, if he was paid under the table and would agree to a slight pay decrease. That suited Nick just fine. He took some ribbing about his failed marriage, but otherwise it was business as usual. Burgers and onion rings. He was miserable, but he liked being miserable, because he believed—and he came to this just recently, in the gas station men's room, which was amazingly conducive to prolonged thought—that everyone was miserable, but only an elite were lucky enough to have the veneer of comfort stripped away to enjoy their misery.

And it was enjoyable. He could feel the words to describe this misery forming inside him, like an embryo waiting to finish so it could be born. He had never been more happy. Or more miserable.

Sybill came into Big Bertha's one day. She smiled at Nick, but didn't seem to recognize him in his new beard and mustache. She ordered a Big Bertha double cheeseburger, deluxe onion rings, and a Coke, no ice. She ate everything and left her paper wrappings for someone else to clean up. Nick was mesmerized by her slovenliness, that entitled American attitude that it was a productive day even if all you produced was trash. Nick let the next batch of onion rings burn and got chewed out by the new manager, who didn't share the former manager's appreciation of Nick's beauty, which was deteriorating anyway due to lack of hot water and too many Big Berthas with extra slices of cheese.

THE LIGHTBULB BURNED OUT in the gas station bathroom. The owner didn't bother to change it, and since Nick and Desmond felt strongly that it was his responsibility, they didn't, either. They brought candles, anchoring them in the hot wax they dripped on the tank behind the commode. After a few days, the tank looked like a shrine, votive lights burning to weird American gods conjured by Nick's brooding.

As was his custom, one day Nick went across the street to the bathroom at 4:00 a.m. It was still dark enough to see the stars, so he propped the door open with a brick and looked out onto the ghetto landscape formed by that peculiar American spirit that hates ignorance, hates excess, and hates misery, yet unwittingly nourishes all three. A creature so large it doesn't feel the parasites feeding on its carcass. A whole nation living the unexamined life.

A chip of his pleasure in the morning fell off, exposing the misery underneath. A palmetto bug, attracted by the heat of the candles, lumbered out from beneath the sink and sat at Nick's feet. Nick reached in his pocket for a pencil and a piece of paper. He licked the tip of his pencil, squinting to examine the point. Slowly, and in English, he began to write his first American poem.

ACKNOWLEDGMENTS

I WOULD LIKE TO THANK Livia Karak from the Passaic Slovak Catholic Sokol for translation, Barbara Flanagan and the novelist D. Keith Mano for their encouragement, and the goddess Serendipity for sending Serge Becker. I acknowledge my debt to Blake Carter for getting me started and keeping me on track. I am happy for this opportunity to thank my agent, David Kuhn, and his assistant, Billy Kingsland, for service above and beyond, and Sarah Crichton, who, like the legendary editors of old, made me reexamine every story through her keen eyes. And thanks and more to my husband and alchemist, Paul Fuhrman—you've changed everything.